THE BETWEEN

THE BETWEEN

A NOVEL

TANANARIVE DUE

HarperCollins*Publishers*

Grateful acknowledgment is made for permission to reprint the following:

Abena P. A. Busia's "Exiles" from *Testimonies of Exile*, Africa World Press, Inc., 1990. All rights reserved. Reprinted by permission of the publisher.

"Running Away." Written by Bob Marley. Copyright © 1977 by Bob Marley Music Ltd. Used by permission. All rights reserved.

Excerpt from "Blessed Sleep" from *St. Peter Relates an Incident.* Copyright © 1917 by James Weldon Johnson. Used by permission of Viking Penguin, a division of Penguin Books USA, Inc.

HarperCollins books may be purchased for educational, business, or sales promotional use. For information please write: Special Markets Department, HarperCollins Publishers, Inc., 10 East 53rd Street, New York, NY 10022.

FIRST EDITION

Designed by Nancy Singer

Library of Congress Cataloging-in-Publication Data
Due, Tananarive, 1966–
    The between : a novel / by Tananarive Due. — 1st ed.
     p. cm.
    ISBN 0-06-017250-9
    I. Title.
PS3554.U3143B48   1995
813'.54—dc20   95-2415

95 96 97 98 99 ❖/HC 10 9 8 7 6 5 4 3 2 1

To my mother,
my guardian angel,
Patricia Stephens Due

I felt a Funeral, in my Brain,
And mourners to and fro
Kept treading—treading—till it seemed
That Sense was breaking through—

And when they all were seated,
A Service, like a Drum—
Kept beating—beating—till I thought
My Mind was going numb—

And then I heard them lift a Box
And creak across my Soul
With those Boots of Lead, again,
Then Space—began to toll,

As all the Heavens were a Bell,
And Being, but an Ear,
And I, and Silence, some strange Race
Wrecked, solitary, here—

And then a Plank in Reason, broke,
And I dropped down, and down—
And hit a World, at every plunge,
And Finished knowing—then—

—Emily Dickinson

Hilton was seven when his grandmother died, and it was a bad time. But it was worse when she died again.

Hilton called her Nana, but her real name was Eunice Kelly. She raised Hilton by herself in rural Florida, in Belle Glade, which was forty miles from Palm Beach's rich white folks who lived like characters in a storybook. They shared a two-room house with a rusty tin roof on a road named for Frederick Douglass. The road wasn't paved, and the stones hurt Hilton's tender feet whenever he walked barefoot. Douglass Road was bounded by tomato fields behind an old barbed wire fence Nana told him never to touch because he might get something she called tetanus, and they couldn't afford a doctor. Hilton knew they were poor, but he never felt deprived because he had everything he wanted. Even as young as he was, Hilton understood the difference.

Nana had been a migrant worker for years, so she had muscles like a man on her shoulders and forearms. Nana always saved her money, and she played the organ for pay at the church the monied blacks attended across town, so she hadn't harvested sugarcane or picked string beans alongside the Puerto Ricans and Jamaicans in a long time.

Hilton worshipped her. She was his whole world. He didn't know anything about his parents except that they were gone, and he didn't miss them. He didn't think it was fair to his friends that they had mamas and daddies instead of a Nana.

Nana always said she didn't intend for Hilton to end up in the fields, that there were bigger things in store for him, so she sent him to school instead. She'd taught him to read before he ever walked through the doorway of the colored school a half mile away. And it was when he came home from school on a hot May afternoon that his life was changed forever.

He found Nana sprawled across her clean-swept kitchen floor, eyes closed, a white scarf wrapped around her head. She wasn't moving, and not a sound came from her. Hilton didn't panic just yet because Nana was old and sometimes fainted from heat when she tried to act younger, so he knelt beside her and shook her, calling her name. That worked by itself sometimes. Otherwise, he'd need to find her salts. But when he touched her forearm, he drew his hand away with a cry. Even with the humidity in the little house and the steam from pots boiling over on top of the stove, their lids bouncing like angry demons, Nana's flesh felt as cold as just-drawn well water. As cold as December. He'd never touched a person who felt that way, and even as a child he knew only dead people turned cold like that.

Hilton stumbled to his feet and ran crying outside to find a grown-up who could help. He was only half seeing because of his tears, banging on door after door on Douglass Road, yelling through the screens, and finding no one home. After each door, his sobs rose higher and his throat closed up a little more tightly until he could barely breathe. It was as though everyone were simply gone now, and no one was left but him. He felt like he'd tried a hundred houses, and all he'd found was barking dogs. The barking and running made him feel dizzy. He could hardly catch his breath anymore, like he would die himself.

In truth, there were only six houses on Douglass Road. The last belonged to Zeke Higgs, a Korean War veteran angry with middle age, angry with white folks, and whom no child with sense would bother on any other day because he kept a switch by his door. Zeke appeared like a shadow behind his screen when Hilton came pounding and crying, "Nana's dead. Come help Nana." Zeke scooped Hilton under his arm and ran to the house.

When he got home, Hilton's childhood flew from him. Nana was no longer lying lifeless on the kitchen floor. She was standing over the kitchen stove, stirring pots, and the first thing she said was: "I wondered where you'd run off to, boy." She looked at Zeke's face and nodded at him, then she fixed her eyes on Hilton. "I'm 'fraid Nana's made a mess of supper, Hilton. Just a mess."

"You all right, Mrs. Kelly?" Zeke asked, studying her face. Hilton did the same. She was perspiring, and her cheeks were redder than usual underneath her thin cocoa-colored skin.

"Just fine. May have had a fainting spell is all. I hope Hilton didn't send you into a fright."

Zeke mumbled something about how it wasn't a bother, although he was annoyed. Hilton barely noticed Zeke slip back out of the house because his eyes were on Nana. His tiny hand still tingled from the memory of the cold flesh he'd touched, as unhuman as meat from the butcher. Nana's smiles and gentle manner frightened him in a way he didn't understand. He stood watching her, his tears still flowing.

Nana glanced at him several times over her shoulder while she tried to scrape burned stew from the bottom of her good iron saucepan. The scraping sounded grating and insistent to Hilton. For the first time in his life, Hilton wondered if Nana might ever do anything to try to hurt him.

Finally, Nana said, "You go on out of the way now, Hilton. Supper's late today. Don't give me that face now, pumpkin. Nana's not going to leave you."

Hilton wanted to take Nana's fingers and squeeze them, to see if the cold was still there, but she hadn't reached out to him and he wouldn't dare touch her if she did. Hilton felt something had changed, maybe forever. He went outside to play with a three-wheeled wagon he'd found, but he wasn't really playing. He was sitting on the front stoop, rocking the wagon back and forth in front of him, but he barely knew where he was or what he was doing. And, as he'd sensed, things were different after that day he found Nana on the kitchen floor. She began to wake up crying out from bad dreams. He watched her get out of bed for a glass of water in the moonlight, her nightgown so soaked with sweat he could see all the lines of her body as though she wore no clothes. Many nights Hilton went to sleep alone because Nana would stay up humming and writing hymns on the porch. She said she did this because she couldn't sleep. Hilton knew the truth, that she didn't want to. Maybe she had met the boogeyman.

It was fine with Hilton to be alone, because it was hard for him to sleep with Nana there. Her sleep breathing sounded different to him, the breaths longer and drawn farther and farther apart until he was sure the next one wasn't coming, but it always did. Once, he counted a minute between her breaths. He tried to hold his own breath that long, but he couldn't.

Nana was confused all the time now. She would get cross with him more easily than before, and she'd smack his back-side for no good reason. One day Hilton was smacked when he didn't bring home cubes of sugar he knew she had never asked him to bring.

This went on for nearly a year, and Hilton began to hate her. He was afraid of her for reasons he didn't know or want to know. She'd never hurt him, not really, and on the rare occasions he touched her now her skin felt warm, but his memory of that day in the kitchen was too strong.

All of this changed the day Hilton took his first ride on a Greyhound, sitting at the back, of course, when Nana and their Belle Glade cousins took him to Miami for the Kelly-James family reunion. Twice before, Nana had stayed home and his women cousins drove him to the reunions to meet his kin, but she decided to go this year. The smells coming from Nana's picnic basket and the wonder of the flat, endless Florida landscape through the bus window were enough to make Hilton forget his fear.

4

The reunion was at Virginia Key Beach, and Hilton had never seen anyplace like it. This was a beach in Miami for only colored people, and folks of all shapes and shades had flocked there that day. Hilton had become a good swimmer in canals near Nana's house in Belle Glade, but he'd never seen so much sand and the trees and a green ocean stretching to forever. He'd always been told the ocean was blue, so the sparkling green ribbons of current were a wonder to him. Anything could happen on a day like today.

No one warned Hilton about the undertow, and he wouldn't have understood if they had, but Nana did tell him he could only go in the water if he didn't go far; this would have been enough if Hilton had minded like he should have. Nana, who was helping the ladies set up picnic tables, pointed to the orange buoy floating out in the water and said he could go only halfway there. And Hilton said "Yes, Nana" and ran splashing into the water knowing that he would go exactly where he wanted because in the water he would be free.

He swam easily past the midway point to the buoy, and he could see from here that it was cracked and the glowing paint was old. He wanted to get a closer look at it, maybe grab it and tread water and gaze back at all those brown bodies on the sand. And it was here that he met up with the undertow.

It was friendly at first. He felt as though the water had closed a grip around his tiny kicking legs and dunked him beneath the surface like a doughnut, then spat him back up a few feet from where he started. Hilton coughed and smiled, splashing with his arms. He didn't know the water could do that by itself. It was like taking a ride.

The buoy was now farther than it was before the ocean played with him. It was off to his left now when it had been straight ahead. As Hilton waited to see if he could feel those swirling currents beneath him again, he heard splinters of Nana's voice in the wind, calling from the beach: "Hilton, you get back here, boy! You hear me? Get back here."

So the ocean was not free after all, Hilton realized. He'd

better do as he was told, or he wouldn't get any coconut cake or peach cobbler, if it wasn't too late for that already. He began sure strokes back toward the shore.

The current still wanted to play, and this time it was angry Hilton was trying to leave so soon. He felt the cold grip seize his waist and hold his legs still. He was so startled he gasped a big breath of air, just in time to be plunged into the belly of the ocean, tumbled upside down and then up again, with water pounding all around his ears in a roar. Hilton tried to kick and stroke, but he didn't know which way was up or down and all he could see was the water all around him specked with tiny ocean life. Even in his panic, Hilton knew not to open his mouth, but his lungs were starting to hurt and the tumbling was never-ending. Hilton believed he was being swept to the very bottom of the ocean, or out to sea as far as the ship he'd seen passing earlier. Frantically, he flailed his arms.

He didn't hear Nana shout out from where she stood at the shore, but he'd hear the story told many times later. There was no lifeguard that day, but there were plenty of Kelly and James men who followed Nana, who stripped herself of her dress and ran into the water. The woman hadn't been swimming in years, but her limbs didn't fail her this one time she needed to glide across the water. The men followed the old woman into the sea.

Hilton felt he couldn't hold his breath anymore, and the water mocked him all around. It filled his ears, his nose, and finally his mouth, and his muscles began to fail him. It was then, just as he believed his entire fifty-pound body would fill with water, that he felt an arm around his waist. He fought the arm at first, thinking it was another current, but the grip was firm and pulled him up, up, up, until he could see light and Nana's weary, determined face. That was all he saw, because he went limp then.

He would hear the rest from others who told him in gentle ways about Chariots to the Everlasting and that sort of thing. One of the James men had been swimming closely behind Nana, and she passed Hilton to his arms. Then she simply stopped swimming, they said. Said maybe she just gave out. Nana's head began to sink below the water, and just as one of the Kelly men reached to try to take her arm, the current she'd pulled Hilton from took her instead. The man carrying Hilton could only swim against it with all his might toward the shore. Many people almost drowned that day.

When Hilton's senses came back to him and he was lying on the beach, caked in gritty sand, all that was left of Nana was her good flowered dress, damp and crumpled at the water's edge.

So what the gifted old folks, the seers, often say is true: Sometimes the dead go unburied.

PART ONE

EXILES

Funerals are important.
Away from home we cannot lay
our dead to rest
for we alone have given them
            no fitting burial.

Self-conscious of our absence
brooding over distances in western lands
we must rehearse
the planned performances of our rites
            till we return

And meanwhile through the years
our unburied dead eat with us
follow behind through bedroom doors.

—Abena P. A. Busia, Ghana

CHAPTER 1

Hilton looked at his watch and winced. Four o'clock. His wife's reception had started at three, and although the lodge was only a ten-minute drive from here, he was late even by Colored People Time standards.

"You got to go, right?" Danitra asked, her arms folded across her chest, not hiding the disappointment on her painted lips. Hilton was intrigued by lipstick, especially this shade as bright as blood, because Dede never wore it.

But then, Dede didn't have to.

"I'll be in trouble if I don't," Hilton said, glancing at the boxes stacked in the empty apartment. Anything to keep his eyes off of her black tank top, which she wore with a brazenness only a woman in her early twenties could. "You're all set here, Miss Thang. I know the elevator's broken, and it's not Buckingham Palace, but—"

"Oh, please," Danitra laughed. "Close enough. This is better than I thought it could get for me, Mr. James. And I won't mess it up this time over shooting up or a man or nothing else."

Metro-Dade police had referred Danitra to Hilton's drug-rehab center six months ago, when the remnants of her stitched-on, store-bought braids hung sloppily from her scalp, her lips were never quite closed and never quite dry, and her arms were swollen from needle tracks. Now her arms had dark bruises from the habit she would fight off all her remaining years, but they were also sculpted with muscles. Her faded jeans at last had a form to cling to, and cling they did.

This was a dangerous place for a married man to be today, Hilton thought. Higher intentions were one thing, but it was a plain fact the woman was looking good, and the two of them had spent the past hour working up a healthy sweat carrying boxes and donated furniture up two flights of stairs to move her and her baby into a place they hadn't known for the infant's entire eighteen-month life: a home.

And Danitra had brains going for her. Even when she used to get high, she never shared needles, which kept her and her baby free of the disease that had decimated his clients who shot up. She had a strength that reminded him of his wife, with a will to match.

All of these qualities added, in his mind, to her general fineness. He couldn't help thinking about what might have happened between them if he were single, which he hadn't been in fifteen years. The bare, airy room felt too small for them both.

She read his mind. "You know, there was a time a man like you would have asked for my phone number. Back before I tore myself up like I did."

"A man like me would ask for your phone number now," Hilton said carefully, to reassure her that she should not be ashamed, "if a man like me weren't married."

"I guess you already got my number, don't you?" She took his hand and pressed it to her chest near her collarbone, where beneath a thin film of perspiration her skin felt touched with fever.

another time, a different doorway
another life

His lips parting slightly, Hilton gently pulled his hand away and patted her firmly on the shoulder. Danitra laughed at the brotherly gesture.

"Don't be looking at me like that, girl. I don't know what you want with an old man anyway."

"Not that old. I don't see no gray in that beard yet."

"You aren't looking closely enough."

"Well, I don't think I'd better look no closer, seeing as you have that ring on your finger and you won't take it off."

Still smiling, Hilton shook his head. Her attraction was flattering. "Damn. You don't give up, do you?" he asked.

"No, sir. That's why I'm standing where I am right now."

He saw a fleeting image of the two of them nude, entwined behind boxes on the carpeting, christening her new home, but he forced the thought away because he felt the heavy warmth of arousal growing beneath his stomach. He took a deep breath and pinched her cheek. "Good luck, sweetheart. I'm late. I'd better leave."

"Yeah," Danitra said, grinning knowingly, "you'd better."

As Hilton climbed into the dented Corolla he'd driven since grad school in the late 1970s, the thrill of temptation buzzed in his mind. Instead of regret, he felt a sense of power over it, knowing he had chosen not to act. He had Dede, who even now was being lauded as a newly elected circuit-court judge, the only black woman in Dade with that title; and together they had Kaya and Jamil, whom only a certified fool would risk willingly. Cute wasn't worth it. Ten times cute wasn't worth it.

He knew and respected men who didn't feel the same carnal allegiances—and he'd heard straight-faced arguments from black friends on how insulting it was to try to force fidelity, a European notion, on the descendants of African princes—but Hilton had already come too close to losing his own tribe from selfishness. Fucking around, as far as he was concerned, was just another form of selfishness. One he didn't dare explore.

The Elks lodge on Northwest Seventh Avenue was flanked by rented limousines with tinted windows and three Miami police cars, sirens flashing, just in case any restless have-nots nearby got ideas about crashing the bourgeois party. Seventh Avenue was otherwise occupied by storefronts badly in need of paint and customers; the Burger King across the street was bustling, but the African-fashions store next to the lodge was nearly empty. Hilton adjusted the kente-cloth necktie Dede bought him from the little shop as he excused himself

13

past the huddles at the lodge door. Inside, he scanned the balloon-filled hall for his family.

He saw Dede immediately, but she didn't see him. She was center-stage with a dozen other black officials wearing name tags, posing for group photographs. She stood among the tallest, a graceful giant with a long neck and a sculpted natural that sloped above her forehead. Alongside her were two black mayors, state legislators, local commissioners, and two black U.S. congressmen. All had been guests in his home at one time or another. Hilton was struck by how impressive the group was and consciously stood a bit straighter when he reminded himself that his own wife was among them. Flashing bulbs lit the room like strobes.

A stage whisper floated to Hilton's ear from behind him: *"Psssst.* Dad."

He saw his daughter waving in her lilac taffeta dress from a table near the buffet line. Her permed hair was curled loose against her shoulders instead of in ponytails, the way he was used to seeing her. Apparently, she'd been allowed to wear a touch of rouge on her cheeks. She'd won many of these little compromises since her thirteenth birthday, or, as Kaya called it, her "teenagehood." Jamil's head popped up from whatever game he was playing crouched under the table. They had inherited their mother's sharp jawbone and long neck, and their faces were smooth and round, looking nearly identical in a complexion mingling Dede's darker shade with Hilton's red-clay-tinged brown.

"You're late, Dad," Kaya observed while Hilton kissed her forehead and massaged Jamil's scalp.

"Watch out for my fade, Daddy," Jamil said, patting his flat hairstyle back into place. Hilton couldn't remember being that vain at eight, or at any age since.

"Mom made a speech," Kaya said, and Hilton's spirits sank. He'd left the house to help Danitra move out of the rehab center before he could listen to Dede practice her speech as he'd promised that afternoon. Now he'd missed the real thing too.

"Uh-oh," he said. Uh-oh was an understatement. "I bet it was good, though."

"Of course it was. She got a standing ovation."

Hilton gazed intently at the group posing for pictures, and Dede suddenly shifted her head and saw him. Not daring a smile, Hilton raised his hand to greet her. Dede's face remained unchanged, unreadable. I'm sorry, he mouthed to her. Her eyes returned to the camera, and she managed an insincere smile for the picture. With her mother on vacation in the Bahamas, Hilton remembered, he would have been especially missed today. Hilton knew he was most certainly, without a doubt, in big trouble.

"I've got an idea," Kaya said, close to his ear. "Say your car broke down. She'll believe that. It's always broken."

"Thanks a lot. I'm glad we raised you to be honest."

"You'd better have some excuse, Dad. She wanted you here."

Sorry, dear, Hilton rehearsed in his mind ruefully, I would have been here for your shining moment, but I was getting a hard-on for one of my junkie clients.

Once Dede joined them, Hilton won a reprieve from her solemn dark eyes in the stream of well-wishers who wanted to shake her hand, who remembered her from when she was only so tall, who'd contributed to her campaign and were so happy to finally see a sister in there. In these situations, Hilton envied Dede for her liquid smile and easy enthusiasm. She lost herself in the warmth of other people in a way he could not, grasping their shoulders, hugging them, taking telephone numbers with relish.

Dede maintained her gracious dignity while allowing an infectious playfulness to peek through. She had a peal of laughter he could usually hear from across the room. Maybe that was the African in her; Dede's mother was Ghanaian and equally effusive. Dede's nature spilled into her campaign, a clean race that found her victorious, despite their bare-bones finances, over an older white man with a recognized name. By the end, Kaya and Jamil were scrawling campaign signs with colored markers.

Hilton held Dede's hand while she spoke to one person after another, brushing her knuckle gently with his thumb; this was half an involuntary impulse to remind her admirers that he'd had the good sense to choose her, half a silent apology. A black Metro-Dade police officer they'd both known for years, dressed smartly in his brown-and-beige uniform, kissed Dede's cheek, then gave Hilton a soul shake. Curtis was a vice sergeant who often steered homeless addicts to Hilton's Miami New Day center with his finesse for ignoring county paperwork. He'd brought Danitra after finding her asleep with a needle in one arm and her baby in the other, beneath the Interstate 95 overpass.

"Watch it, Hil, or I'm 'a take this lady right from under your nose. You know how they like the uniform, right?"

"Look here, you can try," Hilton said.

"Curtis, you'd better go get a plate of food and stop being foolish," Dede dismissed him.

Curt pursed his lips grimly beneath his moustache. He leaned closer to Dede, his voice free of mirth. "You let me know if you change your mind and decide to file a report on that thing. I'll make sure it gets looked after."

"Hold up. What thing?" Hilton asked.

Dede blinked rapidly and squeezed Hilton's fingers hard. She was looking toward Kaya and Jamil, whose heads were bent hungrily over their food. "Not now," she said. "I'll let you know, Curt."

As an afterthought, Curtis pointed to Hilton. "How's that girl with the baby doing? Danitra?"

"She's great. In fact, that's where I was today, man. I got held up moving her into The Terraces."

Hilton was so distracted by his concern over the secret Curtis and Dede shared, wondering what would be so pressing that she would consider filing a police report, that it didn't occur to him until after he'd spoken that this wasn't the way he'd intended to explain his late arrival. In fact, this way was dead wrong. He'd all but decided Kaya had a point, that it might be better to stretch the truth a little bit this time. Dede might see something in his eyes when he talked about Danitra, and the last thing he needed was to rouse in her the beast they'd spent hundreds of dollars in marriage counseling to quiet.

"I should have known," he heard Dede mutter, and he knew the beast was stirring already.

CHAPTER 2

Anyone who lives in Miami or a subtropical climate knows that the color black draws heat, so it's best to avoid it or else squirm with discomfort; in this way, Dede Campbell's dark mocha complexion drew Hilton James. He saw her walking beside a duck pond on a pathway winding across the Coral Gables campus of the University of Miami, a woman with height and nicely proportioned heft and a natural shaved nearly to her scalp in 1978, when brothers and sisters were still growing Afros as high as they could reach. Her loose-fitting dress was bright yellow, dangling against her body's gentle curves past her knees. Even from where he sat on a bench across the pond, Hilton could see she was wearing sandals and had a sterling silver bracelet draped around her left ankle. Silver glistened against her skin as though the precious metal were mined for that purpose alone. Her gait foretold all her ambition, all her confidence, all her promise.

Hilton had come to grad school for two things: his master's in public administration and to find a wife. Not even necessarily in that order. The sisters he'd met in the working world during the two years he'd spent as a teen counselor in Liberty City just hadn't been doing it for him. They could boogie on the dance floor, and he'd found his own sweet corner of ecstasy between hot thrusts in his bedroom, but when it came to conversation and vision he was coming up dry. Forget about sisters, some of his friends told him when he complained, their arms wrapped around white women with blond locks and imaginations fixated on the Congo.

Forget about sisters. He wouldn't forget about this one. He found the bench every day at the same time, waiting for her to pass. Most days she didn't. But some days, especially Wednesdays and Fridays, she did. He followed her at a distance and watched her take steps two at a time into the law school. He'd braced himself to discover that she might be an actress or a music major with her head untroubled by the worldly concerns that consumed his thoughts, but she wasn't. Damn if she wasn't a law student. This was fate, he decided.

He had them married with two sets of twins before he'd even spoken to her or asked her name. After three months he was kicking himself because he hadn't found the nerve to stop her on the path and introduce her future husband.

When he was invited to a black graduate-student mixer at the union sponsored by UM's Black Student Society, he chuckled at the invitation, thinking there wouldn't be more than a half dozen people there. But he knew she would come.

Seeing her there in a white sundress with thin straps, Hilton mustered the resolve to walk up to her. Her name tag identified her, so he tried to sound familiar: "DeeDee, it's great to see you. I've noticed you around. Can I get you a drink?"

She looked at him skeptically, not the way he'd hoped. Her face was wrinkled with a confusion over who this fool was pretending to know her; then she remembered her name tag and raised her long, unpolished fingers to touch it. "DAY-day," she said. "It's pronounced DAY-day. It's African."

Strike one against him. He had to be especially smooth now. "Are you from Africa?" he asked, already counting that question as strike two. Of course she was, with that glorious skin and her natural face pure of makeup and the traces of a clipped accent under all that America.

"My mother is. She's from Accra."

"Ghana," he said quickly, too quickly, trying to impress her.

She smiled, seeing all this at work in his mind. "Yes. Ghana," she said.

Uncomfortable pause. "Would you like a drink?" he repeated.

"Fruit juice, if they have any," she said, looking his face over and then glancing at his name. "And when you come back—Hilton—try to be yourself. I'll like you better that way."

After a year's worth of Earth, Wind & Fire concerts, poetry readings, and black-student meetings, they were engaged. A year after that, no sooner than she'd taken and passed the bar exam, they were married at Overtown's St. John Baptist Church, where Dede had come up. Lionel Campbell, her father, owned a small black weekly newspaper and knew everyone, so the church was filled beyond capacity. Well-wishers who couldn't get in fanned themselves and cackled on the front steps, their voices floating through the walls as Hilton and Dede said "I do."

Years later, describing their introduction, engagement, and wedding, and most especially Dede's rainbow-kissed African ceremonial wedding dress, Hilton related the story like a fishing yarn, remembering each detail, treating it like a dream. He would cling to those details in coming years, when the dream began to fall apart and daily realities took root between them.

Neither of them changed. Dede had always been more quick to anger and had a tendency to snap when annoyed. Hilton had always retreated into silence when confronted, and he'd always had a full schedule of meetings and appointments, squeezing his time with Dede around them. And she'd always felt a need to keep track, asking him where he was at five o'clock, at six o'clock, an implicit reminder that she did not trust him to roam alone. This annoyed him like nothing else.

It didn't help him that his life was full of women. His boss at the Miami New Day Recovery Center, where he had started a job as the head social worker, was a woman; many of the counselors were women; the workhorses at the Miami

Action Coalition, a civil rights group, were women. They called him at home and on weekends, and when Dede complained, Hilton tried to explain that he could not simply tell them, "I don't care who's having a seizure or which building is burning down, my wife doesn't want me to take calls on Sunday. Sunday is our time." Perhaps he should have said it, but he didn't feel he could. He wanted—expected—her to understand that.

Dede had her own brand of commitment, but she was more adept at saying no than he was. Her inspirational speaking appearances or participation in free legal clinics were carefully selected, and she made it a point to inform Hilton each time she turned something down for the family. For the family. It sounded like a curse, the way she said it.

He tried to make it up in other ways, by surprising her with exotic dinner recipes when he could (he was a good cook, as good as she), by arranging flowers and candles in their bedroom, by cornering her for midafternoon lovemaking in the walk-in closet while Kaya watched cartoons in the living room. But all it took was one phone call and Dede's announcing "It's some woman for you" in a tone that painted him as a dog to unravel all the work.

It got worse after Jamil was born. His son's birth coincided with his promotion to assistant director, so just when Dede wanted him at home the most he was staying at the office until eight o'clock most nights. He cut out much of his other volunteer work, he called her on the hour to update her on when he would be getting home, but it couldn't slice through the awful silence when he returned after dark and leaned over his new son's crib and wondered what once-only achievements he'd missed while he was away.

The cutbacks didn't last long, though. As Jamil grew, so did Hilton's schedule of meetings in Overtown, in West Perrine, in Liberty City, wherever the disenfranchised tried to organize and asked for his help. One week he never made it home before eleven. He was spared Dede's wrath only because she was sleeping.

"Why don't you just tell me who you're seeing and get it over with?" Dede said to him when he was in bed one night, dumbfounding him. She was holding a white dress shirt he'd just tossed into the bathroom hamper, her fingers closed tightly around the collar. She pushed the shirt into his face, and he saw the faint smudges of brown makeup, like dried finger paint.

At first he was numb with confusion. What woman had gotten close enough to him that day to muss his clothes? Then he remembered Beatrice Price. "Oh, Jesus," Hilton said, and he couldn't help it: he laughed.

His laughter enraged her. She whipped the shirt into his face so hard that one of the buttons bit into his cheek. "Don't make me out to be a fool, Hilton," she said in a deadly tone.

He might have read her tone and simply apologized, but he was angry at the accusation and at his smarting cheek. "You're making yourself out to be a fool," he said. "I won't answer that. This is bullshit."

"And then you lie," she said in a sweeping vibrato, as though this is what she'd always expected. "You can't be a man. All this time, all the time you spend away, a meeting for this and that every night, all the times I call your desk and you're out—"

"Have you ever heard of field work? I'm supposed to sit on my ass behind a desk all day?" he shouted. Hilton knew Kaya would hear him from her bedroom across the hall, but he couldn't bring his voice down: "So you're checking up on me? Do you follow my car in the mornings too?"

"Whose makeup is it?" Dede screamed back, her dark lips pulled tightly across her teeth. "I don't wear that goddamned paint on my face. Whose is it?"

Hilton leaped to his feet, and Dede drew back from him without fear softening her face. He tossed the shirt to her feet, wishing it could make some awesome noise; he was more angry than he could remember being at someone he loved. "The commission meeting was today, and we got our funding. Commissioner Price gave me a hug, if you want to be jealous of an old bitch who could be my mother. She was congratulating me, which is more than I get from my fucking wife."

The fights began this way, but they didn't end. As Jamil grew from infant to toddler, their fights grew more heated, more painful, until they were a part of the household. The choices were between silence or shouts, and often they chose silence.

Part of the problem, he knew, was that Dede had worried about her father's fidelity before he died a year after Jamil was born; the community's gossip was vicious, and most blacks in town had heard a story about some woman Lionel Campbell had supposedly set up in an apartment. Mr. Campbell knew of the rumors himself and denied them in print before he died, but they were always there. Dede must have had some reason to believe them.

And when Hilton tried to reason her out of her jealousy, asking her what he'd ever done to deserve her distrust, she countered by asking why he couldn't simply come home at night.

Here they reached an impasse. She knew when she married him what his schedule was like, what his commitments to his community were, he said. What did she think the riots were all about? He'd already given up his literacy tutoring, he'd given up his vice president's position at the Miami Action Coalition. Was he supposed to give up everything?

The mood inside their house seeped to every corner; Kaya, at seven, became more irritable, teasing her brother to tears for attention. Hilton began to spank her with a belt, never hitting her hard enough to hurt her, but the ritual of the lashes to her palm made her howl and then sob for hours in her room. Kaya was crying, Jamil was crying, Dede was unreachable.

One Sunday, sitting in front of a television set he was staring at but not watching, Hilton knew he could not stay like this any longer. He found Dede typing at the desk in the den and stood watching her with tears in his eyes. She looked up at him. He simply shook his head, a surrender. She turned away, expressionless, and continued to type. He heard the electric clacking as he walked to their bedroom and began to pack a suitcase, tossing in random shirts and slacks.

"So where should I tell them their father is?" Dede asked from the doorway in a voice unlike the one he knew. He didn't know how long she'd been there.

He couldn't answer right away. He didn't know. "If we can't do better than this, Dede, we can't be together."

"What happened?" Dede asked. "Did we fall out of love?"

Love was the least of his worries; love was burning a hole in his stomach and sucking his mouth dry. "I didn't," he said.

"Neither did I." A whisper.

He clicked his suitcase shut. "Then it must take more than that," he said.

"It does."

Her friends at the prosecutor's office and his friend Stu, a physician at Miami New Day, intervened and insisted they get marriage counseling before he spent all his money at the Holiday Inn and things went too far to turn back. After eight years of marriage, two children, and three days of separation, Hilton and Dede visited the Biscayne Boulevard office of Dr. Raul A. Puerta, Ph.D., family and individual counselor.

Hilton was unhappy with the arrangement, partially because Dede did the choosing, but mostly because he wanted a black therapist—and if not black, certainly not Hispanic. The entire flavor and language of Miami had changed since thousands of Cuban exiles flooded the city from the Mariel boat lift in 1980, and this was the one time he couldn't afford communication problems. While they waited in a room filled with tall stalklike plants and Spanish-language ballads on the radio, Dede told him to be quiet and consider it a compromise because she would have preferred a woman therapist. She'd been told Puerta was good, one of the best in town. And, she added, we need all the help we can get.

Puerta was young and overthin, in his early thirties, with a moustache and round-frame glasses. He was dark-skinned, but not as dark as some of the Afro-Cubans Hilton had seen, who were indistinguishable from any brother on the street. Puerta wore a short-sleeved shirt with a loose tie, keeping cool with a small fan on his desk. He asked them a few standard questions: their names, what they did, about their children, how long they'd been married. Hilton noted his thick accent and grew distracted by the cars he could see through the window, passing by. He began to perspire, slouching in his upholstered seat.

"Let's start with something simple. It's a role-playing exercise," Puerta said, pronouncing each syllable with a care that was both annoying and soothing to Hilton. "I find it helpful for couples to try to view the world through the eyes of the partner. I'm going to give you an incomplete sentence, and you must answer as your spouse would. I'll begin with you, Mrs. James. The sentence is, 'It makes me angry when . . . '"

Now Hilton was paying attention. He watched Dede's face as she searched for an answer. She took a breath, avoiding his eyes: "It makes me angry when you don't trust me," she said.

Damn straight, and say it louder, Hilton thought. Maybe this wouldn't be such a waste of time after all. Puerta's brown-green eyes were now on him. "Your turn, Mr. James. Finish this sentence as your wife would. 'It makes me jealous when . . . '"

Hilton didn't need to think. "It makes me jealous when you care about other people more than you care about me," he said. His voice was unsteady.

The silence in the room felt like the arrival of a new baby. Dede swallowed, looking at Hilton with a sort of awe. Puerta raised his eyebrows, pleased. "Let's talk about that. Do you care about others more than you care about your wife and children?"

"Of course not," Hilton said, and he could feel Dede's unspoken objections surging beside him, but she held her silence.

"Do you think you spend too much time with other people?"

"Yes," Hilton said reluctantly. Beside him, Dede exhaled.

"Why is that, do you think?" Puerta asked.

Hilton sighed, gazing out of the window again. "I don't know. Because I have to. Someone has to. I have to give back."

"Every night?" Dede whispered.

Puerta nodded slowly. "Why do *you* have to?"

This time, the words came to Hilton's mouth from a hidden place, and he couldn't have prepared himself for what he would say if he had imagined it: "Because my grandmother died for me. She drowned for me."

After a stunned second at the sound of his voice, Hilton touched his face, finding his cheek damp with tears. Hastily, he looked away from his wife and the stranger, brushing his face against his shirtsleeve. This room was too hot, too cramped. His heart was pounding a river of blood to his temples.

He'd never told Dede much about his grandmother, about Belle Glade, about the beach. He never thought about it himself. He could barely remember her face.

nana's not going to leave you

"Why don't we try Mondays and Wednesdays?" Puerta asked.

Hilton couldn't speak. "That would be fine," Dede answered for them. He felt her hand slip to his knee.

((

At last, away from the cameras and campaign supporters, they were alone. Without a sound, Hilton eased his nakedness behind the familiar ridges of Dede's body beneath the hot stream of water. She gasped with a start, clinging for the hand grip, then relaxed and rested against him as his hands smoothed a lather across her waist, her belly, and her nipples. He pinched them slightly with two fingers and felt them stand until they were as solid as his own phallus resting against her slippery buttocks. He kissed her shoulder, lapping up the warm water beading there, then craned to gnaw at the spot on her neck that would make her eyes close and her head tilt back to him. He found it. He pressed his mouth to hers and their tongues met, circling.

There was no room in the shower stall for proper lovemaking. Without drying off or wiping themselves free of soap, they dripped across the bathroom's Mexican tiles to the plush carpeting of their bedroom and collapsed there in a heap. The soap helped him slip easily inside of her, and his thrusts were prolonged, measured, as he eased his abdomen back and forth across her most sensitive parts. Their chests rubbed together. Her warmth enveloped him like a slick leather glove, and his thrusts grew more determined as his love ache strained for more, more, and he would have thrust his entire torso inside her if he could. Dede clamped her nails into his buttocks, her mouth loose, her face pliant as all cares vanished save the spell of their touch. With the shower still beating hard, they were careless with their cries when their bodies clenched and heaved.

"Not so loud, not so loud, not so loud," Dede repeated, nearly shrieking the words, until he covered her mouth and they both laughed against each other. They lay quietly a moment while he was semirigid and still nestled inside her, listening for scampering feet or hushed voices near their closed door. They heard none; the kids were supposed to be watching an Arnold Schwarzenegger video in Kaya's room anyway. One of the reasons they'd bought this house was the lure of split bedrooms, with the master bedroom an entire floor plan away from other parts of the house that needed to mind their own business. It wasn't simply through overindulgence that Kaya had her own VCR and color TV at thirteen; it was strategy.

"Talk about a wet spot. Look at that carpet," Dede laughed while she slipped on an oversized Snoopy nightshirt.

"It'll dry," Hilton said, and kissed her nose. "That's the first time I've bribed a judge. What's your verdict, Your Honor?"

"I may have to hear your case again in the morning."

Hilton glanced down at the tent poking inside his silk pajamas. "You can hear it again now." He bumped against her.

With the frenzy of the campaign and the frenzy of the fall season as more homeless addicts came to Miami in search of a warmer climate, Hilton and Dede had not made love in at least a month. That accounted for their eagerness, their tirelessness as they drenched themselves with each other's wet heat on their bed, then on the leather reclining chair near the bedroom's glass sliding door. The venetian blinds painted Dede's body with striped shimmering reflections from the patio's pool while the floodlight outside turned their lair bright green.

Exhausted, they finally crawled beneath their sheets and held each other. Dede's earlier anger seemed far away now. "Tell me about your speech," he whispered drowsily.

"Not now. You've heard it all before."

african-coon-tarbaby-nigger-american bitch

Suddenly, oddly, Hilton snapped wide awake. He raised his head to try to see Dede's face. He could make out the glistening whites of her eyes. "Dede, tell me what that business was with Curt today. What did he want you to file a police report about?"

"It's nothing, baby," she said, rubbing figure eights on his chest with her index finger. "Something at work Friday. I got a letter, some kind of threat. Nonsense."

"Like what? What did it say?"

She sighed, irritable about being pulled from sleep. "Some guy I must have prosecuted for something. Typical racist garbage. You black bitch and so forth and so on."

"Let me see it."

"Hil, it's in my desk drawer. It's not important. The prosecutors get letters like these, you know? It's nothing." Her last words were nearly lost in a yawn.

"I want you to bring it home Monday, okay? I'm going to call you at work and remind you."

Dede mumbled something agreeable. He watched her eyes flicker closed, and he brushed his finger across her cheek. "I'm sorry about today," he said. "I screwed up. I know it."

"Shhhhhh," she said. "You had to do what you had to do."

He felt a warmth pouring through his chest that reminded him of holding Dede for the first time in his UM dormitory, swaying to "Reasons" by Earth, Wind & Fire and falling in love. How could he have forgotten that during their troubled times? How did he imagine he could ever walk out on this?

"Dede," he said, "don't go to sleep. You forgot about it."

Their ritual. They had done it almost every night without fail since he'd undergone two years of therapy alone after their marriage counseling was finished, a habit as ingrained as brushing their teeth, and he felt as though something were missing if he tried to sleep without it.

Half asleep, Dede craned upward to kiss one temple and then the other. "Sweet dreams," she said.

CHAPTER 3

Hilton awakened to find a subdued predawn glow cast across the bedroom, a pristine moment in the day. This was his favorite hour, but he couldn't enjoy it. He had a headache already and a bad feeling about the day.

Just as he believed he had a knack for sensing good, occasionally a vague unease settled over Hilton's psyche, forcing him to try to predict all of the things that might go wrong, and one of them usually would. On a Sunday, it could be as simple as the Dolphins losing their game—although that hardly seemed likely in a home game against the Colts. Still, you could never be sure. He played with the possibilities of fumbles and interceptions that might lie ahead that afternoon, mentally listing the players on injured reserve, but his discomfort grew to a grumble in his stomach and he knew the feeling had nothing to do with football. He decided the family would go to church that day.

The dictate met grumbles from Kaya and Jamil and amazement from his wife. Dede was the more religious of the couple, always wearing a tiny silver cross around her neck, but she was far from devout. The Jameses, who'd raised Hilton, considered God a personal matter and said the only true church was the home. Hilton suspected his adoptive father was agnostic but had yet to ask him. Saying grace was an afterthought at Hilton's own family table and occurred rarely, usually only on holidays when Dede's mother was present. Church was a part of their Sunday schedule only when Dede insisted far in advance, announcing, "We *will* go to church this Sunday" because she didn't want to be absent so long she'd be ashamed to show her face.

So the family's reverently bowed heads as they stood in one of the empty pews near the back of the church belied the arguments and elaborate compromises that had started the morning. Kaya and Jamil had shorts, T-shirts, and roller skates waiting in the trunk of the car to liberate them from starch and lace for their promised trip to the park. Their sullen expressions revealed that in their minds even that hadn't been a fair trade.

Hilton tried to keep focused throughout the service. He still hadn't decided whether or not he believed in God, but if he paid close enough attention, sometimes a sermon would move him to trembling, or an inspired gospel harmony could make him think yes, yes, yes, Jesus. That wasn't likely today. The regular minister, whose sermons were logical and persuasive, was on vacation. Instead, a younger, associate minister who looked about twenty-one was shouting about Revelation's "river of water of life," but Hilton found the message abstract and had no patience for it. The service was more poorly attended than he had ever seen, and Hilton was aware of all the empty space beneath the majestic stained-glass murals. He felt farther from God than ever. He wanted, he needed, to feel closer.

"Jesus offers an open invitation, his door is always wide," the young pastor said in a sing-song voice punctuated by organ flourishes. Hilton believed the man was looking directly at him.

"Some only come calling when they're sick. You know it's the truth. Amen. Some only come when they don't want to lose that job. Amen. Some only come when they feel their hearts are finally wearing out. Someone say amen. Some only come when they know their days on God's green earth are gone and it's time to face eternity. Amen. And they knock on the door once, twice, three times, and say, 'Jesus, I have sinned. Now will you let me in?'"

                    *   *   *

"Daddy!"

Jamil's tearful shout yanked Hilton's head from the pages of the Sunday *New York Times* and Dede's from a Toni Morrison paperback, piercing the serenity of the park. Hilton's heart leaped as he watched his expert-skater son scramble toward them without finesse, nearly losing his balance. Hilton swept his eyes across the park for Kaya. They'd seen her earlier from where they sat beneath the shade of a banyan tree; she'd been skating on the path near the footbridge over a Biscayne Bay inlet. Dede had the same thought. "Where's Kaya?" she asked, sitting upright, pulling off her sunglasses.

"What's wrong, Jamil? Where's your sister?"

"I don't know," Jamil sniffled, stumbling and pitching headfirst over the spot where the paved path met the grass. He was wearing knee pads, but he scraped his right elbow raw in the fall. Dede was first to reach him and take his arm to help him stand, warning him to be careful.

Hilton spotted Kaya skating with an iced lemonade in her hand at the opposite end of the park, and his chest loosened. "There she is. Jamil, what's wrong?"

Up close, Hilton could see that his son's face was tear-streaked with anger instead of only childish upset. "Some bad kids hurt a baby duck," he said. "There's a mama duck and a bunch of babies, and they caught one."

Hilton almost smiled, comparing the degree of actual urgency to his initial fear, but he couldn't look at Jamil without sharing his sense of moral outrage. "Okay, little man, let's go take a look."

Hilton and Dede jogged beside Jamil as he led them on the path and then across a strip of grass near the jutting boulders of the landfill separating the park from the bay that stretched into the Atlantic Ocean. The water was dotted with patient, brightly colored sailboats. Jamil stopped at one of the benches facing the bay. "It's under there. See?"

Hilton kneeled. He saw tail feathers hidden behind a

crushed soda can. When he nudged the can aside, he saw a midsized yellow duckling with brown spots lying on its side. The blue eyes were wide open, but the duckling's neck was twisted. Hilton didn't have to touch it to know it was dead.

cold

"Where's the mommy duck?" Dede asked Jamil, rubbing his neck gently. Jamil didn't answer, wiping new tears from his face. He apparently hadn't seen the duckling this closely until now, and it confirmed his worst fears. Jamil loved animals. His hay fever prevented them from keeping pets other than parakeets, but Jamil cared for the birds conscientiously without being told.

"I'm sorry, Jamil," Hilton said. "You were right. Those were bad boys, whoever did this."

"The mommy is in the water. See?" Jamil said, pointing. A white adult duck paddled in the water a few feet out, nibbling at bread crumbs still floating near her. A line of four ducklings, one of them colored in striking black, followed her. She was oblivious to her missing ward.

"What happened?" Kaya asked, breathless, skating behind them.

"Jamil saw some kids kill a duckling. The poor thing. And that's a felony in this state," Dede said.

Kaya bent down to take a look under the bench. "Gross," she said.

Jamil's eyes suddenly narrowed as he gazed back at the park, and he pulled from Dede's grip to launch himself back onto the path. His legs pumped with speed and determination.

"Where's he going?" Dede asked.

"Maybe to those boys over there," Kaya said.

Fifty yards out, Hilton saw four boys ambling down the path away from them with a basketball. Two were white, two were black, and they looked tall from where Hilton stood. All but one were bare-chested, wearing cutoff shorts that reached their knees. Jamil pitched toward them and skidded to a stop after circling in front of them. Startled, the bigger boys stopped walking.

"Hil . . . I don't like this," Dede said.

"Stay here," Hilton said. "Those boys aren't little."

As Hilton neared him, he heard his son confronting the preteens, telling them the duck was dead and they had no right to do that. What gave them the right to do that? His voice was clear and resolved in a way Hilton had never heard. Fearless, even.

"Yo, man, I didn't kill no duck," the tallest black boy said, pointing to a wispy-haired blond boy. "You talk to this crazy motherfucker about that shit, all right?"

The blond boy took a step toward Jamil and cocked his fist back in a threat. "Faggot, I'll kick your little ass. Get out of my face."

"Oh, no. There won't be any of that," Hilton announced, and four surprised faces looked up at him. One of the boys, sensing trouble, began to walk away and bounced the basketball unhurriedly as he walked. The rest stepped away from Hilton and assessed him. Hilton's stance was threatening, shoulders forward, the way he'd learned from the teenagers he once counseled—boys who were old beyond their years. Hilton's frame was slight, but he was six-two and could make his eyes look menacing. Diplomacy, on the streets, was the last resort.

"Man, you'd better check this little shrimp," the blond boy told Hilton. "He came over here talking shit."

"In the first place," Hilton said, "you shut that filthy mouth in front of me. And the second thing is, if I ever see any of you killing animals in this park or anywhere, I'll call the police. How would you like it if somebody broke your little necks just because they felt like it? And believe me, somebody could."

"I didn't kill nothin'," the tall black boy protested.

"You just remember what I said. And if you think this is a joke, just try me. Just try me one time."

Hilton still had the touch. The boys grumbled sullenly, but

none had the nerve to look Hilton in the eye or to make a move to walk away until he backed up a step.

"Come on, Jamil," Hilton said.

Hilton heard catcalls as he and Jamil made their way back toward the bay, but nonetheless he felt good. Angry and frustrated, but good. Jamil's confrontation with those boys had been impulsive and dangerous—especially since one of them might have been armed—and he would have to tell Jamil that one day. One day. For now, he said, "That took guts, little man. I'm proud of what you did, standing up like that."

Jamil smiled, but the smile faded quickly. He had been disturbed by what he'd seen, and he was silent as he and Kaya unlaced their skates and the family packed Dede's Audi to go home. The sun was still blazing white high above the horizon, but the day didn't seem so nice anymore and there was no reason to stay. Yes, Hilton reminded himself, he'd known since that morning that unpleasantness was waiting. Jamil had seen violence, death, lack of remorse. Big lessons for a third-grader.

"So I guess Dad really told those boys off, huh?" Kaya asked Jamil in the backseat, clicking on her seat belt as Hilton started the engine. There would be no teasing, no fighting for space between them today. "At least the other ducks will be okay."

"Hil, let's stop at Dairy Queen on the way home," Dede said. With the radio on as he turned onto South Dixie Highway to head south, Hilton heard the day's first bit of good news: near the end of the first half, the Dolphins were already ahead by fourteen points, thanks to two Marino touchdowns. Colts, zero.

"See? The Dolphins are winning, Jamil," he heard Kaya saying.

Traffic on the three-lane highway was clogged for a Sunday, and Sunday drivers were the worst because they all drove like they were sightseeing or looking for somewhere to have dinner after church. Hilton pulled behind a black hearse in the center lane to try to move faster, but he regretted the move almost immediately. He couldn't see past the hulking vehicle, and this lane was as slow as the last. In fact, the hearse seemed to have slowed purposely. Staring at the white curtains tied neatly in the hearse's back windows, Hilton drummed his fingers against the steering wheel and fought not to curse. He hated traffic, especially at a crawl.

"My drama workshop is going to do a musical," Kaya announced, "and we're going to put it on at a big theater downtown for all the schoolkids. And I'm going to play one of the leads."

"Great. When is that?" Dede said.

Hilton, seeing an opportunity as a red Honda Civic sped past and cleared the fast lane, tried to dart around to the left of the hearse. No luck. The hearse's blinker came on with slow, deliberate flashes, and the vehicle wandered left in front of him, still leading. "Dammit," Hilton whispered. The hearse was hideous to him, an older model with its black paint faded and bubbled from years under the sunlight. It looked as if it could be from the 1960s, and it probably had no business still puttering around.

"Will you stay in one lane?" Dede said.

"I can't see past this thing. I hate that."

"You're already doing the speed limit. Stop tailgating."

Three things happened simultaneously: the radio erupted with cheers as a Dolphins defender picked off a Colts pass bound for the end zone, Jamil laughed because of something Kaya whispered in his ear, and an irate driver somewhere to the right of their car bore down hard on his horn and sustained it until Hilton and Dede turned their heads to see what the commotion was. These things happened in the space of less than two seconds, and Hilton allowed the road to escape his eyes for less time than that.

"Dad, *watch out*."

Instinctively, Hilton planted his foot on the brake. As the car fought to stop, he saw the hearse's rear bearing down on them. He jammed harder on the brake, and the tires screamed and the car began to skid before bucking to a stop.

The jolt threw his family's weight against their seat belts, their arms reaching for anything they could grab, and rapped the top of Hilton's head against the windshield with a loud *thunk* before he was thrown back against his leather seat. *nana won't leave you*

stop running, hilton
is he breathing? lord have mercy

For a moment, sitting inside of the car reeled to a stop on South Dixie Highway, Hilton was aware of everything and nothing. Orange and black shapes danced before his eyes against the sunlight, and his ears were plugged against what sounded vaguely like faraway men's and women's voices. He thought he smelled salty air. Then he smelled the pungence of charred rubber and saw cotton-thin wisps of white smoke rising from his front tires. Everything looked familiar, like something he had known once, but it all felt different. Where was he?

Then he heard the halting voices of his wife, his daughter, and his son, in that order. The radio said the interception was no good because someone was offside, and Dolphins fans were booing. And the thought came, as though it were miraculous: I'm in my car.

Hilton's eyes were riveted to the hearse's back curtains directly ahead of him, the only clear reality. The fabric wasn't white at all, he could see now. The curtains were cut from a faded pattern that might have been pretty once, and they were held in perfectly pleated canopies across the windows by ribbons of a matching pattern. While Hilton studied them, a pale hand appeared in the left window and pulled a curtain away to expose darkness inside. No light was penetrating, it seemed. Then, as distinctly as if the layers of glass from his windshield and the hearse's back window had vanished, a man's head appeared from behind the curtain. He was wearing dark glasses and a black cap, and his face was wan and appeared impatient. He could be any age. The dark glasses stared back at Hilton for what seemed like a long time. Hilton felt beads of perspiration forming at his armpits and his testicles. He thought the man might smile at him, and his stomach curdled as though he would be sick.

how many times

"Hil, are you all right, baby?" Dede asked, her voice in near-panic because she had asked more than once. She touched his cheek.

do you think you can die?

The face in the window was gone, and the hearse's back curtains were drawn. Hilton tried to blink away the electrified shapes tumbling through his vision. He suddenly realized he had a dizzying headache, and he touched the top of his head to see if he was bleeding from the bump.

"I'm fine," he said quickly. Hilton glanced in his rearview mirror at Kaya and Jamil, who were both wide-eyed but didn't seem badly shaken. "The flight crew's okay?"

"A-okay," Jamil said, giving him a thumbs-up.

"Dad, they said in my science class you could have flown through the windshield at forty miles per hour even though the car stopped. Did you know that? A projectile traveling at—"

"Hush, Kaya," Dede said.

Hilton's vision cleared. He snapped the radio off and grasped the steering wheel firmly, replaying the near-crash in his mind. The hearse had stopped at a red light, that was all. He'd looked away from the road. He was lucky no one was hurt. He still felt sick to his stomach. Nerves. Nerves were jumping all around the car. Hilton took a deep breath and attempted a laugh. "Sorry about that," he said.

The hearse began to move. Slowly, cautiously, Hilton raised his foot from the brake and began to follow, straightening the car. As soon as he had a chance, he would change lanes. He didn't want to stare at those curtains and the silent, shadowy man inside.

"Fasten your seat belt," Dede said. "You want to get killed?"

The day, as Hilton had known since that morning, was a complete loss, and his headache was worse. Dede examined his head once they were home and suggested he visit a doctor the next day, but he said he was fine. While Dede began to brown some ground beef for dinner, he overheard Kaya talking to a friend on the kitchen phone: ". . . and then the car stopped just like that, *errrrrrrgggghh*, and Dad bumped his head on the windshield." Jamil was in the living room, leaning across the sofa to stick his finger inside the birdcage so Abbott and Costello could peck seed from his fingertip. He was lost in an eight-year-old's thoughts. Hilton wanted to say something to him, but he didn't know what. He didn't have the energy, not tonight.

And the Dolphins let him down, Hilton found out when he turned on the radio on the living room stereo to hear the final score. The Colts had turned the game around to win, the announcer said, with a final score of 28–13. Twenty-eight to thirteen. It couldn't be. Before downing three Extra-Strength Tylenol and going to bed before dark because of his headache, Hilton called the sports line to check the score again: 28–13. So not only were the Dolphins sorry enough to lose to the Colts at home, they somehow managed to lose their fourteenth point too.

Hilton lay alone in the fading sunlight and tossed fitfully under the sheets for nearly twenty minutes before he could sleep.

CHAPTER 4

The loose gravel crunching beneath his shoes on the unpaved road sounds like finely crushed bones. He walks through a wall of light until he sees the slanted roof of the wooden house, the porch wrapped in vines, two front windows adorned with red sheer curtains. No one is waiting beyond the curtains. He walks past a crippled red wagon to climb the wooden steps, which shudder slightly beneath his weight. The door hangs ajar from a twisted, rusty hinge. Inside, he sees all the things he knows; the old green couch covered with an afghan to hide the threadbare upholstery, mason jars filled with summer flowers, a small wooden table for two polished to a shine behind the couch, the portrait of the white Jesus with cascades of flaxen hair on the wall. He likes this room, but he cannot stay here. He can smell supper burning, and he sees a thin cloud of greasy smoke floating above him. He must go to the kitchen.

He sees a heap of women's clothes on the kitchen floor, with a bulky shape unmoving beneath the tangle of skirts, dresses, and shawls. He kneels and pulls the clothing aside, one article after the other, to disinter whatever lies there. He knows this dress with the interwoven daisies, this white lace shawl, this purple head wrap, this long calico skirt. He lifts the skirt to his face, and he smells talcum powder, bleach, a hint of a lemon fragrance. More hurried now, he casts the clothes aside until the heap shrinks to nearly nothing.

Then he uncovers her face, fat-cheeked and calm, her crown of Seminole-touched gray hair in limp strands across her forehead, eyes closed, lips drawn. She is sleeping. He shakes the heap to try to wake her, but she does not move. He throws the remaining clothes aside and reaches for her arm, but he finds only dry bones that come apart at the joints at his touch. The sleeping head is attached to a pile of dirty, brittle bones collected inside a flowered dress. The head's eyes fly open, and there is nothing inside the eye sockets except holes where he can see through to the back of her skull and its crisscrossing cracks.

He has never run so fast. He flies through the kitchen, past the couch, down the porch steps and stumbles to the unpaved path lined with identical houses as far as he can see in either direction. He bounds up the steps to the porch next door. He should be able to get inside here, but he cannot. He shakes the doorknob, but it is sturdy. He bangs on the door and shouts for someone to let him in. No one comes. He runs to the house across the street and finds the door locked again, and no one answers his cries. The same obstacle waits at house after house stretching down the road. He checks his pockets for keys because he knows he should be able to open these doors, all of them, but his keys are gone. How will he get back home? How will he find the right house? Why will no one let him in?

"...James, J-A-M-E-S ... Hilton, H-I-L-T-O-N, like the hotel ... "

He hears unfamiliar voices but doesn't know where they are coming from. He hears them behind this door, and then the next, and the next, a chorus of unhurried murmurs.

"...black male ... three twelve '56 ... What was wrong with those fuck-up Fins today? ... come mierda ... Up by fourteen zip, and the fucking Colts ... look at this face ... Jesus ... Is this one slice and dice or on ice? ... Check the M.E.'s form ... Shit, this face ... I swear and be damned ... You said you wanted a hamburger, right? ... Very funny, you sick fuck ... "

No voices behind the next door. He tries the doorknob and it clicks open. But this is not his house. The door opens to a long, brightly lit hallway with more doors on either side. He has never been here before, so he knows he is lost.

41

The first door he tries gives in to him. He is in an immaculately clean men's bathroom decorated with potted palms like the ones on his patio. The walls and floors are white and glistening. He walks to a mirror above one of the sinks; there are mirrors behind him as well, so his reflection stares back at him in an infinite assembly of Hiltons.

But no. They're not identical, they're not reflections. A line of men stand there with glowering eyes full of hate. Most of them are spattered in thick, congealed blood from head to foot, but Hilton recognizes his own face on each menacing figure. There are dozens of them. Hundreds.

An eerie rasp floats above him as their lips move simultaneously: "Your time is gone, too. Stop running, Hilton." Hilton stands frozen, blinks to clear his eyes, and stares hard at himself in the mirror. Thank God. The other Hilton figures are gone.

But he has no mouth, he realizes as he glances back at his reflection. This is not his face after all. His brown eyes peer back at him from behind a mass of exposed white bone, caked pinkish brain tissue, and blood-soaked flaps of skin hanging from his jaw like a half-worn Halloween mask.

The sight makes him collapse to the cold floor. The smell of ammonia is nearly overpowering. He closes his eyes to wish himself out of this room, but when he opens them he is still on the floor beneath the sink. He weeps and tries to moan, but again there is no sound.

Behind the polished drainpipe he sees the scrawl of handwriting in black Magic Marker, lone nonsensical graffiti marring the clean wall: unborn seeds of your insidious kind, of monkey-men. *The incomplete thought jars him, makes him shake. This time he is able to scream at last.*

The dreams.

Hilton caught his breath, frozen in bed, listening to the erratic drumbeat pounding inside his chest. His mouth and throat were so dry he had to struggle to swallow. His sheets were wrapped tightly around his feet, binding him like ropes. He touched his face, and his fingertips glided against perspiration. His left cheek was also sore; he'd scratched his face in his sleep somehow. He had been holding his face, clinging to it, when he woke up. That much he remembered.

Dede was gone already, and the morning sun splayed brightly onto the floor from under the patio door's closed venetian blinds. Eight-thirty, he saw after glancing at the bold red numerals on his digital clock. Of course she was gone. She began prosecuting cases at nine most mornings, and her routine wasn't likely to change even after her swearing-in ceremony in January. Dede always joked that as a judge, she wouldn't hear any cases before noon.

The dreams.

With a start Hilton sat up and reached for a pen and a scrap of paper on his nightstand to take notes the way Raul had instructed him during therapy. Already, with each moment of consciousness and the clearing of his mind, the dream seemed as far away as forgotten childhood temper tantrums. He wrote one word, *Nana*, then stared at the word and crossed it out. He couldn't be sure. That was speculation, not memory. He didn't know what images the dream had brought him; he only knew he was still so shaken that his wrist felt weak even now as he tried to write.

Staring at his haggard face in the bathroom mirror, especially his deep brown eyes, Hilton felt a last shiver of uneasiness before he splashed himself with water. Anger and frustration grew in his belly. After confronting memories about Nana and her drowning death, he'd had five years of peaceful sleep. Why would the dreams come back now, when he thought he was free?

He'd been plagued with bad dreams since childhood. Hilton's earliest memories of his life with the Jameses, once he moved in with them in Miami's neat, middle-class black neighborhood of Richmond Heights, was Mrs. James in curlers and her pink housecoat, sitting on the edge of his bed, applying a cold towel to his head and telling him to try to sleep, that she'd keep the dreams away. But she couldn't.

His screams woke up the household. The dreams were at their worst in the beginning, when Nana's death and his living arrangement with these kind strangers in their seemingly palatial home were still new and unfamiliar. His night visitors came in earnest in March, right before his birthday. Bedtime was an ominous thing to Hilton as a child, and not much more welcome when he reached adulthood and no longer believed in vengeful creatures under his bed with gleaming red eyes and an appetite for black children.

In college, he tried friends' tranquilizers and sleeping pills, which only made his dreams worse. He felt more trapped than before, his dreams playing before him unfettered in drug-enhanced colors. So he relied on avoiding sleep, using coffee and NoDoz to force himself to stay awake working on papers or watching vintage late-night television programs like "I Love Lucy" and "The Honeymooners" until his eyelids flickered in a half-sleeping state that left him exhausted by morning but at least allowed him to rest without dreams.

He could never remember them. Sometimes he'd have a feeling of déjà vu during the day, but no solid memories. He mentioned the dreams to Raul Puerta when his individual therapy began after three months of marriage counseling, and the psychologist was fascinated. He was a dream buff, he said.

"Your unconscious is speaking to you in a language you cannot understand," Puerta said with his deliberate accent, which sounded almost lyrical to Hilton after the passage of time. "As soon as you wake up, write down what you can remember about them, anything at all."

This exercise was a failure until that March, near his birthday, when the dreams increased in frequency and intensity. He began to wake up to find his own handwriting scrawled on the notepad beside him, notes written hastily before he blinked to full wakefulness. Usually, he had written one or two words: *Choking. Water. Running.* Then he saw a new word: *Nana.* When he read it, he nearly dropped the notebook.

"What is this Nana?" Puerta asked during Hilton's excited telephone call, which caught the therapist having his early-morning *café con leche* at his desk before his first client arrived.

"That's what I used to call my grandmother. I haven't thought about that term in years. The Jameses always called her Grandma Kelly, so I did too. Now, all of a sudden, this word pops back."

"Do you remember the dream?"

"No, no, of course not. But seeing this paper made me remember something. I think . . . I think that when I was young, I was afraid of her."

"Did she beat you? Mistreat you?"

"Nothing like that. It was a childish fear, a sinister fear. I'm not sure why. I think it had something to do with sleeping. Maybe it's just Nana in my dreams, coming back. And I remember something else about her."

"Go on. No need for suspense."

"I think Nana used to have bad dreams too."

It wasn't much, but to Hilton, whose memories before his life with the Jameses had become so fuzzy they were nearly nonexistent, it was a breakthrough. He was so excited that day, he could barely concentrate at work. He couldn't understand why Raul insisted on waiting another two full days until their scheduled appointment to talk it out. Hilton had begun to rely on his therapy, he realized. And maybe it was finally beginning to make a difference.

The road was not as easy as he had hoped, however. After his initial flashes of Nana's memory, the bulk of her remained unfocused. He could frame her face a bit; the straight white hair (the Jameses had told him she was half Seminole), her jowls, her skin so leathery and etched with lines, so different from his. But there was little else, and the more difficult the memories were to grasp, the more convinced he was that Nana held secrets that could unlock some of his.

After a month or so, Puerta suggested hypnosis, and Hilton

was skeptical. "What are you going to do, wave your wrist-watch in front of my face?" he asked.

"No, I don't need props," Puerta said. "This is a hobby of mine. I can induce a hypnotic trance with my voice alone. If you are indeed blocking as much as you say, hypnosis might help. We may also see if it can help you remember your dreams."

Hilton hesitated, telling him he would think about it until their next session. As much as he wanted to remember the woman who had raised him until she died saving his life, he wasn't sure he wanted to remember his dreams. Their clutch on him seemed to transcend his sleeping state, bringing fears he could nearly touch even while awake. On the worst nights, he would wake up and find he had soaked through his pajamas in a cold sweat. He'd been surrounded by sights, smells, and sounds that were so real they weren't like dreams at all. He didn't want to go back to that place under hypnosis or any other time, if he could help it.

The first time, he had trouble relaxing, so Raul couldn't hypnotize him properly. The next couple of times, he couldn't coax Hilton to recall any details about his dreams even in a hypnotic trance, although he'd dreamed each night before. Finally, while Hilton was under hypnosis, Raul asked him about Nana.

"She's waiting for me," Hilton had said. Listening to his own voice on Raul's cassette player later, he marveled at how much he sounded like himself, yet he couldn't recall their conversation.

"Where is she waiting?"

"At the house. We live on Douglass Road, and I'm late. She don't like it when I be late." (Hilton cringed, listening later. Under hypnosis, he'd lapsed into the childhood grammatical habits the Jameses worked diligently to pound out of his head. Instead of a professional Miami man, he was once again a countrified child).

"Tell me about Nana, Hilton."

"She's old."

"What else?"

Long pause. "Wait, I'm 'a go find her. I think she's in the kitchen. She always be in there cooking."

"Well, then, go find her for me."

Longer pause. On the cassette, Hilton heard his voice lower to nearly a hush. "She's laying on the floor. She ain't moving. Maybe she fainted, 'cause it's so hot in here. I wonder how come it's so hot in here."

"Did Nana faint?" Raul asked. Hilton sucked in his breath hard but didn't speak. "What's wrong with Nana, Hilton?"

"Nana's dead," he said in a tight voice.

"Are you at the beach now?"

"No, in the kitchen. She on the floor, she ain't moving. And when I touch her . . . ."

"What happens when you touch her?" No answer. Raul waited a moment, then repeated the question patiently. "Tell me, Hilton."

"She feel cold. Her skin feel cold, and hard. Her arm don't move up when I pull on it. She don't feel like Nana. She dead now. I got to go get help. Nana's dead now. She dead."

"Where can you get help?"

"I'm 'a run down the street, but ain't nobody home. Nobody's home but that mean man on the end who likes to beat on little kids, but I got to find somebody. So he comes with me. He comes with me when I say Nana dead."

"What does he do?"

"He don't do nothing."

"Why not?" Raul asked him.

"Cause Nana ain't dead no more."

Raul clicked off the cassette and looked at Hilton, whose breaths were shallow after listening to his childhood memories recited back at him. This was a creepy feeling to him, tampering with his past, and he didn't like it. The words on the tape chilled him, as though he'd awakened from one of his dreams.

"There's more," Raul said, "but nothing is very informative after this point. We can try it again some other time. I must

47

say, your hypnotic recollection is remarkable. Do you remember these incidents now?"

Hilton shook his head. "Not yet. I do remember an old Korean War veteran down the street who used to beat kids with a switch for no reason, even if they just knocked on his door . . . " He paused. Where had that come from?

"I suspect that it will begin to come back to you," Raul said, unable to conceal his satisfied smile at the session's progress.

"That's fine for you, man," Hilton said, "but I'm not sure I want it to come back to me after hearing all that."

"Oh, come now," Raul coaxed. "A child's misunderstanding. Your grandmother's skin was probably clammy after she fainted, and you believed she was dead. It's understandable you would be surprised to find her conscious when you returned. She then became a ghost to you, and perhaps that's why you learned to fear her."

Hilton's fingertips tingled as though they were being dipped in icy water. He clamped back his thoughts because he didn't know how they would sound to Raul: what he had felt with his child's hands so long ago wasn't clammy skin, it was flesh as lifeless as rubber. There had been no misunderstanding. Nana was dead that day. He'd known as a child, and he knew it now.

He understood then why he had buried her memory. He decided that although he would try to remember all he could about his childhood during his therapy, he would not agree to further hypnosis. It was best not to search for something he wasn't prepared to find.

CHAPTER 5

"Mr. James, we have a problem."

This greeting had replaced good mornings at the Miami New Day Recovery Center when Hilton arrived each day. The center's twenty-eight-bed expansion was a chaos of transferring addicts to new sleeping quarters and coordinating plans with the contractor, who was to begin work next week. All this, and the last grant from the city wouldn't be approved until the next afternoon's commission meeting. And Hilton had dealt with government enough to know never to count on cash until it was in the bank.

His assistant director, a beefy and excitable young Muslim brother named Ahmad, blocked the doorway to Hilton's office with his six-foot-four bulk. "The newspaper is on the phone," Ahmad went on, "and that's not the worst of it. Some citizens council is all stirred up, saying they're going to the commission tomorrow to protest the expansion."

"They're protesting now?" Hilton asked, taking a pile of messages from his secretary's desk. Wanda, who was talking to a caller on her telephone headset, looked up at him with a smile, shrugging. "There isn't a residential neighborhood in a mile's radius of this place," Hilton pointed out.

"You know that. I know that," Ahmad said, stepping aside so Hilton could toss his worn leather briefcase on top of his desk. "The newspaper wants a comment. I said we have to clear all comments with you."

Hilton considered it a moment, longing for a second cup of coffee. "Wait. I've got something better. Tell the reporter to come here at—" He flipped through his schedule book, finding it crammed with tasks for the day. "One-thirty. I'll give them a tour of this place and show them what we do."

"Have you seen the facility today?" Ahmad asked, hesitant.

"You all just have to get it straight, and we'll explain we're doing some relocating. You've got four hours."

"Yes, sir," Ahmad said, always eager for impossible tasks, which was a prerequisite in this field.

"I've warned you about that 'sir' business. I ain't your damn daddy," Hilton called after him, feigning anger.

"Sure sound like him, though," Ahmad shot back.

Miami New Day operated with an award-winning format; the semiprivate center split its eighty beds for men and women between homeless addicts and paying clients who couldn't afford pricier hospitals or who were willing to give up frills for results. The center was created in 1972 with a trust fund from a Miami Beach socialite whose son died from a drug overdose, and who blamed his death on a lack of treatment facilities. In her will she set aside more than a million dollars to get Miami New Day running; the center still relied on dividend checks from investments made by its original board of directors, but it also received public funds because it took referrals from the state social service agency.

A client had committed suicide ten years before, but the center had run relatively free of tragedy since then. Only a small fraction of clients returned to Miami New Day after their treatment ended, and counselors provided follow-up visits to make sure they stayed clean. More and more clients, men and women, were turning up infected with the HIV virus, however. More than once, Hilton had attended the spare funeral service of a former client who kicked a drug habit in time to get sick and die. Their brief, troubled passages made Hilton wonder if some souls weren't born doomed to misery.

Since his appointment as director by the board three years before, Hilton had gained a reputation for cleaning house. He knew which counselors still had a genuine commitment and which were merely putting in time for their paychecks, and he had no patience for the latter. He'd replaced four staff members and brought in Ahmad from the state agency. He did so despite reservations from the board, because they'd worked well together, Ahmad himself was a former addict, and he worked long hours to do any job right.

Hilton had high standards but didn't have the budget to pay well, so he tried to compensate by making the working conditions pleasant; his staff had a carpeted lounge with a microwave oven and vending machines, he allowed them to work flexible hours, and the center had weekly staff meetings so that no problem could go too long undiscussed. Hilton let his staffers know they weren't alone in their battles; since he had experience as a counselor, he spent much of his time working with the clients, learning their names and gaining their trust. One thing marriage counseling instilled in Hilton was a compulsion for open communication. Whether at home or at work, he knew that anything left unsaid was far more dangerous than spoken words could be, no matter how hurtful. His staffers joked that if the coffee machine was broken, he would call a meeting to discuss how they felt about it.

In his search for more coffee, Hilton found the staff lounge empty except for the white-coated back of Dr. Stu Rothchild, a physician who had worked at Miami New Day two days a week for several years. Stu was Hilton's age, in his late thirties, completely bald at the top of his head but with bright red hair everywhere else, extending to his face in a matching beard. Stu always played Santa Claus at the center's Christmas party for addicts and their families because with powder in his hair he was a ringer. He greeted children with a twinkle in his eyes and an inside joke: "Shalom. Merry Christmas." Hilton heard Stu muttering about the lack of decaf when he sat at the table.

"What's this rumor I hear about somebody protesting us?" Stu asked. "Are they going to have a sit-in and march around the building singing 'We Shall Overcome'?"

"Who the hell knows?" Hilton said. "Man, I don't even want to talk about it. I hope this doesn't fuck up our grant."

"I don't see why money is a problem. You should have plenty of campaign contributions left over," Stu said, joining Hilton at the table with a smile. Stu was Hilton's closest friend at the center and as a result knew best how to provoke him.

Hilton glared. "I know that's a joke. We spent our savings on that campaign. Good thing the kids don't have any crazy ideas about going to college."

Stu squeezed Hilton's hand affectionately. "I'm pulling your leg, boss. A little levity."

"Yeah. Very little."

Stu sipped his coffee, then kneaded his freckled forehead as though he had a headache. "I do have some bad news, though, since you're here. About Antoinette."

Antoinette was sixteen, and she'd been fifteen when she came to Miami New Day to try to kick her crack cocaine habit. Stu tested all new clients for the HIV virus; this girl's results came back positive, and Stu diagnosed her with early symptoms of AIDS. The slight teenager's face didn't change when he told her, and she calmly announced she'd like to stay and get clean. That was all she wanted. Her boyfriend had died the month before, and he finally confessed in the hospital that he had AIDS, she said. He didn't like condoms, so she'd been sleeping with him for two years without them. The amazing thing was, Stu told Hilton later, she said it without a trace of anger in her voice. Antoinette was slightly thinner and with shorter hair than Kaya, but her sweet nature and intelligence reminded Hilton of his daughter.

"I don't want to hear this," Hilton said.

Stu nodded, glassy-eyed. "She's back at Jackson Memorial with fluid in her lungs. She may pull through it again, but there's not much they can do except keep trying to drain them because there's so much tissue damage. I stopped by to see her yesterday, and her uncle is still being a prick. She's not getting any visitors, not a card, no flowers. It'll break your heart, this kid in a hospital room by herself with four walls to stare at all day, not knowing if she'll live or die."

"I'll post a notice to let the counselors know," Hilton said, and he cleared his throat to regain his voice. He would never get used to seeing kids dying. Never. "You think I can hold off for two more days? I probably can't make it there until Saturday."

"I'll warn you if I think she's deteriorating."

Hilton didn't speak for a second, and Stu simply stirred his coffee. "Goddammit," Hilton said finally.

Despite Dede's cautioning, Hilton ended up involved in his clients' lives outside of the center; he'd found himself helping Danitra move into her new apartment Saturday because one of his counselors couldn't make it and Hilton didn't want her stuck trying to move by herself. Now, this weekend, Antoinette.

"Just go when you have time," Stu said. "You can't save the world all by yourself. And you're not looking well yourself, Hil."

"No?"

"You're wearing some mean bags under your eyes."

"Oh, yeah," Hilton said, still preoccupied with thoughts of Antoinette. "I haven't been sleeping much this week."

"Well, you know my spiel on that," Stu said. "You can't take care of anyone else if you're not taking care of yourself. Right?"

Hilton smiled at his friend. "Okay. Right. Now, lay off."

By four-thirty Hilton was several hours behind in his work. Between the reporter's tour, inquiries from his contractor, and attempts to reach the mayor for reassurances, much of the paperwork he had planned to read that day, including a grant proposal that needed to be postmarked by morning, was still untouched on his desk. While he was on his telephone holding for the contractor, Ahmad walked into his office and dropped a new stack of papers in front of him. "A petition," Ahmad said, turning to walk out. "Next we'll be getting threatening phone calls." Hilton scanned the blur of signatures.

your herd won't live

On impulse, he raised his eyes and locked them on the framed family portrait before him on his desk. His family posed for a new photo each summer because the children changed so much each year, so this one was barely three months old; they all looked exactly as they had last weekend at the park, except that they were all smiling in front of a hokey meadowland backdrop. *unborn seeds*

Gazing at his family huddled together, their round faces and smiles, Dede's hand on his knee, Kaya and Jamil side by side, Hilton felt a searing sadness, a claw at his insides. He sat up straight in his chair, hung up on the contractor's office, then dialed Dede's number.

"Sorry, Hil. She's away from her desk."

"Is she gone for the day already? Is she in court?"

"She was just here. I think she's in the powder room."

Hilton knew that if he didn't leave a message with the secretary now, he would forget as he had all week. "Just tell her to remember to bring home that letter she mentioned last weekend."

"Oh, that nutty one?" the woman laughed. Hilton couldn't remember this woman's name, although he'd dealt with her for years. He wanted to tell her there was nothing funny about it, and that only his friends could feel free to call him Hil. Most of all, he was annoyed Dede had shown the letter to her office as a joke.

"The one with the threats," Hilton said patiently.

"No problem, Hil. I'll leave a note on her desk."

CHAPTER 6

Hilton lived at the end of a cul-de-sac just east of the boundary—and accompanying higher property taxes—of courtly Coral Gables, on a street where even at midday ficus trees and live oaks blanketed everything beneath them in shade. His house was bordered from the street by a waist-high wall built thirty years before from pure coral rock that had turned brown and crumbled slightly, and the house had coral-rock arches at the end of the path leading through the yard to the front door. Bougainvillea hedges with bouquets of pink blossoms grew against the house like a crown of colors.

They'd never have afforded the four-bedroom house with its Spanish-tile roof, swimming pool, and polished wooden floors if the old widow selling it hadn't liked his family instantly. She couldn't keep her fingers from pinching Kaya's cheeks, which made Dede tense because she recoiled when she believed whites were treating her children like objects of amusement. But this woman was sincere, if a little conde-scending, and the house had them enchanted, so Dede held her tongue.

The woman told them how happy she was to see a fine young black family, how she'd been brought up by a black nanny in Virginia, how she'd always hired blacks to clean for her and became such good friends with them, how her husband had marched with Martin Luther King. "I know you all think I'm a silly old fool," the woman had said, tears glisten-ing in her rheumy eyes, "but I know what struggle is all about. If Aaron were alive today to see you here, he'd be tick-led pink. Tell me what you think you can pay, and let's talk about a price."

Now, after dark, the bright solar lamp Hilton had installed soon after they moved in cast a surreal light over the house and painted shadows from tree limbs and leaves across the walls. Through the living room draperies he could see the blue glow of the television set. Dede's Audi was already parked in the gravel driveway; Hilton pulled up behind it and sat a moment in an awe-inspiring solitude in which even the crickets didn't stir. He broke the spell by opening his car door and slamming it shut.

Jamil cornered him to talk about his after-school soccer game while Hilton sat at the small kitchen table and wolfed down leftover African beef stew, which Dede made with a taste of peanut butter for flavor. (He'd balked when he first heard the recipe, but he'd loved eating it since the first time he tried it.) Then it was time for "The Simpsons," so Jamil excused himself to watch television after assuring Hilton he had finished his homework and had left it on the kitchen counter for inspection. Hilton didn't hear a fight about which child would watch the big TV in the living room and who would have to go to Kaya's room, unusual for a Thursday.

"This stew is something else, my queen," Hilton said to Dede, standing to kiss her when she wandered into the kitchen wearing a loose-fitting African housedress and a casual head wrap. This was her time for freedom; she never wore African clothes in court or at her office.

"Did you see the rice Kaya made on the stove?"

Hilton patted his stomach, which was taut from overeat-ing. "It's right down here. Where's Kaya tonight? Rehearsal?" When Dede sat at the table and looked at him with a search-ing smile, Hilton expected news of the rape case she'd been arguing for weeks. "A verdict?" he asked.

Dede shook her head. "More important," she said. "Kaya got her period today."

Hilton stood still, aware that his face must be frozen in a comical expression of bewilderment. "Already?" he asked.

"She's thirteen, Hil. All her friends got theirs by last year, so thank God she finally did. You know how children hate to be different."

Hilton sank back into his chair. In the short time since they'd lived in their new house, Kaya had grown from ten to thirteen, and what an immense difference that small journey made—the difference between "Daddy" and "Dad," and now the difference between a tree-climbing child and an appearance-conscious young woman biologically equipped to make a new life herself.

"I see you getting misty over there," Dede teased. "We went through the same thing on her birthday. She's a teenager now."

"How's she doing?"

"She's nauseated and a little shy about you and Jamil, so she's doing her homework on the patio. She had a little accident at school, but I told her it's nothing. A spot of blood on her dress, and I'm sure no one noticed except her friend."

"You womenfolk catch hell coming and going, don't you?"

Dede laughed ruefully. "Coming and going. That's right."

Hilton picked up a newspaper and walked through the kitchen's French doors to the east end of the patio. Its paved pebbles glistened in the moonlight, and reflections from the lighted pool swam everywhere in shimmering designs. The screened-in patio was a man-made jungle, with palms lined against the screen and air plants clinging to trellises. The wispy, spiderlike air plants fascinated Hilton with their ability to thrive without soil or real roots. They were so odd, so heroic.

He saw Kaya sitting at the white wrought-iron patio table at the opposite end, furiously at work on an essay. She wore her permed hair in two long ponytails that rested against her shoulders, a hint of Nana's ancestry, and she still looked quite childlike to him at that moment.

Gingerly, as he always did, Hilton walked to the table at a

careful distance from the edge of the pool. Water. He wouldn't have purposely sought a house with a swimming pool, but he couldn't bring himself to sour the deal on the house after it had won Dede's heart. And it was glorious; thirty yards long, eight feet deep at its deepest end, with elaborate, Roman-style steps leading to the shallow end. Black tile spelled out in four-foot letters the name D-E-E at the pool's bottom, the previous owner's tribute to his wife; Hilton was amused by the similarity to Dede's name, and he usually told visitors that workmen had misspelled *Dede* when the pool was built. The coincidence was nearly uncanny.

The few times Hilton had been coaxed into the pool, he felt a gripping lethargy when he held his breath and plunged below the surface. His limbs grew heavy, frozen, and he invariably ended up choking on the chlorinated water. As though something intended to keep him there. Dede told him it was psychological, but Hilton was convinced it was more than that. Like that day on the beach, with the undertow. It was best to keep his distance from the pool.

"Hey," Hilton said, taking the chair beside Kaya's.

She didn't look up or stop writing. "Hey."

He struggled a moment with words, then exhaled. "So your mom told me about your little adventure at school today."

Kaya rolled her eyes theatrically. "Great. She's already called everybody else in the world and told them."

"I'm not everybody else in the world, you know. I'm your dad. No secrets, remember?"

She looked at him as though she couldn't imagine a more foolish statement from an adult's lips. "You're a guy, Dad. Guys don't like to hear about this stuff."

He was silent a moment, acknowledging her point. The less he had to know about menstruation, whether Dede's or Kaya's or anyone else's, the better. "Right. But you didn't mind me being a guy when we built that treehouse, or when we used to go to ball games. Remember? The only Dolphin Jamil knew about was that damn Flipper. So it was just you and me. No secrets."

"Yeah, yeah . . . "

They hadn't attended any ball games lately, and the days of treehouse-building were long past, Hilton thought. He'd been fifteen when he lost his virginity, only two years older than Kaya. Soon she'd be showing up at the door with hormone-crazed young punks with their arms around her waist and their minds inside her pants, just the way he'd been when he charmed his girlfriends' parents with his smile and erudite conversation. Hilton and Dede had believed in frank sex education from the time their children were old enough to ask questions, but this would be new territory. Yes, the time for secrets had begun now. Secrets were the first wall between parents and children. Children, in the end, were only adults in disguise.

"You feeling okay?" Hilton asked.

"My stomach hurts some. I hope I won't have PMS like Mom," she said, and they both laughed. "Don't tell her I said that."

"I won't, princess," he said. "Listen, Kaya, I know you've got a busy schedule with drama workshop and the mall and your friends, but why don't we do something this weekend?"

Again, that look like he was crazy. "Like what?"

"Well, we could go to a movie. We could go horseback riding . . . " Kaya sighed, so he went on quickly: "Or not. You pick something. Just a couple of hours."

"You're not going to talk to me about sex, are you?"

"Not the whole time, no."

"Dad . . . " she said, turning her attention back to her homework.

He reached over to take her pen to prevent her from writing. "No, I'm being for real, Kaya. Let's do something Saturday. We'll do any movie you want."

Kaya looked at him questioningly a moment, but he knew she understood. Yeah, I love you too, Dad, she said with her soft brown eyes. I didn't mean to grow up so fast, it just happened like that. Now leave me alone so I can do my work. "Okay," she said.

‍（

Sorry, the dispatcher apologized for the third time, Sergeant Curt Gillis hadn't been raised on his radio yet. He was doing a night shift at the projects, and he might not return his messages for several hours. Was it an emergency?

Hilton paused. He wanted to say yes, it was an emergency, but how could he? Curt was in the thick of crack dens and drug busts, and Hilton was calling from the serenity of his bedroom near the City Beautiful. "Just tell him to please call me when he gets a chance," Hilton sighed.

He'd been about ready to go to bed, even contemplating back rubs with Dede to help them both relieve stress, when she found him in the bathroom and gave him a single piece of paper. "Here it is. I didn't forget," she said.

Now, after hanging up the phone, Hilton sat in the bedroom easy chair beneath the light of an upright lamp with the letter in his lap. Once again, he raised the folded paper with its perforated edges to read the words that had ruined his night:

> Am I to believe it is mere coincidence they sent an African-coon-tarbaby-nigggger-American bitch to persecute me? And you, the child of Ham's clans, marked by Satan himself, beholding me with contempt and irreverence, your insides raging with unborn seeds of your insidious kind, of monkey-men?
>
> Do you believe I'm only a monkey, too, adept at the art of mimicry? You are wrong, sadly wrong. You and your herd won't live to mock me further, nor will your offspring ever grow up to taint and murder mine.

"Don't keep reading that, Hil. You'll just make yourself crazy," Dede said from where she lay in bed. "I can't have you sitting up there with that light on, baby. I have cross-ex with my rapist tomorrow, and it's late."

Hilton's eyes were glued to the neat words on the computer printout. The paper was a high grade, and the printer of superior quality. Those might be the only clues; there would be no hope of lifting fingerprints from this, since so many had touched it before now. "You don't know how much I wish you'd kept the envelope."

"It may be on my desk somewhere, but I'm afraid it might have gotten tossed," Dede said in a small voice. "There was no return address, I remember, because I looked. It was post-marked from central Florida somewhere. Maybe it's from the Raiford prison."

Yes, Hilton, thought, he hoped to God it was from the prison. But would they allow an inmate to send a letter like this? Perhaps it was smuggled out. Or perhaps the sender was a free man walking around who had casually slipped it into a streetside mailbox.

"He's dangerous. He's sick, and he's dangerous."

Dede exhaled slowly. "I just didn't want to confront it, you know? I think that's why I made a joke out of it. I have to deal with ugliness fifty hours a week, like that scum now who's on his way to convincing the jury a sixty-year-old woman is lying about getting raped. I didn't want to bring it home with me. I didn't want it to touch you or Kaya or Jamil."

"It does touch us, Dede," Hilton said, his eyes traveling across line after line of the hateful words. Each time he read it, he was stunned by the menace presented so calmly, so professionally. The sender had even spelled her name correctly in the greeting: Mrs. Dede James, Attorney-at-Law.

"I know. That's why we're not in the book," Dede said.

"People can find you when they really want to. I don't have to tell you that. And he knows you have children—that's what I don't like."

Dede chuckled into her pillow. "Shoot, Hil, you know folks figure all of us black women have babies. He doesn't know. And what makes you so sure it's a man? Could be a woman."

No, Hilton thought. It was a man, without a doubt. And as much as he wanted to believe it was from a lifer at Raiford, he also knew the man was free. He was free, and he was close.

"Turn the light off, Hil," Dede said.

After a moment, Hilton reached up to turn off the floor lamp, leaving the room in darkness. He sat in the chair, the letter still in his hands, and waited for the telephone to ring. He could hear the bathroom sink dripping intermittently, then the click and hum of the central air-conditioning unit. These were sounds he had grown used to in his nightly flight from sleep. Soon he would hear Dede's breaths slow until they were long and deep, interrupted by occasional snores.

Hilton wondered why it was so dark until he remembered no one had turned on the floodlights outside to brighten the patio. He stood and fumbled for the switch beside the venetian blinds, glancing through the sliding glass door. There, outside, he saw a light above the pool. Not the electric lights controlled by the panel; he saw a murky, phosphorescent gray-green mist that appeared to be rising from the pool like steam.

Hilton's hand froze above the light switch as he pressed his nose to the door, not breathing. What the hell—

A woman. She seemed to be hovering above the pool. But no. She was standing ankle-deep on the surface of the glowing water, hands at her sides, returning his gaze. The dim light made the lines of her face look harsh, etched in charcoal. She wore a patterned dress, flowers. Her straight hair was silver, fine, whipping gently around her face in an unseen breeze. Hilton felt his head and chest swelling. Nana.

Instinctively, he flicked on all three light switches and flooded the patio with beams from all sides. Now, the pool blazed with a white light beneath the still surface, the manmade light he recognized. The mist, the woman, were gone.

Jesus. He was hallucinating. He'd spooked himself thinking about that letter, sitting in the dark. His limbs feeling weak, Hilton retreated to the chair and sat listening to his amplified heartbeat. He would still be in the chair two hours later, wide awake, when Curt finally called and Hilton recited the letter to him from memory.

"Damn," was all Curt could say. He offered none of his

usual jokes, and he sounded tired from his shift. "Yeah, man, bring that to me at the station tomorrow. I'm on at four. I'll have one of the plainclothes look at it."

"This scares the shit out of me, Curt," Hilton said, his voice low so Dede could drift back to sleep. And seeing my dead grandmother stroll across the swimming pool, he thought.

"Don't sweat it, man. It might not be anything."

"But be honest: It sounds like something, doesn't it?"

"I'll tell you what, I've never heard nothing like that," Curt said. "But, hey, it's probably a whole lot of bullshit, some crazy cracker blowing steam. Now get your ass to sleep. Some of us have work to do."

CHAPTER 7

The child's desk he sits in is too small for him, and his knees feel cramped. Afternoon light pours through all the classroom's rows of open jalousie windows, so everything around him is sharp and focused. He can read every state on the This Is Our U.S.A. *map hanging above the teacher's pinewood desk, he can see his classmates' names from the week's best drawings posted on the walls. Mrs. Robertson's bouncy, feminine script covers the chalkboard with words spelled in syllables:* di-no-saur, hur-ri-cane, cre-ma-tion. *The date, she has written, is May 1963.*

Mrs. Robertson is not in the classroom. He thinks everyone is gone until he notices a little pigtailed girl three rows ahead of him, who raises her hand and stands up although there is no one to call on her. She begins to recite the state capitals breathlessly, one after the other, facing the chalkboard.

He sees a spot of blood the size of a nickel on the back of the girl's beautiful taffeta dress, so he tries to whisper to her. "Pssssst," he says. "Hey, little girl."

She ignores him. She has reached Tallahassee, Florida, and Atlanta, Georgia, in her recitation.

"Hey, girl, you're bleeding," he says, more loudly this time, and she stops and whirls around. Kaya is wearing lilac ribbons in her hair that match her dress, and she looks lovely.

"You're bleeding, honey," he says.

Surprised and embarrassed, Kaya presses her palm to her chest. "Daddy?" she says, as though she can't see him. When she moves her hand away from her chest, blood has seeped through the fabric to leave a perfect palm print in bright red.

"Jesus, Kaya, you're bleeding," he says, alarmed now.

She gazes down the front of her dress, where blood is soaking from her chest in spots that grow and darken, creeping down to the belt tied around her abdomen, the fabric sagging beneath the liquid weight. He can smell the hot, coppery scent now; the air in the room is heavy with it. The front of her dress is drenched in red-black, dripping from the hem to a small puddle on the floor. Kaya watches her dress with wide, unblinking eyes. She screams and stamps her feet in panic, then screams again and shakes her foot when she steps in the sticky puddle. "Dad-deeee . . . " she sobs.

He stands and tries to hold her, to touch her, but he cannot. He can only watch her frantically try to brush the blood away, clawing at her dress in a dazed wonderment. "Daddy, help me," she sobs, choking. "Dad-deeeee!"

He has no voice. Still screaming, a wounded sound that shreds his soul, Kaya runs past him through the classroom doorway, and a heavy door slams shut behind her. He tries to open it, and it is stuck at first; when he finally pulls it free of the frame, he stumbles into darkness. He can still hear Kaya's cries in the distance, winding away from him. He calls for her, his own voice strained from sobs.

The darkness nearly paralyzes him in its vast emptiness, numbing his reason. He could stop fighting, he realizes, and simply float into the darkness. He is so weary he feels pain in his joints when he tries to move, but each time he considers surrender he hears Kaya's frantic, frightened cries ahead, closer than the last time. Daddy is coming, he says in a choked whisper. Daddy won't leave you alone.

He bumps into new doors and struggles to open each one; each leads to darkness more complete, more enveloping than the last. He is breathing in gasps now. The darkness is as dense as liquid, and he cannot breathe at all. He is drowning in it. He is drowning.

Finally, he heaves his weight against a door that opens freely, momentarily blinding him. He is on his patio, and now he can see the brightness glowing from the green floodlights. He recog-

nizes the potted palms and air plants, each in their proper place. Kaya is hunched over the white wrought-iron table, her back facing him.

Yes, now I remember, he thinks.

"Hey," he says, and she does not answer. Then he notices the unmistakable dripping beneath her chair, feeding a blood puddle that is growing and snaking its way toward the swimming pool. Even the pool's lapping waters are tinged with red, bubbling and hissing in a mist. He runs to Kaya to hold her.

Kaya's cheeks are sunken in a death mask, her skin frightfully pale and paper-thin. Her shriveled arms cradle a package wrapped in brown paper and tied neatly with twine. The box is addressed to him with a bright red marker in a handwriting he believes he knows. He nearly collapses to his knees when he sees the package, and he lunges to try to take it, but he can't wrestle it from her grip. Her open eyes are lifeless, her irises glazed and clouded white.

From nowhere, an unseen hand wraps itself around Hilton's throat, gently at first, but then seizing him so tightly that all air is blocked, siphoned out of him. He feels himself shrinking to nothing. He cannot move to see whose hand it is, and he is powerless to fight. "Hey, bro," says a voice he will know soon. "I'm afraid I don't know nothing about birthing no babies."

Hilton can see nothing now except darkness that grows steadily more dense as the last of his air seeps away. The hand won't free him. He is drowning again, in blackness. "Help us, Daddy," Kaya pleads in a voice that belongs to the dead.

Hilton felt a warm hand on his forearm, and he jolted to wakefulness with a cry to fling it away.

"Hilton, what's wrong? Wake up."

Dede's voice. He sat up straight on the living room's leather couch, clutching the armrest as he gasped deeply to breathe. His heartbeat pulsed hard from his neck's carotid artery, and he could feel his chest constricting. He glanced at the snow flickering on the screen of the television set, then the faint light creeping through the front window's curtains.

Dede's African masks, crafted from wood and leather, glared at him from the walls as though they could leap down. Dede was bent over him, her face shiny and puffed from sleep. It took him time to realize Dede was talking to him.

"What?" he asked, still trying to catch his breath.

"You looked like you stopped breathing," Dede repeated. She pressed her palm to his chest, where she could feel his heartbeat. "My Lord, Hil. It's like what happens to babies. Remember what the pediatrician said that time? When we're sleeping, we sometimes forget to breathe. Most people wake up when that happens, but sometimes infants don't. You didn't wake up, not until I came."

Hilton stared at Dede, riveted by her moving lips and her words that seemed to follow a split second after. "We're always closest to death when we're asleep," he mumbled. "You know that."

"What?" Dede asked, her eyes widening.

Suddenly, as his mind began to clear, Hilton couldn't remember exactly what he had said to her or why. He'd felt such a certainty before, with that voice that didn't even sound like his own, but now the words fluttered in his ears like nonsense.

"You're not awake yet," Dede said finally.

"A . . . a bad dream," he said hoarsely. "What time is it?"

"I don't know, something before six," she whispered. "Get up and come to bed, Hil. You're going to wake the children out here. I could hear you all the way across the house."

Hilton nodded, wiping perspiration from his face with both hands while he sat up, but he didn't move to stand just yet. He always needed a brief time for readjustment, to remind himself that whatever horror he'd seen in his sleep wasn't real, that he had escaped it. Again, vague scents and sights seemed to linger around him, waiting to lash out.

dad-deeee

"Where's Kaya?" he asked, his voice still strained.

Dede didn't hear him, or she ignored the question as the

mumblings of someone only half-awake. She smoothed her hand across the top of his closely cropped hair, a soothing massage.

"How long have they been back?" she asked.

Hilton blinked several times. He hadn't wanted to tell her about the dreams, thinking if he didn't, they might vanish again. The truth was, they seemed worse each night; and his birthday, when they were usually at their worst, was still four months away, in March. He sighed and sank back against the couch's softness, which earlier had betrayed him and lulled him to sleep. "About a week," he said.

"Like before?" she asked.

He nodded. Dede turned the television set off, then sat beside him on the sofa and tapped her fingers against his thigh. Abbott and Costello were stirring beneath the bedsheet draped over their birdcage, fussing softly at each other. "I don't like it when you dream," Dede said. "It reminds me of a bad time. I don't want that again."

He kissed her nose. "It won't ever be like that again."

"You can't go without sleep, Hil. I wondered why you'd been staying up so late. It's been so long, at least five years. I never even thought—"

"Maybe it's stress, or I'm just worried about that letter we gave to Curt. I hope so."

Dede hesitated. "Do you think you should—"

He squeezed her knee, then stood up. His legs felt unhinged, waterlogged. "I promised Raul a Heat game sometime next week," he said, reading her mind. "I'll bring it up when I see him."

"I hope you will. Or maybe a regular doctor. The way you breathe when you sleep has always worried me," she said.

Hilton started to follow her down the hallway toward their bedroom, but he paused when he saw the sliding glass door leading from the family room to the green-lighted patio. He turned and padded back to the living room, then to the hallway that led to the study, Jamil's bedroom, and then Kaya's.

Her door was nearly closed, but it was still ajar. He pushed it open slowly, careful not to allow the hinge to creak. Kaya's walls were plastered with posters of her favorite television and rap stars, and the clothes she had worn the previous day were thrown across the back of a chair. All that was visible of her in the mound beneath her blankets was a single ponytail. He wanted to touch the mound, to see his daughter's face, but he dismissed the urge as irrational. No reason to wake her. She was there, just as he'd known she would be. Whatever poison had touched him from his dream was poison in his mind only, and it had no potency in the safety of his home.

Still, his pounding heartbeat hadn't slowed. Just dreams, he reminded himself, and he gently tugged the door to his daughter's bedroom until it clicked shut.

CHAPTER 8

Jackson Memorial Hospital, a sprawling drab-colored complex wedged along busy streets near the expressway in northwest Miami, was the only hospital equipped to receive the county's most badly injured accident victims; it also served the county's indigent, who could spend hours in gurneys in crowded hallways waiting for a bed.

Antoinette Grays had her bed in a room by herself, the receptionist told Hilton after a few strokes on her computer keyboard. Hilton recognized the wing from the heavyset woman's directions because he had visited there many times before; it served AIDS patients exclusively.

Hilton put his arm around Kaya's shoulder and began to steer her out of the way of people with dazed and overburdened expressions who shuffled through the hospital's lobby. In their faces he could see all of their details still unsettled, all of their fears unresolved, their irritation acting as sole sustenance to push them through each hour. Newcomers at Miami New Day often wore the same expression, lost and angry.

"Tell you what . . . I'll drop you off in the cafeteria, you grab a quick lunch, I'll run to Antoinette's room, then we'll get to the movies before two," Hilton told Kaya.

"You're crazy. Haven't you heard about hospital food, Dad?"

"Do you want to hang out in the waiting room?"

She turned her eyes upward. "Can I go in with you?"

The question surprised him, so he had no ready answer.

Hilton pulled her closer and patted her shoulder as they neared the elevator. "Why would you want to do that?"

She shrugged. "I've never met anybody with AIDS."

"It's no fun, Kaya. I know you're a young lady now, but this is a wing even a lot of grown-ups avoid. I guess it's human nature to run away from death. That's why people like Antoinette don't get enough visitors."

"Wouldn't she like to see another teenager?"

Hilton smiled at her, jabbing the elevator button. Kaya definitely had a point there. Antoinette had dropped out of school and grown up so fast, so hard, he couldn't think of another young person in her life. "Maybe she would. Are you sure about this? This is something you really want?"

Kaya nodded, although her lips were tight with nervousness. The elevator's bell rang and the arrow lit up in green before the door slid open. Hilton sighed. "Okay then, princess. I'll explain a few things to you when we get up there. It's not like a regular hospital wing."

The only other nonpatients on the floor today were nurses organizing charts at the nurses' station, talking over each other's voices. Through door after door they passed, Hilton and Kaya glanced at solemn men and women staring up at their mounted television sets or asleep, curled up. The faces were gaunt, cheerless. Most of the rooms were bare, with no efforts made to personalize them.

Miami New Day had sent Antoinette a bouquet of brightly colored carnations, and they were the centerpiece of the table beside her bed, where they glowed in the shaft of light from her window. Two slightly deflated red helium balloons were taped to her wall by their strings.

The only view from Antoinette's window was the wall of bricks and rows of windows from the building next door or, if she had been able to stand and peer downward, an alleyway. She'd been watching a "Sanford and Son" rerun when they came in, and the mounted television set ran in silence above them while Hilton and Kaya pulled chairs up to her bed.

Antoinette's arms were strung to two intravenous drug pouches, and tubes ran from her nose to an oxygen machine to help her breathe. With the dexterity of experience, she found the button to raise her bed so she could see them better. Antoinette wore her hair in a short jheri-curl style that looked dry and brittle for lack of care. Though she appeared thinner than ever to Hilton, her face beamed as though she weren't sick at all.

"Look at you, all fixed up like what's-his-name, Dr. Huxtable on 'Cosby' or somebody," Antoinette said, half laughing although she sounded weary. He heard congestion bubbling in her chest when she breathed.

"Do you think this look is me?" Hilton asked, running his fingers along the paper mask covering his nose and mouth. Both he and Kaya wore masks and gloves as a part of the wing's regulations, a protective measure designed for the patients, not the visitors. Their germs could be deadly to an AIDS patient robbed of basic immune defenses.

"Uh huh," Antoinette said, conserving words.

Hilton squeezed Kaya's hand. This visit was hard for him, and he wondered now if it had been smart to bring his impressionable daughter. "This is my oldest, Kaya. She wanted to come up and see you. We're going to the movies today."

Antoinette glanced at Kaya shyly, then looked back at Hilton. "What you gon' see, Mr. James?"

Kaya answered before he could, explaining that they hadn't decided between the new movie with hip-hop artists Kid 'N Play or a Walt Disney cartoon. Kaya wasn't sure about the cartoon; too babyish, she said. She was thirteen, but she wasn't allowed to see too many R-rated movies yet, she said.

After swallowing with apparent effort, Antoinette said, "I like Kid 'N Play. I hope I get out before they stop showing that."

Without a beat of hesitation, Kaya asked, "Which one do you think is cuter?"

Antoinette shook her head. "They both look good to me,"

she said, and suddenly their conversation sounded like two schoolmates chatting over lunch in the cafeteria. Kaya went on to talk about how her friends liked Kid because he was "red-skinned," as they called him, but she didn't believe people look better just because of a lighter complexion. She asked Antoinette if she agreed.

Hilton listened to their conversation, transfixed and momentarily mute. He'd never seen Kaya so self-directed, so deft in social relations. He knew she had to be nervous and sad and sickened just like he was, but he could hear none of those things in her hurried, casual tones as she tried to draw conversation out of Antoinette. Kaya's eyes smiled above her mask, enabling the barrier between them to disappear. Antoinette told Kaya she liked Luther Vandross, and her favorite song was "A House Is Not a Home." Hilton didn't know these things about her, would never have known. They sounded like instant friends.

And he could see the difference on Antoinette's face, softening her gaunt features, making the worried lines above her forehead vanish, if only for a time. The more she spoke, the less labored her words and breathing sounded.

"Where's your uncle today?" Hilton asked during a lull.

Antoinette clicked her tongue against her teeth. "I dunno. Jail, could be."

"You haven't seen him?"

"He needs to get his behind here and fill out a form, that's what the nurse said. And our phone been shut off. I ain't calling over there no more."

"Where's your baby brother?"

"With his godmama, I guess. She called here once for something, but they had took me out for tests." She sighed. "He's all right. I'm 'a go look after him soon as I get out. She stay way up by Northside. The L bus go up that way, with a transfer."

"How old is your brother?" Kaya asked.

"Eight," she said.

"My brother is eight, too."

73

"For real?" Antoinette asked, and the two shared friendly gazes again. Antoinette's straight teeth, and one gold cap with a star imprinted on it, glistened against her skin. Hilton wondered if this was the last time he would see her smile.

Hilton and Kaya were still at Antoinette's bedside, in their imaginations, twenty minutes later, while they stood in a downtown Miami movie line and heard babbling conversations about film trivia, the Lotto jackpot, and whether it would still be sunny enough later to go to the beach. Hilton was kicking himself for taking Kaya to Jackson. He'd fought back tears himself when they told Antoinette they had to leave, thinking how silly it seemed to go to a movie when so many lives were confined to bare rooms like that one. This had been Kaya's day, and he'd ruined it for her by making it too heavy. Again, he'd blurred the line between work and family, and family had suffered.

An apology was forming on Hilton's lips when Kaya poked his kidneys to get his attention. "Antoinette's really sick, right?"

"That's right."

"And she probably won't leave the hospital, right?"

Hilton paused. "Could be, honey," he said.

"But does she know that?"

"I'm sure she does, Kaya. Antoinette watched her boyfriend die, so she knows what's going down. She's so sick that she can't walk anymore. Even if she leaves, she'll need a wheelchair."

The usher took their tickets and directed them to a theater at the far east end of the multiplex. The previews of coming attractions hadn't begun, and they easily found seats in the dim light of the half-filled theater. Kaya leaned on the armrest closest to Hilton and fingered her popcorn without eating.

"But Dad, how come she said that stuff about going to get her brother and taking the bus and everything? And she said she wanted to come see this movie, remember?"

"I remember."

Kaya sounded pained. "How come?"

Hilton wrapped his arm around Kaya's shoulder and leaned closer to her, sighing. None of the patients he'd visited in that wing had ever even spoken the word *AIDS*. "A lot of people who are dying, even when they know they're dying, pretend they aren't. They keep on planning just like they would if they weren't. It's called denial."

A woman with a mane of African-style braids and holding a toddler in her lap snapped around to gaze at them, as if offended by Hilton's words, then she remembered herself and turned back to face the screen. Hilton understood her surprise. Death had no place here today. Death was not something to be explained to children like a confusing plot twist.

"So she knows she won't ever really go on the bus," Kaya said, uttering the words like uncomfortable shoes she was trying on for the first time.

"That's right. She knows."

Hilton tried to force himself to laugh at appropriate spots during the movie, but it was hard. Kaya was unusually silent. She brought the silence with her when they pulled out of the parking garage of the Omni International Mall and drove toward Interstate 95. The sun, as someone had predicted earlier, had been smothered by dark cloud cover as a prelude to a fall-afternoon rainstorm. Miami never saw snow, but it got enough rain to more than make up for it.

Unexpectedly, while they waited at the traffic light near the overpass to the expressway, Kaya blurted, "Maybe I won't go to the arts school next year."

The county school system had special schools, designed for desegregation, that also gave children a chance to specialize early in arts, sciences, and languages as enticement to make them take long bus trips away from their neighborhood schools. Kaya was a straight-A student, but she'd been bent on going to South Miami Middle School so she could study drama during the week. But her best friend wanted to attend an inner-city science school farther north, so Kaya had also toyed with the idea of going with her.

"And do what? Science?"

She nodded, gazing out of her window through rain droplets dyed red from the stoplight above them. "I get good grades in science," she said. "I dissected my frog better than anyone."

"But you get good grades in all of your classes. You can do anything you want, really. What made you think of that?"

Kaya didn't answer right away, and when she did, she was indirect. "It's terrible there's a disease like that, where people can't even see your face when you visit because you're wearing a mask. And kids get it, and everybody gets it."

"It's terrible, all right," Hilton said.

"If there were more doctors and they really worked at it because they really cared, I bet they could find a cure for that disease," Kaya said.

"They do care. They'll find a cure within your lifetime."

"Some doctors are researchers, and that's all they do."

"Yep. That's right," Hilton said.

"I could do that," Kaya said after a pause.

Hilton gazed at her, and he realized he was feeling a sadness completely isolated from any thoughts of Antoinette or his nostalgia for Kaya's lost childhood. "Of course you can," he said, but his throat was dry and his words sounded like lies to him for a reason he couldn't grasp. "You can do anything you want."

The traffic light turned green, but a black motorcycle officer in a fluorescent rain jacket and rubber boots scooted into the intersection and thrust out his open palm toward Hilton. His flashing blue light lit up the underpass and the bundles of clothes and furniture that belonged to the invisible homeless who lived there. The moustached officer sounded his siren in a spurt to warn other traffic to stop.

Then a procession of headlights began, with a long shiny hearse passing in front of them first, then two limousines, then a stream of cars filled with blacks in Sunday hats and dark suits and hidden faces. Hilton thought of the Dennis Miller joke about funerals, about how the police stop traffic for you the one time it doesn't do you any good. That was what life was about, empty gestures. It was one of Hilton's favorite jokes, but the memory of it left him feeling hollow. The line of cars seemed endless, and Hilton felt a growing certainty as each new car passed that all of the mourners' forlorn eyes were watching him.

CHAPTER 9

"Oye. Over here, man."

Raul's voice was unmistakable even over the drone of noise inside the Miami Arena, which was packed for the Heat's game against the Orlando Magic. Raul was decked out in his black satin Heat jacket with its flaming basketball logo, and he stood and waved his trademark Mets cap to Hilton with a grin. The hat and jacket clashed, but Raul never went to a game without his badge of loyalty to his hometown Mets. As usual, Raul had lucked into good seats, putting their eyeline directly above the press table with a perfect view of center court.

Hilton was still marveling at their seats as Raul embraced him warmly and squeezed his forearm in the affectionate way Hilton had noticed in some Hispanic men, treating one another like brothers. Hilton was more reserved, but he was used to Raul's hugs. Raul's arms were still lanky, but the years since they'd first met had widened his middle with a slight paunch. "Sit down. Taste your Coke."

Hilton sipped from the large paper cup Raul offered and had to catch his breath. His soft drink was drowned in rum, and no doubt a dark Puerto Rican brand. His throat felt singed.

"I don't get how you sneak that eighty-proof in here every time," Hilton said, and Raul tapped his jacket pocket while keeping his eyes surreptitiously straight ahead, as though he carried nuclear secrets on his person.

"You have your talents, I have mine," Raul said. *"Mira.*

There's Shaquille O'Neal, looking cocky tonight. I'd yell something, but we're too close. He might kick my ass."

"Hell, *I* might kick your ass. The Heat's my boys, but Shaq's the man now. Don't get crazy on me."

"Fucking traitor."

"Damn straight."

Hilton's friendship with his former therapist was as unplanned as it was unlikely. Several months after his therapy ended, he and Dede ran into Raul at a wine-and-cheese reception sponsored by a nearby bookstore following a poetry reading by a Puerto Rican writer Dede admired. Raul seemed to avoid them at first, but Hilton insisted on cornering him because he felt a genuine affection and respect for the man who had stopped his nightmares cold. Two months later, Hilton thought of Raul when Miami New Day needed a therapist to volunteer a few hours a week. He called Raul to ask if he knew anyone who might be interested. Raul said he had some free time on Wednesdays, and he would be happy to do it himself. He came three times, until Hilton could hire someone full-time to make up for the staff shortage. As compensation, he invited Raul to a Dolphins home game with him; Stu had backed out on him, and he had complimentary tickets for Miami New Day.

Raul shook his head firmly, clearing his throat into his fist. "Oh, no. *Gracias*, but no. I have a strict rule about not socializing with former clients." He was obviously a sports fan, however, because he eyed the tickets hungrily even as he demurred. "I don't suppose those would be good seats, your comp seats. You might get a nosebleed in those seats, no?"

Hilton assured him that Miami New Day was well-liked by a major corporation that provided very good seats. Fifty yard line.

Abruptly, Raul's head stopped shaking. He sipped delicately from his cup. "Ah ... well, those would be good, wouldn't they? Quite good. Yes. It's really a shame about this rule of mine."

"There's no statute of limitations?" Hilton asked. "It's been nearly a year, man. What's past is past. Besides, I owe you. I promise never to talk therapy."

For more than four years, Hilton had kept that promise. Despite his urge to seek advice, he remembered that promise again as the Heat and Magic players flailed their arms in the air for first possession of the ball, and a lucky swipe landed it in a Heat player's sure hands.

"You're good with your drink?" Raul asked him.

"Damn, man, I can only drink one at a time," Hilton laughed. Hilton had never felt he needed Raul for anything other than friendship, and he was a good friend to have; non-judgmental, curious about things he didn't know, and with a bizarre sense of humor: once he showed up at a Heat game with black lace women's panties draped over his head like a tam. He did it straight-faced and with no explanation, except for saying that a beautiful woman was bound to tap him on the shoulder and demand to have them back. It didn't work, but it was good for stares. If a woman's gaze lingered too long, Raul asked, "Did you lose these, miss?" He almost got punched out many times that night. Hilton could hardly believe this was the same man who had so skillfully guided him from the prison of his dreams.

And he had accomplished more than that, even. Raul had helped Hilton save his marriage, and he'd allowed him to talk to Nana. Toward the end of their sessions, after weeks of preparation, Raul scraped an empty chair across his floor and rested it directly in front of Hilton. Then he told Hilton to talk to the chair, to talk to Nana, to imagine that she was there before him.

After all of their hypnosis and soul-searching, with Raul taking him back to the beach, back to the monstrous under-tow, Hilton was ready to do it. He faced the chair and could almost see Nana's tall, well-built frame there. She was not smiling in that picture of her in his mind, but he was no longer afraid of her.

"Nana," Hilton began in a husky voice, and he paused a moment to let his words frame themselves without forethought. "It was my fault, what happened. You told me not to go out too far, and I didn't listen to you. I disobeyed you. And then"—his throat was hot, closing itself tightly—"and then you drowned, and it was my fault. I'm sorry, Nana. No one knew you told me to stay close to the shore. No one knew how bad I was. The Jameses gave me cake and toys and a beautiful house, and I didn't deserve it. I killed you. I didn't mean to, but I killed you."

Hilton could barely speak for his tears. He'd never vocalized these thoughts before, he'd never remembered them. But, yes, he'd been a scrawny eight-year-old kid pampered and nurtured, in his view, for the act of killing his grandmother. No wonder he had nightmares. No wonder she haunted him in his sleep. He couldn't tell anyone how he felt, that he had murdered her, because he was afraid the Jameses would turn him out or send him to jail. They were such good people, they would never understand such a bad thing.

As an adult confronting his youthful logic in the face of an empty chair, Hilton realized how he'd tortured himself as a kid. As soon as he spoke, he could almost hear Nana's voice reassuring him, saying: Hilton, you was just a child. Children don't always listen, because they just don't know what's best. You didn't kill me. What happened was an accident. Nana knows you're sorry. Nana still loves you, Hilton. You can't make up for me by doing for other people. Do for yourself, do for your wife, do for your children. I swam out to save you that day so you could have a whole life of your own. Don't live that life hurting over me.

Just live.

Soon after, the dreams were gone. He felt a relief that brightened all of his days, as though he'd ducked around the corner from bullies who would never chase him again.

And now, unexplained, they were back. Not to mention his eerie, wide-awake hallucination the other night. Hilton stared at the basketball court with heavy eyes, barely registering a Heat three-point shot that tied the game. He didn't even know what the exact score was, or if O'Neal was still on the court. Raul was hooting gleefully beside him, but the other sounds in the vast indoor arena sounded far away. Hilton drank the last of his rum and Coke and rested the empty cup beside his feet. He should know better than to drink on an empty stomach.

Hilton was annoyed by the too-loud whispering of a man and woman sitting behind him, the kind of pompous conversation spoken to be overheard: ". . . but let's just say I don't have to fly to L.A. next month. Say we shoot in Orlando. That still leaves us four, five weeks to edit. We're not dead in the water *the way they found that poor orphan child . . . And no lifeguard . . . Course not, just us coloreds . . . Brought him down from Belle Glade way . . . You knew Eunice Kelly, who was raising him after her daughter ran off . . . died of an attack, just like that, some kind of heart ailment . . . That's what I'd heard . . . boy found her in the kitchen, dead-cold . . . Lord have mercy . . .*

"*. . . His cousin Melva brought him to Virginia Key, wanted to see if somebody from the family could . . . Oh, well, no sense worrying 'bout it now. . . . Water was plain deadly, Matt said . . . The grandmama dead last year, now the boy . . . Damn shame . . . This world ain't right, just ain't right . . .*"

"Are you fucking crazy?" Raul asked Hilton, nudging him.

"What?" Hilton mumbled, stirring.

"You're asleep at a fucking game. Now I've seen it all."

"I'm not sleeping. Go to hell," Hilton said, but he knew from his familiar heartbeat thudding at his temples that he'd been sleeping, that he'd been dreaming. He glanced around him at the cheering faces, at men waving their game programs with wide-mouthed shouts as the players bounded toward the Heat's end of the court. He looked to see whose voices were speaking behind him; he saw a blond-haired woman wearing a black dress and sunglasses, even indoors; the man beside her wore his graying hair in a ponytail. They were huddled close together, discussing details of some film project. Hilton stared a moment, then looked away. He hadn't expected them to be white, for some reason. He hadn't expected to see a man, or a woman so young. He'd expected someone else.

"What's the score, then?" Raul taunted. "And don't look."

"All right, all right. I was sleeping. Lay off, huh?"

"You're better off asleep. Twelve unanswered points. And this guy misses . . . *Oye, maricón!*" Raul's voice rose to a shout as the basketball bounced wildly off the backboard.

Hilton stared hard at Raul. He hadn't noticed how much his friend's hair was thinning, that he was combing it to the side to make his scalp look less sparsely covered.

"What are you looking at? Too much rum for you, I think."

"Where's your Mets cap?" Hilton asked suddenly.

Raul touched the top of his head, then shrugged and turned his attention back to the game. "Left it tonight. Couldn't find it. De-fense, de-fense! They call that defense? Jesus Christ."

The screams and shouts in the arena roared a moment in Hilton's ears as though he were in a sound tunnel of pulsing waves. He leaned over to examine the floor, finding crumpled hot dog wrappers and a discarded program. Then he glanced at Raul's lap, where Raul held tightly to his cup still half-full of rum and Coke. No Mets cap.

"You were wearing it when I came in. You took it off and waved it to me," Hilton said.

"Are you here to be fashion consultant, or are you watching the game? I can't believe you were sleeping," Raul said, not looking at him. His voice was slightly slurred. "I think you're still sleeping."

Hilton sighed, annoyed at Raul's tipsy dismissal. "Maybe so. I can't sleep at night lately."

Raul shouted and jumped from his seat as the Heat grabbed a skillful rebound from a missed O'Neal shot. The noise coiled around Hilton's earlobes, and he shook his head to clear it. No, he would never again drink on an empty stomach. He needed to find a hot dog, or he'd doze through the rest of the game. He tried to remember if he'd dreamed that Raul was wearing the Mets cap, but he knew he hadn't.

He could still see the blue corduroy fabric and orange logo waving in Raul's hand. That part had been real.

The Heat never made up the dozen points, and the gap had widened to fifteen by the time the final horn sounded. O'Neal had been in amazing form, a treat to watch from so close. Hilton forgot his troubles through the end of the game, but he was still irritated with Raul as they made their way out and found the line for the men's room, by an unspoken understanding that they both needed to piss.

Raul had an excited conversation with a Spanish-speaking man ahead of them in line, then he bumped his shoulder back against Hilton to get his attention. The sound of flushing urinals and toilets from the stalls echoed against the walls, making it hard to hear him.

"You say you're not sleeping? Why not?"

Hilton shrugged. "I'm not sure."

"Dreams?"

Hilton met Raul's reddened eyes, which were concentrated on him as though the sober therapist inside had snapped to life. Hilton only nodded.

"Bad ones?"

"Just like before."

"Shit," Raul said.

As they always did, they had both chosen a parking lot blocks from the arena because it was cheaper, so they joined the stream hurriedly making its way through the glass-littered streets of the Miami ghetto where the incongruous pink arena had been built. The homeless and the nameless lingered in shadows around them, their eyes studying the well-off intruders who lit up their unhappy streets with headlights and laughter so late at night.

"How long?" Raul asked.

"Couple weeks."

"You feeling okay?"

"It's getting to be a strain. I'm wired at work from not getting enough rest. Dede wanted me to talk to you about it. Maybe I should come in."

Raul made a thoughtful sound but didn't speak.

"What?" Hilton asked.

"Call me Monday. I have a name for you."

"A name of what?"

"A therapist. She's good, if that's what you're looking for."

Hilton stopped walking, stunned, and Raul fell ahead of him by three paces before Hilton jogged to catch up. "No thanks. I'm not going through this whole routine with somebody new. Let me just come in for some hypnosis or something, man."

"*Lo siento mucho . . .* " He shook his head.

"What are you talking about? You know me."

"Exactly. I know you as a friend. You're not my patient, Hilton. That relationship is over now. I cannot work that way."

"What we did before worked, Raul."

Raul shrugged. "If it had worked, I don't believe you'd still be having the dreams. You have some unresolved issues."

Hilton laughed. "You sure sound like my shrink now."

"Call me. I'll give you her number, and I'll give her your file. If therapy is the route you want . . . "

"No way. If it's not you, no therapy."

"You may not need it. It may just be stress."

The elderly, sallow-skinned parking-lot attendant yawned, seeing them, and unlocked the padlocked fence to allow them to walk inside. Raul greeted him in Spanish, and the man responded grumpily. From what little Hilton could understand, the man said he was ready to go home because it was too cold outside. *Hay mucho frío,* he said. Raul drove a red 1970s Mustang convertible he kept immaculately shined, and it glistened beside Hilton's beat-up old Corolla. Hilton knew he needed a new car, and he'd always said he couldn't afford it, but the truth was that he hated to let go.

"How's Dede?" Raul asked while they lingered beside the Mustang, and Hilton recognized the veiled inquiry into the state of his marriage. Raul couldn't help being a counselor, even when he tried.

"Good. Very good."

"What about work?"

"You're not charging me by the hour for this conversation, are you?" Hilton asked.

"Fuck you," Raul said, turning to fit his car keys into his door. Hilton laughed, watching him fumble to open the lock.

"You okay to drive?"

"You're asking me? You're the one who passed out during the game. I can drive fine. I live right across the bridge in Little Havana. This is not drunk. You've seen me drunk."

"I know that's right."

Hilton still stood beside the car while Raul started his engine and the car roared flawlessly to life, as though it were new. Hilton was sorry the night was over, that he'd have to find his way home and crawl into bed beside Dede to face his simultaneous desire to sleep and to remain awake, the two yearnings that fought within him each night. Right now, he simply wished he could sleep. He wished Raul could pop him into a quick hypnotic trance and make his problem disappear.

"Any undue stress in your life?" Raul asked.

"Well, a weirdo sent a death threat to Dede's office a couple of weeks ago. Called her a nigger and said he wanted to kill her and her family. We're having the police look it over."

Raul nodded, pursing his lips, then he smiled at Hilton. "Two weeks, you say? It sounds like that's enough to give anyone nightmares. Wouldn't you agree?"

He was right, of course. That was the simplest answer. Yet it wasn't the right one, Hilton believed. He wished he could explain why he felt that way, but he couldn't explain that any more than he could explain how he'd seen Raul wearing his Mets cap when he insisted he'd left it at home, and he wasn't wearing it now.

There was simply too much, lately, he couldn't explain— even to Raul, whom Hilton had hoped could give him answers. He hadn't realized how much he'd hoped for Raul's help until now, with his hands grasping the cold metal of

Raul's car as though he were afraid to release it. *dead-cold*

He felt afraid of everything tonight; afraid to drive through the grim, skeletal streets of Overtown; afraid of facing the empty stretch of U.S. 1, which had been blocked by fire engines and ambulances from a nasty accident earlier that night. He could still see the fresh image of a man with a bloodied shirt being pulled gingerly by paramedics from the driver's side of a crumpled Honda; he'd stared so long, trying to see the man's face, that the line of cars behind him blared a symphony of horns.

Most of all, he was afraid to sleep, and going home meant sleep would come. If he were still in therapy with Raul now, Hilton realized, he would be breaking the primary rule. He was holding back. He wasn't being honest. Short of begging, however, there was nothing left to say, and the cool air was uncomfortable. The old parking attendant was right to complain. It was a bad night.

"It's probably the letter," Hilton said. "You're right."

"You see?" Raul said, winking. "That's a hundred bucks. I'll mail my bill. *Buenas noches, compadre.*"

"Yeah. Good night," Hilton said, his spirits lower than he could remember in a long time.

CHAPTER 10

"Hilton! You get back here, boy. Do you hear me?"

A sharp voice he knows pierces through a cacophony of rhythms playing in his brain. He tries to open his eyes. He will answer her this time instead of hiding. "I'm coming, Nana," he says.

He sees nothing except fluid spots of every color swimming before him in a broth of darkness. Tiny voices fly at him in flurries, tickling his ears. Nana's aged voice is no longer with him; the voices he hears now sound like sinister mimicries of his own. They hurt his ears, and he tries to bat them away.

"How many times," says one voice, fading in and fading out from one ear to the other, "do you think you can die?"

Another voice explodes in a cackling scream that comes from everywhere. "Do you think you can keep dying forever?"

He covers his ears, but the flurry of voices penetrates his flesh as if he has none. He doesn't know where he is. "All I want is peace," he says. "Please just let me have peace."

The flurries race through his head, and the spots swimming before him lurch into a mad dance. He is taunted by old voices, young voices, strangers and loved ones, the remembered, the forgotten. The last voice is a kind one at last, Nana's: "Hilton, there's no peace where you're at," she says, her words laden with the sadness of a dozen lifetimes.

"Child, you done swum out too far."

PART TWO

Even a spirit looks after his child.

—Ghanaian proverb

CHAPTER 11

> Question: What do you call a baby nigger?
> Answer: A niglet.
> Question: What do you call Dede James's two little
>   niglets?
> Answer: Dead.
>
> I hope you've studied for your final exam. I am your
> judge, Your Honor. My sentence on you won't be com-
> muted by a wall made of coral or a nigger house built of
> bricks. I'll huff and I'll puff, and I'll blow your house
> down.

"Where are the kids?" Curt asked Hilton quietly, slipping the plastic-encased note back into Hilton's hand. This note was neatly typed like the rest, but it was worse than the others. It had been delivered in person.

"They're at Dede's mom's," Hilton answered gloomily. "We told them Grandma Kessie wants them to spend the night. Kaya knew something was wrong, though."

The two men stood in the doorway of the Dade state attorney's systems researcher's office at the timeworn justice building downtown. Dede, uncharacteristically still sporting her black judge's robe, sat across from a gray-haired man taking patient notes while she spoke to him in a voice very unlike her own, shaken and small and frightened. The prosecutors' offices were deserted except for the four of them. There was a somber hush here tonight.

"Are you and Dede spending the night at home?" Curt asked.

"We haven't talked about that yet," Hilton said.

This note, the fifth in two months and by far the most cryptic, had been delivered in a business envelope addressed to The Honorable Dede James in her chambers two floors below in the justice building. When she called Hilton earlier, she'd told him she happened to see it on her secretary's desk just before she planned to leave for the night. Hil, he might have been right there when I was alone, Dede said. He slipped in somehow. This isn't some nut upstate anymore. He's come back to Miami.

The bailiff hadn't seen anyone, and the secretary had left at six. Dede called her at home, and she said she didn't remember seeing a letter or its carrier before she left.

"Baby, do you want some water or a Coke or something?" Hilton called during a pause in her discussion.

"There's coffee," offered Jerry, the white-haired analyst, whose accent was more reminiscent of Brooklyn than of Miami. Practically everyone in the city was a transplant from somewhere else.

"I'm okay," Dede said, but she didn't sound or look okay. Her eyes were red, her voice was nearly gone, and she was kneading her fingers under Jerry's desk.

Watching her, Hilton felt so angry he imagined himself choking the letter's author to death bare-handed. "Son of a bitch," he muttered, and Curt patted his back.

"So what are we looking for here, case-wise?" Jerry asked Dede. "We've pulled files for all the major crimes you've been on since '90. What else do we need?"

"Everything," Dede said firmly. "Every case."

"Every case? You were here twelve years. When you started, you were on fifty-odd cases a week."

"I only want the cases that went to trial," Dede said.

"No," Hilton spoke up urgently. "Plead-outs, too. Anyone who did any kind of time."

Jerry whistled, scribbling on his yellow legal pad. "What I'll need to do is write a computer program. I'll key cases using your name. That's easiest. So tell me what I'm looking for."

"Every case, misdemeanors and up. Convictions and acquittals. Men and women. Whites and Hispanics. We don't need to look at blacks. Hilton? Do we?"

"It's a white male," Hilton said, stepping closer to her.

"I want to look at everyone," Dede said in that same tired, scraping voice. "Can you group them according to their expected release dates, major crimes first, white males first? I'll just prioritize them."

"Sweetheart, I can do anything you want," Jerry said.

Dede's eyes were anxious. "How long on this, Jerry?"

"I can have a written request on the state attorney's desk Monday morning. I need permission to run a program like this."

"I'll call her at home for you right now," Dede said.

Jerry smiled back at her warmly, cocking his head to peer closely into her eyes. "Dede, I know you're shook up, but listen to me. I've been here fifteen years. I've heard guys screaming you-motherfucker-this and I'll-rip-your-balls-off-that right in the courtroom. Sure, they're pissed at the person trying to send them up. You know how it goes. And judges get it worse than ASAs. But not once has anyone followed through, or even tried. Not once."

"I know," Dede said, nodding with closed eyes.

But there's always a first time, Hilton thought to himself. He stood behind Dede and began to rub her shoulders, then rested his chin atop her soft Afro. "We'll get him, baby," he promised.

Wall made of coral. Hilton didn't want to panic Dede, but he thought of something he knew he would have to share with Curt as soon as they were alone. He'd smelled an overpowering stench of urine on the front porch the week before; they all had. Dede thought a neighborhood dog or cat had tried to claim their house as territory, but now Hilton understood the urine had been human. The racist bastard had pissed on their porch, probably while they slept, only a few feet from Jamil's bedroom window. Maybe he'd wanted them to know he'd been there.

"You two going home tonight?" Curt asked.

Dede didn't answer. Hilton rubbed Dede's shoulders harder, to fortify her. "Nobody's chasing us away from our home," he said.

"Great fucking way to start the new year," Jerry sighed.

((

When Dede and Hilton pulled up to their house at nearly nine o'clock with Curt trailing in his Metro Police car, a blue-striped white Miami Police car was already parked at the curbside with the driver's side door open, a faint light illuminating the faces of a black woman and blond-haired man inside. As Hilton climbed out of his car and Dede snapped off her Audi's headlights, he could hear the beeps and squawks from the parked car's police radio. He sat with Dede on the coral wall while Curt and his police cousins exchanged words. No one unusual in sight, they said. All quiet.

The cold night air seized Hilton and made him shiver with the utter unreality of it all, seeing the police car parked beside the covered aluminum garbage can that sat at his curb each Friday night and had sat there long before this madman began stalking his family. This simply couldn't be.

Hilton invited Curt inside, ostensibly for hot cocoa, but under the pretense of admiring the way they'd decorated in the year since his last visit, Curt casually surveyed the house. Curt wasn't Hilton's closest friend, but he knew about wiring and had helped him install lights and an electric garage-door opener (which was rarely used, since the garage was buried in clutter) in exchange for beer and laughs some time back. They were both Alpha men, both sons from middle-class families, both committed to hard work to try to make life in Miami better for black people. Curt was obsessed with protecting the innocent, and Hilton wanted to save lost souls. That combination and chemistry worked between them. Even if Curt did hate the Dolphins.

Curt commented on their closet space while he peeked

behind clothes, then he moved on to peer out through the sliding glass door at their patio. He glanced inside each bedroom. By the time he sat to drink his cocoa in the living room, every light in the house was on. For the first time in hours, Hilton felt safe and back in control.

When Dede excused herself to call her mother's house from the kitchen, Hilton told Curt about the urine on the porch. Curt laughed, wiping cocoa from his moustache. "Well, white folks been pissing on us all these years. No sense stopping now, I guess."

"I'm telling you, man," Hilton said.

"You need a twelve-gauge. That'll really give the SOB something to wet his pants about."

"That's what Dede was just saying. She wants a gun."

"And I told you about that security dog my cousin is getting rid of, right? He had some K9 training, but he didn't cut it. He's antisocial but smart as hell. And loyal to whoever's got the bag of Gravy Train."

"That's what counts. Lemme know when we can look at him."

After Curt left with a promise to call the next afternoon, Hilton sat on the living room couch while Dede stretched out with her shoes off and lay across the length of the couch to rest her head on the soft of his thigh. He draped his arm across her shoulder, rubbing her forearm gently. He'd put a Marvin Gaye CD on the stereo, but they weren't hearing the music. All they heard was the silence of Kaya's and Jamil's absence. It seemed an invisible intruder had entered their home.

For a long time they did not speak. Hilton couldn't remember why they had argued at breakfast, and he had forgotten all of the work on his desk that had seemed so urgent right before Dede's call. Only this mattered now, and it would probably be like this for a long time to come.

"My first weeks on the bench ... I'm already so overwhelmed, like I have to prove something because people are just waiting for me to mess up," Dede sighed. "Now this.

Why is this happening now?" She sounded like a little girl.

Hilton had no answer, and he didn't try to make one up.

"How did he find out where I live?" Dede wondered aloud.

"Jesus, Dede, what do you think? Real estate records, driving records, voter registration. The damn newspaper published your birthdate in that profile, remember? With a name and a birthdate, there's a hell of a lot people can find out."

He sounded callous, even to himself, but he couldn't disguise his frustration. She'd never taken the threats seriously enough. He wished she'd been more careful when she talked to the reporter, that she'd used her head. Hell, the story even mentioned that they lived near Coral Gables, and mentioned Kaya and Jamil by name. It was a wonder it had taken the son of a bitch this long to find them.

"We have to tell the kids," Dede said, her voice nearly lost again. "It's time now."

"Tomorrow. When they get back," Hilton said.

She exhaled deeply, and he felt her head rise and fall on his lap. "I'm so numb, so drained. I think I'm going to bed."

"It is getting late."

She tugged at his pant leg. "Will you come with me?"

Hilton paused a millisecond too long before answering, and his silence seemed eternal. "Sure I will. Give me a few minutes."

She released his pants with a yank and pulled herself to her feet abruptly, walking toward the hallway. "I just thought, after all this, it would be nice for my husband to hold me. I'm not going to force you," she said.

"Now what's that supposed to mean?" Hilton asked. He didn't have the energy to stand and walk after her. He wasn't in the mood for a tantrum, so he let his head rest on the sofa back and he stared up at the countless patterns etched in the popcorn ceiling. They hadn't made love in ages, but he hoped that was far from her mind tonight. Sex would be a chore now, not a comfort. "I said I'd come. I'm coming."

She paused in the hallway's track lighting and faced him.

"Will you stay the night, or do you plan to slip out at two A.M. and sit in front of the television?"

"Oh, Jesus . . . "

"Just answer me. I don't want you there if you plan to get up. That wakes me up. I know exactly when you leave."

Hilton's temper flared. He could feel Dede's yearning for a healing hand even from across the room, and he was yearning too, but her selfishness made him angry. "You know I can't sleep. I'm supposed to lie there awake all night?"

"Just forget it, Hilton. I'm not going to beg my own husband to spend the night with me." Her voice cracked at the end, betraying the approach of tears, but he didn't move to follow her into the bedroom. No, she would have to cry, then. She was the one who chose not to understand. She didn't know what it meant to have the dreams. To her, sleep was an escape; he snorted out loud, imagining such a thing. She didn't know how lucky she was.

The sound of her sob, muffled through the wall, surprised him with its depth and intensity. He felt guilty, cruel. After a night like tonight, was it really so selfish for her to want him there with her? Was it really such a sacrifice? His thoughts were growing muddled. Dede was right in what she'd been saying about him; he was changing, in small pieces. He was losing himself.

"Baby, I said I'm coming to bed, okay?" he said, sounding overly gentle. But when he tried to open their bedroom door, he found it locked.

Hilton walked through the house, turning off light after light until only one lamp in the living room threw a pale yellow glow across their white leather furniture and scuffed wooden floor. He sat a moment listening to Dede's sobs from the back of the house, his eyes stinging each time he heard her solitary pain pitch to a wail. Then he found the remote control and switched on the television set. Ten-thirty. It was time for "The Jeffersons."

CHAPTER 12

Dede's cries fill up all of the space around him and create space of their own, woven from threads of pain, despair, desperation. She sounds as though she has been pierced in half, peering at death's face. She needs him. They all need him.

"Dede, I'm sorry," he says. "Where are you?"

In an instant when his mind is overrun by images and sounds, he is plucked from the living room and finds himself standing in the middle of a busy highway in the overpowering light of day, making him shield his face with his palm. He recognizes a Chevron gas station and a Lexus dealership and knows he is standing between lanes on South Dixie Highway in a sea of shining cars. Gridlock. Sunlight bounces from chrome all around him in a bright glow. The drivers are pounding their horns, but he can hear Dede's cries inside the noise, calling to him. She is screaming his name in a chilling rote, repeating it like it's the only word she knows.

He tries to search for her face through the windshields, but all of the cars' windows are charred black; he can't see inside even when he presses his face to them. He tries to open the car door of a black Audi that looks like hers, but the handle flips out of his hand uselessly, locked. The next car is also locked, and the next. None of the drivers respond when he taps on the windows. The car horns blare in his ears.

". . . Head-on crash . . . Did someone call for help? . . . whole front end is smashed . . . There's children . . . Jesus, where's Rescue? . . . Woman's screaming her head off . . . driver is history, a goner . . . "

No, he's not supposed to be here wandering on the roadway,
Hilton realizes. He has to turn away, go back. But back where?
He hears Dede's screams rising again, then falling in a near-
hoarse hysteria, calling his name between sobs. Again, he tries
to open a car door that won't yield to him. The lines of cars are
endless, bumpers touching and nudging, three lanes in each
direction as far as he can see. He should not be here. But where
does he belong? Where is Dede?

Her screams make him shiver. Those screams tell him she is
beyond comforting, beyond consolation or salves. He only
wants to see her. He continues his search beneath the heat that
makes his feet drag across the asphalt and forces him to gasp
to breathe. The carbon monoxide from the cars, heavy in the
air, is choking him. He is drowsy. Sleep.

Up ahead, towering above the smaller cars, he sees the grill
of a worn, ancient black hearse with headlights beating defi-
antly into the sunlight. All of its windows are black too, but he
begins to run toward it because he knows he has seen this
hearse before.

He can hear Dede's screams more loudly as he nears the
awful hearse with its phantom driver. He is not the only one
running toward it, he sees. Doors from cars on all sides of the
hearse are being flung open, with people he knows and yet does
not know jumping from their cars to follow Dede's screams. A
player is offside against the Colts, a radio announcer is saying.
The Dolphins. From a radio, he hears a violent wave of boos.

". . . omigod, omigod, omigod . . . I've got a cellular in the
car . . . Get them out . . . "

Hilton's limbs feel drained, and he stands motionless on the
roadway as people push past him as though he isn't there. A
car has crashed into the back of the hearse, splintering the
back windows around the perfect white curtains. He cannot
discern the make of the car behind the hearse because its front
is mangled, crushed against the bigger vehicle. A man, the car's
driver, is hugging what was once the hood of his car, his arms
spreadeagled across it like the embrace of a tender lover. A
jagged hole is shattered in the windshield from where the man

once sat, and his passage left the glass coated in blood.

He is a black man. His face is unseen, twisted toward the opposite side, held by tangled bloody shreds of his neck. Hilton believes he knows him. Yes, he must.

Dede's next scream seems to be in his ear. "Hillll-ton!"

There she is, sitting in the car's passenger side, within an arm's reach of lifeless legs dangling through the glass. Her hands are clamped to her cheeks in horror, her seat belt binding her chest. Through the windshield's spiderweb of cracked glass, he sees her face streaked with tears and her mouth twisted in an unspeakable agony. Then there are more screams, from the back of the car. Kaya and Jamil are there, wide-eyed (he has seen those saucer eyes before), with Kaya pounding her seat as though she is insane, trying to claw her way from the car. Jamil is whimpering like an animal, arms wrapped around his knees as he rocks in place beneath his shoulder strap. Their roller skates are thrown haphazardly across the seat. They're wearing seat belts, both of them. Good kids, he thinks. Good kids.

"Dad-deeee . . . " one of them cries, or both.

He has seen this day, lived this day, sometime before.

He sees his yellow sports Timex on the dead man's limp wrist, the waterproof one Dede gave him for his birthday two years ago that can flash the time in London and Los Angeles and Madrid. He sees his imitation snakeskin belt winding through the loops of the dead man's jeans. The dead man is him.

He is frozen, speechless. Even his thoughts have fled.

He feels eyes watching him, so he whirls around to look at the hearse. He sees someone beyond the back window's curtains, a pale powdered face in black sunglasses and a cap emerging from the cool darkness of the vast vehicle's interior. The man raises his hand and beckons him in a slow, languid gesture. His thin-lipped smile is assuring, nonthreatening.

Come, the man mouths to him with an exaggerated motion of his lips. Hilton hears a voice that fills his senses, though no sound could possibly reach him through the glass: you see now that you must come.

Come.

Hilton's shoulders drop, and he nearly staggers to his knees on the hot roadway because he is so tired. Dede's voice is beginning to sound far away, and he can no longer hear Kaya or Jamil as he watches the hypnotic hand. What is he doing here? He should be resting inside the coolness, releasing himself to it.

What's done is done is done is done.

He takes one step toward the hearse, then another. With each step, his limbs feel lighter, more free, his breathing is easier. So this is all, he thinks. This is all.

Something jars his focus as he lifts his leg to take the third step toward the hearse's soothing call. A white Jeep to the right of the hearse has a vanity license plate, which he reads in a shocking instant. The bright green letters of the Florida plate spell out one word: NIGLET.

No, not yet, he remembers. You forgot about him. You forgot about Charles Ray.

When the name sinks into his psyche, he sees a grin so evil it is nearly unhuman, ageless rows of teeth gleaming with an ancient hatred. The grin of a man who would steal lives, who walks with no other purpose.

Suddenly, the screams from his family pour into his ears with the force of a shattered dam. When he looks at the hearse again, he sees three pairs of hands scratching for life against the glass. The powdered man's face is gone; instead, Dede stares back at him in a face knotted with fear, mouthing his name in wretched silence.

CHAPTER 13

"Can we name him, Daddy?"

"He already has a name. His name is Charlie," Hilton said, wrapping the leash around his palm with a yank so the seventy-five-pound dog would sit after his parade in front of Dede and the children. Obediently, the German shepherd rested on his haunches and took shallow breaths while a huge tongue swung from his mouth; the dog's sleek coat was all black except for a gray and brown patch on his forehead. Charlie looked up at Hilton expectantly, waiting for his next command, ignoring the others. They were gathered in the front yard beneath the sprawling branches of the ficus tree.

"Is he really a guard dog?" Jamil asked, leaning in to study him.

"He just retired. Go on and pet him, Jamil. He has to get used to all of us because he'll be living with us now."

Kaya didn't look impressed, her arms folded across her chest. She'd begged for a cat many times, and this apparently was not a welcome substitute. "For good?" she asked.

"Probably. We'll see how things go."

Uncertainly, Jamil extended his small fingers toward the dog's mane of bushy fur that looked like a muffler around his neck. Charlie eyed him warily.

"Just do it, Jamil," Hilton said. "Dogs can sense when you're scared. Pet him. Hurry up."

Charlie submitted to the kneading of Jamil's fingers without reaction or movement, as though affection were something the animal tolerated rather than craved. He kept his brown eyes on Hilton.

"He's not very friendly," Kaya observed.

"He's not supposed to be friendly," Hilton said.

Kaya made a face, and Dede hugged her and brushed her cheek against Kaya's. "Remember, Charlie's not like a regular pet."

"No kidding."

"You pet the dog, too, Kaya," Hilton said. "Pet him so he can get used to your scent. I'm going to teach you to walk him, too. Go on."

"Yeah, right," Kaya muttered, not moving.

Hilton snapped to look at her, and she froze with the knowledge that she'd gone too far. Even Jamil looked nervous, continuing to rub the dog's fur.

"What did you just say?" Hilton asked. "Is this funny to you? Is this a joke?"

"No, Dad," Kaya said softly, forcing herself to meet his eyes.

"You want to make light of someone threatening this family?"

"No, Dad," Kaya said, her voice unsteady this time. She shifted her weight from foot to foot, rolling her eyes skyward as though he were a fool. Ungrateful little—

Hilton felt a foreign impulse to hit her, but he didn't move. "Then pet the damn dog like I told you to and stop giving me your lip, or I'll knock that sass out of you. Move your hand, Jamil."

Hilton glanced at Dede, and he saw in her face that she believed he was being too rough on them. But she kept her mouth shut, thankfully. For once, this time she would trust him to take care of business and work with him instead of against him. Lately, even that seemed too much to ask of her. What had gotten into her? All weekend she'd been undermining him, questioning his logic with childish objections until he found himself asking: Is it me?

Was it so unreasonable to want the best alarm system

installed in the house, no matter what the price? Was it so outlandish to teach Kaya and Jamil how to load the shotgun and show them exactly where he would keep the boxes of rounds, so long as they knew the weapon wasn't a toy? And no, until further notice, the kids would not be allowed to stay at their friends' houses after school until the end of the workday like they usually did. Dede's mother had agreed to pick them up each day, and that was that.

Now he was even getting resistance from Kaya, who was usually a faithful and clear-thinking ally. Only two weeks before, at Antoinette's funeral, he'd felt like he and Kaya were friends who understood each other. She'd been so composed, even through tears, holding his hand during the church ceremony. Other mourners sat around them, but he'd felt as though he and Kaya were the only ones who were really there. Everyone seemed to be gazing at them rather than at Antoinette's frozen face in the open casket, as if the church mourned for this father and daughter. He'd felt dazed even hours after the funeral, but Kaya's resilience buoyed him.

Now Hilton felt alone. They just didn't get it, none of them. They didn't appreciate what he was doing for them, what he was going through. Hilton was so angry, his head ached.

"Daddy, how come somebody wants to hurt us?" Jamil asked. Already, after a moment's contact with the dog, Jamil suppressed a sneeze. Allergies. Well, he'd just have to deal with it.

"Because some people are jerks," Kaya said in a tone Hilton believed was meant for him. He let it go, not glancing her way.

Dede sat on the edge of the coral wall facing them, stretching her bare legs out beneath the dress she wore, an African fabric made up of a swirl of purple shades. "I send a lot of people to jail, Jamil. They don't like it, so they make threats sometimes. This man is especially mad because he doesn't like people like us, African-Americans, because we're not like them."

"Like that dumb kid behind our house who called me 'nigger' that time," Jamil said with a sour face.

"Just like that," Dede said.

Hilton and Dede had debated at length about whether they should move into this neighborhood, where no other blacks were in sight. They'd lived farther north before, in an all-black neighborhood slowly on the decline as drugs began to creep in. They'd had a choice between taking this older house or moving into a new development in the north area that was home to professional black families; the charm of a coral facade and hardwood floors won over the bland new house, but the move hadn't come without incident. One neighbor tossed his garbage into their yard for a month, and then Jamil ran crying into the house one day because a bigger boy had called him a nigger. When Hilton confronted the boy's father, his neighbor studied him with indifferent eyes and mumbled something about kids being kids. Hilton hadn't exchanged words with their bordering neighbor since.

In some ways, Hilton had felt that earlier incident was a good lesson for Kaya and Jamil—and maybe they could learn from this new crisis. Racism was out there, and Hilton figured it was better for his kids to grow up knowing it rather than fooling themselves into thinking everything was wonderful because they could drink from any water fountain or sit in classrooms next to little white kids. Maybe, in the end, this son of a bitch after them was doing his family a big favor. He'd make them stronger.

"Is he going to come here, Daddy, and try to get us?" Jamil asked, looking up at Hilton with eyes as expectant and trusting as the dog's.

dad-deee

Hilton's jaw hardened; he felt the reassuring tautness of Charlie's leash. "No one's going to hurt anybody in this family," he said. The next words came unprompted: "As long as I'm alive."

Hilton tensed and whirled around from where he sat on the couch when he heard a shuffle of footsteps behind him in the living room's darkness. Instinctively, his hands curled into tight fists until he saw Dede standing behind the couch in her Snoopy nightshirt. She hadn't worn it since . . . he couldn't remember. A better time. In the soft light from the television set, he saw her tired features, a face that had once made him smile when visiting his imagination during the day. The only thing Hilton felt keenly now was his own weariness.

Dede tossed a blanket on the back of the couch that landed with the scent of the cedar chest where she kept linens. That smell always reminded him of Nana's, where everything was old and familiar. And safe.

Dede kept her eyes straight ahead, focused on the television screen. "I fixed you a cot in the study and bought you an alarm clock," she said tonelessly. "Please sleep in there so the kids don't keep finding you here. Kaya asked me today what was going on with us."

Hilton blinked. He knew she wasn't trying to pick a fight, but he felt irritated. "What did you say?" he asked.

"What should I have said?"

Hilton puffed out his cheeks and exhaled slowly, staring at the TV. His brain and heart felt empty. In time, he could make things better between them. In time. Now he could barely take care of himself and he had too much to worry about. He had his hands full just making sure Charlie was tied properly, the alarm was set, the gun was loaded at his feet, all the doors were locked. He was thankful, when he glanced behind him, to see that Dede was gone. "I love you more than this world, Dede," he said, so softly he could barely hear himself even in the stillness of the empty room.

CHAPTER 14

Hilton was jolted awake when the door to his office opened with a sharp crack against the wall, and Stu strode inside wearing his white coat and a stethoscope.

Hilton was too tired to sit up straight. Since it was only Stu instead of Ahmad, who would have been crushed to find his boss this way, Hilton glanced up at him from the same position he'd been sleeping in; his head cushioned on his arms folded across his desk. Only Wanda knew how often he took catnaps, since she had to redirect his calls when he pulled his door closed with a nod in her direction. Thirty minutes at a time did it, usually. He'd found that he wasn't so prone to dreams at the office, and the naps gave him just enough energy to muddle through the day.

Only three o'clock, Hilton saw on the wooden wall clock above his doorway. Jesus, it had been three o'clock forever.

"Gee, sorry to wake you," Stu said, grinning. His coat pocket was still bulging with the sandwich Hilton had seen stuffed there earlier that afternoon.

"Out with it, Stu. I had a rough night."

"So I see," the physician said, gently easing a handful of papers onto Hilton's desk. "These are reports on six new clients. I need your John Hancock, and we're in business."

Hilton rubbed his eyes to clear them, then glanced at the papers and the names scrawled on them. Garcia, Jesus. McKinsey, Mary. Peterson, Sahara. Sahara—exhausted or not, he couldn't forget a name like that. He pushed the papers back toward Stu.

"Get lost. I just signed these, man. You getting senile?"

Stu slowly worked on a piece of chewing gum in his mouth, crossing his arms as he gazed down at Hilton quizzically. "Afraid not, boss. These are hot off the presses."

Hilton continued to read the reports and nodded with each familiar word. "Right. All six HIV negatives, one diabetic. Sahara is pregnant. I've got all this."

"You got all this when?"

"When you brought your butt in here fifteen minutes ago."

Stu shrugged, smiling. "Maybe you dreamed you read it. That's handy. To the untrained observer, it looks like you're sleeping, but you're actually hard at work."

Hilton stared at Stu hard. "Look, don't mess with me. I don't know if you've noticed, but I'm not in the mood."

Stu's smile vanished, and he sat in the chair across from Hilton's desk. "As a matter of fact, I had noticed."

"I've signed these papers."

"Then where are your signatures?" Stu asked.

Hilton glanced at page after page, where the line left for the supervisor's signature was blank on each. He flipped each page more quickly than the last, his heart beginning to thud as though a dream had followed him somehow. When he looked up again at Stu's eyes, he saw raw concern glistening back at him.

Hilton swallowed hard. "I signed these," he repeated. "You told me Sahara is in her third month. That sandwich in your pocket is ham and cheese. I made a joke about it not being kosher. Quit playing with me."

Stu leaned closer to him, his blue eyes unblinking. "Hil, what time do I come in on Wednesdays? At three. I just got here. All of Sahara's gestation information is in that report, and you know I eat ham and cheese every day."

Hilton rested against his chair back, rubbing his face. He could feel the walls of his office constricting around him, as though his world would shatter at any moment. "No," he said, mostly to himself, "this is bullshit. First Raul, with that Mets cap, and now this. Something's not right. This is fucked up."

When he looked at Stu again, studying him carefully, Hilton sat up straight. The stethoscope hadn't been around Stu's neck the last time he'd seen him, he was certain. It had been in his pocket. Stu had played with it while they spoke, he recalled. Yet, he couldn't have simply dreamed up Sahara's name, her pregnancy. He couldn't have. Why did these bizarre incongruities creep in while he slept?

"How long have we known each other, Hil?" Stu asked.

"A long time," Hilton said, breathing deeply.

"When have I ever butted into what isn't my business?"

"Every chance you get." Hilton failed in his effort to smile.

"Be serious. Never. I've never done that. But I have to say something, because I think it's my business. You don't look well. You're sleeping at your desk. You're highly stressed."

"I've got those, you know . . . those threats," Hilton mumbled. "It's a little rough at home, you know?"

"All right, I realize that. That's why I haven't said anything. But I've been hearing things here and there, from this person or that. Just talk, I thought. They say you're slipping, you're moody."

"They can go fuck themselves," Hilton snapped.

Stu extended his hand. "This is what I'm talking about. It's not like you. All these years, I've never seen you like this. What I'm saying is, you need a break. Everyone takes vacations." Hilton found a pen in his desk drawer and began to scribble his signature on the reports, hearing the far-off pounding from the construction on the new wing, which was still several weeks from completion. Vacation. That was a good fucking laugh, all right. He needed a vacation from his whole life.

"Hil, I know you've got everything here to deal with, the threats against your family, then Antoinette's death—"

Hilton lifted his pen to silence Stu, meeting his eyes less than kindly. "I'm sure I signed these once, and I just signed them again. I think you have some patients to see, and I have a meeting downtown."

Stu's eyes dimmed with disappointment. "Just trying to help."

"I don't need help. I'm fine. I'm cool."

"One last thing, then. I think you and Dede are taking on too much trying to throw that party next week."

Hilton couldn't argue with his logic, but it was out of his hands. Dede had been talking about hosting a party to thank her campaign supporters since the November election, and he'd promised her a party by the end of January. They stood to lose hundreds of dollars in catering if they canceled now, she'd reminded him—money they already couldn't afford—and she would consider it uncouth to fail to show her appreciation in a timely way. It was too much of a struggle to remain civil during his arguments with Dede, so he'd given in rather than shock her with the obscenities that usually flew through his mind.

"Stu," Hilton said patiently, "you asked me how many times you'd butted into what wasn't your business. Only once. And this is the time."

Stu blinked and sighed, standing up, then gathered his reports with a nod. He was hurt, Hilton knew. "Okay, boss. I'll let it rest. I just have to say I'm worried about you, that's all."

Amen, brother, Hilton thought. You and me both.

((

Traffic was light on Northwest Seventh Avenue in midafternoon, but Hilton was catching red lights at each intersection and nodding off while he drove. Each time his bleary eyes flew open, he told himself he was asking for an accident, driving like this. This couldn't keep up, going without sleep.

He heard a siren wailing in the distance *coming to get you, to take you where you belong, the way you should have gone from the first, the way everyone must go* and then a screech of brakes ahead as two cars nearly collided. He was at a red light again, his eyelids drooping.

"... *ain't nothing worse to me than a tiny coffin this size, some child's life trapped inside that never got lived ... you never know what the boy could'a been, could'a done ... just won't know ...*"

The traffic light still burned red when Hilton opened his eyes. He shook his head to wake himself, to fend off shrouded voices babbling beyond his consciousness. His armpits were stinging from new perspiration even as the car's air conditioner blasted his face in his effort to stay awake. Maybe he needed to see Raul, to insist on help. Maybe he should try to take a long vacation. Or maybe, he thought, he just needed to pray to somehow pull himself together.

The red light was interminable. Hilton was certain he'd seen the red DON'T WALK sign flashing for pedestrians in the intersection, indicating the light would change soon, but now the yellow box proclaimed WALK with confidence, as though the stoplight's entire cycle remained. Maybe he was simply losing his mind. In some ways, Hilton decided, that would be a relief.

Hilton glanced through his passenger window and realized that he was stopped directly in front of the cool green-colored twin towers of The Terraces, Danitra's apartment building.

WALK, the pedestrian sign still read. He hadn't checked on Danitra since the day he helped her move in, and he didn't know what state the counselor had found her in during follow-up visits. Would she be at home at three-fifteen on a Wednesday afternoon?

WALK. Wouldn't hurt to take a look.

Hilton didn't remember Danitra's apartment number, but he knew she lived in the end unit on the third floor of the east tower. He climbed the steps slowly, thoughtfully, remembering the reason he hadn't come back; Danitra had made a pass at him that day. Perhaps that was part of the reason he was here now, but he wouldn't have thought to visit if the light hadn't stopped him there, if the light had changed just a moment sooner, if he hadn't been conveniently poised in the building's driveway. What a string of tiny coincidences had brought him here, he thought. And of course she would be home. He knew she would be there.

"Baby's sick, so I took off from work," Danitra explained when she saw him, after hugging him warmly, tightly, in her doorway with a squeal of delight. "And Lord, I'm glad. Ain't you something in your suit and tie? Come on in, Mr. James."

The apartment, once bare, was now decorated with artificial plants, rugs, and framed posters in shades of pink and fuchsia. A woman's place, he thought, noting the flowery artwork. Danitra herself had gained some weight and looked healthier than ever before, her hair straight and pulled back in a rubber band. Her needle tracks had nearly faded by now. She wore shorts and a long T-shirt that read FLY, her full breasts unrestrained beneath the thin cotton. He could see their quivering silhouettes when she moved, capped by upright nipples.

She leaned over him, smelling of baby powder, and cleared away some books after offering him a seat at her table, explaining that school was going fine. She said she was still studying nursing, although the work was hard. When she brought him a glass of Coke, he noticed she had brightened her face with peach lipstick. The color was lovely on her, like sunshine.

"You ought to be 'shamed, taking this long to call on me," Danitra scolded, sitting across from him.

"Girl, my life has done gone crazy," he said, allowing his country-tinged vernacular to surface since he was away from corporate America, in the company of a sister. "You know I would have been here before. I didn't forget you. You're looking good."

"You too," she said. "A little worn out, but just as fine as you always did look."

They talked about Miami New Day, about her son, about how she fought her cravings for drugs, all the while gazing deeply at each other with unspoken words much less mundane. Danitra leaned on her elbow and paused a moment. "You know what? I'm 'a ask you something that ain't none of my business," she said.

"I've had plenty of that today, so you might as well."

Her dark eyes seemed to burrow inside of him. "Is everything okay with you at home?"

He swallowed the last of his soft drink, realizing that he must look like hell. All of his troubles would be clearly written on his face for someone bent on seeing them. "Fine," he said quietly.

"You don't sound like it's fine."

"As fine as it's going to get."

Her warm hand found his, and Hilton's fingers didn't move beneath hers. Between her touch and heavy stare, he was so filled with desire that every nerve in his body was charged and riveted. His eyes wandered to her chest again, and his lips parted slightly as he imagined how her breasts would taste to darting flicks of his tongue. He'd been starved for a woman's juices, it seemed, for years. A desperate erection fought against the binds of his slacks.

"I have to go." The voice jumped to his lips from nowhere.

"You have to?" Danitra asked, cocking her head.

He chuckled, his first laugh in a long time, at the thought of how easily Danitra was seducing him. Yes, he wanted to be seduced, but he had reached a point where the thrill of fantasy had ended, and a dangerous, real longing had slipped into its place.

"I purposely stopped here on my way to a meeting. That way, I have to go. Pretty damn smart, ain't it?"

"You think I'm a whore, huh?"

"Oh, no," he said earnestly, squeezing her fingers. "I think you're smart. I think you're determined." He paused and licked his lips because they felt parched suddenly. "I won't lie. I think your body is hot enough to send me straight to hell. But I know I'm not telling you something you don't already know."

Danitra nodded at him. "I'll tell you where I'm at, Mr. James," she said. "I got work, I got school, and I got Terrance. That means I'm not a woman anymore; I don't got time for it. Got to get paid, got to hit the books, got to be a mama. I can't be chasing after all these fools trying to move in with that 'yo, baby, yo' mess, and the next thing you know, somebody's hitting on your child or touching them or who knows what. I don't got time for none of that." She blinked several times. He was surprised to see her near tears.

"But see, every once in a while I miss that feeling when a man slides his hands from one end of your body to the other. I miss that. I miss that feeling when a man's hot breath is in your ear. I ain't gon' lie, neither. I ain't after nobody's husband, and I ain't trying to break up nobody's home, but when I look at you, Mr. James, I remember how much I miss being a woman."

Hilton was certain Danitra must be able to hear his pounding heart even from where she sat, that her sharp eyes could read every thought surging through his brain. He'd never cheated on Dede, never even seriously considered it. Not with the redheaded freak he'd met at Curt's party, not with the fine sister at the city manager's office who always called him Billy Dee and invited him for drinks ("strictly business," she said) whenever she knew Dede was out of town. Fifteen years, and he'd always said no. No. No.

Suddenly, those years didn't matter. His desires for Danitra, to swallow her aches, to spread his own over her nakedness, felt larger than that. This could be the one thing to save them both from their private miseries. Hilton was a prisoner, he realized. Nothing could make him leave this room. Already, his mind was constructing excuses for the city officials who were no doubt waiting for him at a meeting that could be worth thousands of dollars for Miami New Day.

Danitra stood up just beyond his reach. Her powder smelled sweet and light, tickling his nose. She folded her arms across her chest, hiding those tantalizing nipples.

"But you know what?" she said. "I know you say you got a

meeting, and I know you're an important man, so I'm 'a let you go this time. Even though I know you want to stay. I ain't gon' get nobody in trouble, so you just go on."

Hilton's muscles relaxed, and he remembered to keep breathing. Lord Jesus help, she'd shown mercy on him. He caught his breath and stood up, uncreasing his pants. Danitra would plainly see the signs of his arousal, but that didn't matter to him. He did not move toward her because the slightest movement would shift the balance between staying and leaving, he knew. He must leave now.

Danitra still held his gaze. "I'm here after six most days, all day mostly on Saturday and Sunday," she said. "I just want you to have something to remember me by, so you won't walk out and never come back."

With that, she whipped her T-shirt over her head in one deft movement, revealing her light brown nakedness beneath, her cocoa-colored nipples more full than Dede's, pinched and stiffened.

Hilton could only stare. "Girl," he whispered, "I wish you wouldn't have done that."

Danitra cupped her breasts in her hands and closed her eyes, just seconds before Hilton was upon her and began to explore her with his mouth. Danitra's hand made a skillful journey between his thighs, finding its way to the spot where his need for her longed to breathe. "I'm sorry, Mr. James," she said against his neck. "I almost let you walk out of here, too. I came just that close."

"Shhhhhh," Hilton breathed as his tongue found her nipple and replaced her words with tiny moans from her smooth, lovely throat that stretched toward the ceiling. He wriggled out of his suit's jacket and allowed it to drop to her floor.

CHAPTER 15

For his entire drive home, Hilton had heard nothing but sirens. The moment he left Danitra's apartment, racing against the deepening orange daylight because he couldn't stand the idea of remaining with her after dark, his car's rearview mirror was filled with the red-and-white flashing of sirens. An ambulance was racing behind him, darting between traffic and closing in with its deafening wails before he pulled off the road and wondered, for an awful moment, if it meant to follow him. It drove past.

Then, as soon as he hit southbound I-95, he got tied up in the snarl of onlookers gazing at a crash clogging the northbound lanes. A minivan was turned on its side, swathed in flashing red lights from emergency vehicles of all sizes. Hilton forced himself to drive past without looking at the crushed van or searching for signs of its unlucky passengers. By the time he had passed it and his lane began to speed up, he realized that his knuckles hurt from clinging so tightly to his steering wheel. His mouth was dry.

Pull it together, brother, he thought to himself. You're on your way home to your wife and kids. Tonight of all nights, he had to chill out.

For the first time all day, Hilton was wide awake. His mind was in full action, quizzing him: Where had he been? Why hadn't he called home or the office since he left? Simple. He'd felt burned out, so he canceled his meeting and went for a drive.

One major fuck-up: he'd left his jacket at Danitra's. Okay,

simple again. He'd forgotten it at the office. No problem.

He sniffed himself for Danitra's scent, which still lingered heavily in his nostrils and made his loins feel tight with the memory of arousal. He glanced down at himself to check for stains, for lipstick, for any sign Dede's eyes would devour. Clean. Good.

He was all right. He could do this.

As traffic eased and he began making good time, Hilton even ventured a smile at himself in his mirror, remembering Danitra's fingernails traveling across his bare spine and her hungry mouth wrapped around him in a way Dede had never mastered, drawing such howls from him that he'd woken her baby up. He was sure he even felt better, much better. So much for the stress Stu had talked about; he'd found the perfect stress relief.

Hilton's mood changed as soon as he turned onto his dark street and saw a Metro-Dade police car parked at the curb in front of his coral wall, nearly blanketed in shadow. Jamil's Huffy racing bicycle was abandoned, lying on its side in the driveway behind Dede's car near the edge of the street. Jamil would never leave his bike out like that.

you never know what the boy could'a been

Something was wrong. This was some swift retribution exacted upon his family to punish him for straying. Like a series of close-up photographs, his mind flashed him images of their bloody carcasses propped up in a grotesque imitation of a family pose on the sofa, and his own blood seemed to thicken in his veins.

Hilton leaped from his car, met by barks of recognition from Charlie, who was behind the fence in the backyard. The barking sounded clipped and urgent, feeding Hilton's fevered mind.

"Dede?" he cried, flinging the unlocked front door open.

Jamil and Kaya were watching television on the living room sofa and looked up at him, startled. Jamil halted the pencil sketch of a race car he was drawing in midstroke.

Kaya was sipping fruit juice through a straw, her legs crossed as he'd imagined her the moment before; but this time, in reality, there was no blood streaming from her empty eye sockets.

"Hi, Daddy," Jamil said. "I'm sorry I left my bike outside, but Mom got scared and said to come in right now—"

"Where's your mom?" Hilton asked.

"In the kitchen with Sergeant Gillis," Kaya said, and glanced up at him pointedly. "She tried to call you."

Niglets. Hilton barely heard her as a roar of silence rose in his ears. He stood without moving, gazing at his two children whose foreheads protruded slightly like his own, whose eyes reminded him of Nana's. Jamil's missing tooth. The sheen of Kaya's braids. He was seized by the startling sensation, almost a certainty, that he was dreaming.

Jamil snapped him from the trance. "We got a letter from that guy again, Daddy," he said.

Hickory dickory dock,
Time's running off the clock,
For a nigger brood,
Their little dog too,
And a judge I'll make suck my cock.

This time, the note had been delivered via the United States Postal Service into the James family's black mailbox directly beside their front door. The plain white envelope was typed, with no return address, postmarked from Coral Gables. The single piece of paper folded inside contained only those five lines, centered on the page with care.

Closer, closer each time.

"Sure is a methodical son of a bitch," Curt said in the kitchen, guzzling a can of Coke. "Man, I don't know, guys. A letter to the house? I know we've filed complaints with Miami PD, but suddenly I'm thinking about the FBI and wondering if maybe we shouldn't be worried about a letter bomb. Remember the last note, what he said about blowing the house down?"

Dede was wearing a bright yellow suit from work, sitting at the kitchen table with reading glasses she rarely wore. She was sorting through her copy of the computer printout from the state attorney's office, her list of the hundreds of men and women she'd prosecuted during her career. Dozens of names had already been highlighted and investigated, but she was always examining the list as though she expected one name to suddenly jump out at her.

"I think that's all nursery rhyme crap," Dede said, sounding far less shaken than she had after receiving the last threat. She'd become a veteran at fright now, and she'd learned how to nourish herself with it, growing stronger. "Just like this hickory dickory dock nonsense. What are we looking for, a highly educated poet who's also a munitions expert? I think we're giving him too much credit, and that's the problem. We've probably already interrogated him and let him slide. I'll bet he dunks fries at Burger King just like these guys we've talked to."

Hilton stood over the sink, rubbing cold water across his face to absorb the perspiration that had been dripping from his brow since he arrived at home. While his family was here dealing with this maniac, he'd been out fucking one of his former clients. His hands still trembled slightly from his nightmarish vision of finding Dede and the children assembled in a death embrace.

"Suck his cock," Dede muttered, annoyed. "It'll be the last time his cock is sucked or anything else, that's for damn sure."

Her words, directed at the letter's author, seared into Hilton's conscience. Danitra's mouth had brought him to a panting orgasm less than an hour before, and even now his imagination still paraded images of Danitra's lips, her tongue, her breasts before his eyes against his will. All of his mental preparations for seeing Dede had been shattered; if she confronted him now, he would be too nervous to lie with any credibility.

"From now on, maybe you'd better not open any letters

from folks you don't know," Curt said. "Just to be safe. Ain't that right, Hilton?"

Hilton nodded, still facing the sink while cold droplets from the running water splashed his slacks. "Yeah. Sounds right."

"Isn't Charlie trained to sniff out bombs?" Dede asked Curt.

"Sure is, but you don't want to take that chance, Your Honor."

"Well, I'll be damned if I'm not going to open my own mail."

If Dede was expecting an argument from Hilton tonight, she wouldn't get it. He remained silent, concentrating on slowing his breathing so he could hold a normal conversation without looking as unsettled as he felt. His neck tingled as though the letter's author was in the room with them, watching them, and he felt helpless to strike out against him. He was too weak.

Charlie, the alarm, the gun—none of it would be enough. Nothing could stop someone bent on hurting them. And how could he be a man if he wasn't strong enough to protect his own family? He had already failed to turn his back on temptation, and it might be that simple to fail again. Hilton felt hollow and useless. He tried to wash the feeling away beneath the stream of running water.

"You with us, Hil?" Curt asked.

Hilton waved toward them and nodded. "I just thought the worst when I drove up and saw the car outside. I'm all right."

Even without seeing them, Hilton sensed that Curt and Dede must have exchanged a look then. Curt was probably puzzled, and Dede most likely shrugged off her frustration. I don't know what's happening to him, her look must have said. He's cracking up.

"Don't let him get to you, man. That's what he wants."

"I know," Hilton said, forcing a small smile and dragging himself to the table to sit beside Dede. He met her eyes for a split second, then looked away from their searching and patted her hand. "I'm okay, baby."

Dede sighed, flipping through the pages on her printout. She was probably plenty worried to see him losing his cool, but she would never question him in front of Curt. She would save that for later, he knew.

"I'm so sick of this searching on and on, not knowing," Dede said. She muttered something in her mother's first language, Ga, a tongue Dede spoke only in phrases and which Hilton could not understand. "It's like my mother says . . . How would that translate? 'An enemy you know is a friend compared to the enemy you don't.'"

"Maybe this is bigger than us," Curt said.

"No," Dede said, sounding as firm as Hilton might. "I don't want it bigger than us. I don't want it in the papers. Next thing, someone will be questioning whether I'm fit to serve, if I can be objective. Let's keep up the questioning, starting with . . . "—she sighed again, scanning the rows of names— "Lord, who knows? This next row of felonies. Craig Farrell, Lee Eric Frank, Charles Ray Goode, William James Grace . . . "

charles ray

Hilton's head snapped up, and he leaned over to follow the trail of Dede's finger across the names. "Wait up," he said. "What was that name? That Goode name?"

"Charles Ray Goode. Aggravated battery. He got time served and two years' probation," Dede read. "I don't even remember him. I'm not getting a face. I remember Grace, though. He tried to rape a high school girl, and he got out last year—"

"It's not him," Hilton said, taking the printout from her fingers so he could peer at the name. His heart was pounding until his body felt unsteady, half from giddiness, half from fear. "This one. Charles Ray Goode. Curt, get this down."

"I'm getting, I'm getting," Curt said, reaching for his pad.

"Hil, it looks like the judge practically let him off. Goode didn't even do any real time."

"His birthdate is . . . " Hilton paused his reading, his mouth stilled a moment. ". . . March twelfth, 1956."

"That's your birthday," Dede said, surprised.

"How 'bout that?" Curt said, chuckling. "But remember— just 'cause y'all have the same zodiac sign doesn't mean this is the one we want, Hil."

"He's the one," Hilton said hoarsely. "I don't know how I know. I just do. Curt, man, I feel like I'd know him if I saw him in a lineup."

"Good thing one of us does," Dede said, looking at Hilton with a gentle, worried skepticism.

(

A rare moment of peace had settled over the house.

Hilton had said his good nights to Jamil and Kaya, taking a moment to sit with them on the sofa and ask them about their lives. He'd had no idea Kaya had been cast in a professional play at the Coconut Grove Playhouse, a musical, nor that she'd told Dede she'd made up her mind to study science instead of drama. He hadn't known Jamil had qualified for the county's program for gifted students, and that he'd nearly gotten into a fight at school the week before because a classmate called him a liar. He had his mother's temper. Hilton listened to them, one arm around each, and marveled at how precious and wonderful their little lives were. Their world was so different from his. What a blessing to be so young, with their lives free of real fear or betrayal or paralyzing sleeplessness, all things that just might come with time.

After sending Kaya and Jamil to bed, Hilton went outside to tie Charlie to the tree in the front yard and then surveyed the property with his shotgun, as he did each night. He searched the shadows where hedges from his neighbors' yards grew against his back fence, then the shed, the patio, the garage. Everything was silent, free of any signs of tampering. Afterward, he made his way inside, carefully locking all the doors, leaving on all the floodlights until the house was encircled in brightness.

In the hallway, Hilton could see the sharp light from the reading lamp streaming from Dede's bedroom. He stood with his gun and took a deep breath, then he peered through the doorway. She sat in bed reading a hardbound law journal, writing notes on a legal pad. She looked lovely to him, even with her hair covered by a faded scarf and in her round-frame reading glasses.

"May I come in?" he asked. The bedroom no longer felt like his. Dede nodded but didn't answer. She closed her book and gazed at him. Hilton rested the gun against the wall near the nightstand, then walked to the closet and began to undress. First, he hung up his white dress shirt. Next, he folded his gray pinstriped slacks on their crease and rested them across a hanger he carefully slid between his other clothes.

"Where's the rest of that suit? That's your best," she said.

"I left it at the office," he said with ease, too much ease. Before now, he'd never had any opportunities to discover that he was, indeed, an adept liar. He sat at the edge of the bed, near her feet. "I'm sorry I wasn't at work when you called."

"Wanda told me about your meeting."

"I canceled it," he said without a pause.

"She told me that, too." Hilton sensed a hidden pain in Dede's face, but it was impossible to guess its source. There had been so much pain lately.

"Aren't you going to ask where I was?" Hilton asked. Dede looked at him but stubbornly refused to answer. He kneaded her foot beneath the blanket. "Work has been hard for me, piling up, and I can't handle it. I took off and drove around. Back roads, mostly. I'm trying to get myself together, Dede."

When he saw her uncomfortable concern for him reflected in her face, his skin began to burn with guilt. He rubbed his neck, wishing he had the courage to be honest, wishing he'd had the strength to remain true to her, true to himself. "I'm a mess, Dede," he said, blinking, staring at his lap.

"You said you were going to see Raul."

"I know."

Her voice drifted to an urgent hush: "Hilton, it scares me to see you like this. Even Wanda asked me what's happening to you. I said I don't know. I don't know what to do. I try not to think about it, hoping it'll go away and I'll have my husband back. But it doesn't. Every day I look at you in the mornings and I can barely remember who you are. Who you were. You're a man who lives here, you walk with that gun, you're watching over us all the time like some sort of guardian angel. But other than that, I don't know you. What's happened?"

He shook his head, unable to speak.

"Promise me you'll get help," Dede said, sitting up, her bleary eyes sweeping over his face. "Promise me."

"I promise," he said, barely audibly.

"Should we cancel the party Saturday?"

"No," he said quickly. "It might be good for us."

Dede ventured a small smile, patting the mattress beside her. "Come," she said. "Lie with me. As long as you can, lie here."

He turned off the light and climbed into bed beside her, and her arms greeted him like a long-sought sanctuary. He could melt in these arms. He rested his head across her chest and felt her breathing, waiting, as heat gathered in the spots where their flesh met. But he couldn't bring himself to touch her. He didn't deserve to touch her like a husband, no matter how much he wished he could and how much he knew she wanted him to.

I'm sorry, he mouthed into the darkness.

Finally, after a moment, he heard Dede's long, wounded sigh of resignation before she kissed one temple and the other. "Sweet dreams," she said.

CHAPTER **16**

Hilton explores the warm, welcoming space between Dede's legs and parts them, sliding himself on top of her with a steady pressure until her insides swallow him. He breathes a sigh and fervidly burrows his way against her flesh, retreating until he feels the heated ringing at his tip—never further—and then easing back inside until the ringing spreads throughout his loins.

"I'm sorry, Dede," he says. "Never, never again."

When she does not answer, he wonders if she is angry. He wonders if she refuses to stir to punish him, or if she is veiling her own pleasure to torment him.

He closes his eyes, his buttocks pinched from strain, and buries himself inside of her again. He kneads her stiff nipples with his fingertips. He can already feel the surge of his seed, a creeping from his testicles through the pulsing length of his organ. Not now, he thinks. This is too soon. A bit longer.

Her grasp around him is more tight now, a second skin lulling him helplessly to the edge of his endurance. Not yet, not yet.

The grip snatches tighter still, so jolting that he pauses in midstroke. It is pain, he realizes. Dede is so parched that he is scraping himself raw inside her. Is he bleeding? The heat he feels is entirely his own; Dede's flesh has grown cold, and he feels it coiling through his system with a spasm.

Hilton gapes at Dede's face. The eyes that meet his are so wide they look propped, glazed in a lifeless love stare. When he touches her, the skin does not yield to his fingertips; instead, his *hand drags across her flesh. Her body beneath him is stone.*

Hilton screams, flinging himself from her and cradling his tender nakedness in a fetal curl on the bed.

"There's no joy in fucking the dead," a voice says from the darkness. His voice. He looks up and sees a Hilton figure facing him from the leather reclining chair. The figure is wearing Hilton's silk pajamas, his hands folded in his lap.

A second Hilton figure, this one dressed in Hilton's pinstriped gray suit, is adjusting his kente-cloth tie in the bureau mirror. He looks over his shoulder to glance at Hilton, grinning unkindly. "Unless, of course, you like that sort of thing. Some people do."

"Fuck you," Hilton says, feeling brave somehow. "All of you." A third Hilton figure pokes his head from the bathroom, holding a dripping razor in his hand. His jaw is lathered with shaving cream, but the lather froths red from the runny, exposed flesh peeling from his face. One of his eyes is obscured by the flat crush of bone that was once his forehead, leaving him to gaze around him in a grotesque, exaggerated squint.

"How many times, Hilton?" the squinting Hilton figure calls. "Twice? Three times? How many times do you think you can die?"

"You can't keep hiding," says the Hilton figure at the bureau. "You don't belong here. You remind me of a tree knocked over in a storm, its exposed roots gnarled and shriveled black—"

"That keeps dropping seedlings," sighs the Hilton figure in the chair, grim-faced, flipping through Dede's legal pad.

"What's another name for a dead tree?" calls the horrid Hilton figure in the bathroom.

"Firewood," says Hilton at the bureau.

"Kindling," says the Hilton in the chair, his face filled with menace. "So how do you like that? A dead tree dropping seedlings. Everything is growing wild, no control. And your hiding is all for nothing, mind you, because those seedlings will choke soon enough. We've found someone to do some weeding."

"Who says it's impossible to find good help?" chuckles the Hilton at the bureau. "Charles Ray's dreams are like yours, easy to find. And he's so willing."

"He'd have almost thought of it himself."

"And a poet, at that. Very nice touch, we thought," says the Hilton in the chair, still glaring.

Hilton draws the sheets up over his naked body in the bed, blinking back tears. "Leave us alone," he says, begging by now. "Why can't we just be left alone?"

"No," says the Hilton in the chair, pointing an accusing finger. "You leave us alone. Are we your puppets?"

"You're offensive," says the Hilton figure in the bathroom, scraping at his torn flesh absently with the razor. A slice of skin the size of a bacon strip drops to the floor.

"You've made us an abomination."

"Imagine the gall, the cowardice, to run the way you do," says the Hilton in the chair. "To expect to keep dying forever. Opening doors that aren't meant for you."

Hilton sees a flurry of movement behind the blinds pulled across the glass sliding door, and a small black boy wearing only cutoff shorts runs from his hiding place. He is Jamil's age or a bit older, but he is not Jamil. He is so familiar. His skin is caked in glowing grains of sand.

"There's a pool outside!" the boy cries. "Can we go swim?"

"That's enough swimming for you," says a woman's voice. Hilton realizes that it is Nana, not Dede, who now lies beside him in the bed. Nana reaches over to stroke Hilton's hand with a warm touch.

"Just a little swim?" Hilton asks her for the boy, clasping Nana's hand.

"No more swimming," Nana says kindly, her warmth drawing him closer and closer until he is wrapped in her arms, unafraid. The three Hilton figures have vanished. Only the boy remains, standing at the bedside with a smile and wondrous eyes gleaming with his innocence. Dried algae is tangled in the boy's matted hair. Hilton is mesmerized by the sight of him. His eyes, his innocence, remind him of . . . he can't remember . . .

"Stop fighting, Hilton. It's wrong to fight," Nana's voice says from all around him, a tunnel. "I was wrong, too. I thought it was all for you, but I left you a curse, not a blessing."

Those eyes. The boy's eyes. The eyes of the unlived.

"Jamil?" Hilton calls desperately, a near-scream. "Kaya?"

In the darkness, no one answers. There is no one to answer. His words bounce against nothing and echo back to his ears.

Hilton woke up to the sound of his own cries, finding himself curled in a ball on the floor of the study, his boxer shorts cleaved to him in a bath of icy perspiration. He'd rolled off of the pallet Dede fixed for him, knocking over his makeshift plastic-crate nightstand and the clock. The room seemed to be trembling, but Hilton realized it was only his own fierce heartbeat. His chest felt so tight, so tight. Jesus, had he been breathing? One of these days, if he weren't careful, he might die in his sleep.

He didn't remember leaving Dede's room. He didn't remember allowing himself to sleep. Gasping, he sat straight up and reached for the shotgun he always kept beside him, feeling certain that they were still watching him, mocking. They were . . .

Who? Who was watching him?

Hilton tried to catch his breath, but it grew to a sob in his chest as he buried his face in the carpet of the empty room. No one. No one was watching. Only he was in here, with what little was left of his sanity.

"God, don't leave me like this . . . " Hilton sobbed, finally acknowledging that in the loss of all hope he, like all men, was seeking refuge in a power he'd never dared allow himself to believe in. "Please, God, please . . . oh Jesus, help me . . . "

What had he done? Whom had he harmed, to deserve this? He'd tried to live a good life, that was all. He'd tried to be a good father, a good husband. He'd tried.

you don't   belong
come, hilton

Hilton sobbed harder, feeling the gun's cold metal barrel in his slippery palm. He could end it all now, he could plant the gun in his mouth. That would be so much simpler, if only it weren't for Dede and the children. He couldn't leave them. Not now.

"Please, Jesus, show me the way . . . " Hilton begged, the muscles in his arms unsteady. "Show me the way . . . This life is worse than death . . . It's worse . . . Is this hell I'm in? Why, God? Why?"

An answer came to Hilton in a word: Danitra. Suddenly, a small sense of hope crept inside of him. He couldn't undo it, but he could try. He could begin his penance.

Hilton turned on the light and tore through his desk to find his message pad, where he'd taken at least one message from her months before, the day they made plans to move her to The Terraces. Yes, here it was. He continued dialing even as he glanced at his clock, which was lying on its side, and noted it was three o'clock in the morning.

The phone rang four times. He heard muttered profanity and a baby's cries. He didn't recognize the woman's voice, which was distorted from sleep. "—dammit . . . Hel-lo?"

"Danitra?"

"Yes," she said, clearly annoyed. "Who the hell is this?"

"It's Hilton James."

There was a long pause. "Mr. James?" she asked, confused. "What . . . I . . . What's wrong? What time is it?"

His heart was pounding still. "I'm sorry to call this late. I didn't mean to wake up Terrance. I needed to talk to you."

". . . Talk to me?" she muttered. "I don't . . . "

"I had to apologize to you about today. It shouldn't have happened, and it can't happen again. I can't sleep."

Danitra sounded alarmed. "What you mean, Mr. James?"

"I had no business over there today. Can you understand?"

Now Danitra exhaled with an exasperated sound. She didn't speak, so Hilton went on: "I left my jacket by there, too. Can you leave it on your doorknob for me when you go to school? I just want to grab it, and then that's that. I'm sorry to be like this, I know you'll think I'm a dog, but I made a mistake. A big mistake."

This time when Danitra spoke her voice sounded more clear, more like herself. "You're drunk, ain't you?"

"I know what you must think, me calling like this. But—"

"I think you better just get off this phone and sleep it off or something, Mr. James. You ain't making no kind of sense."

"I just need my jacket."

"I ain't got no goddamned jacket," Danitra snapped.

"Did you look for it? I think it's— "

"Look," Danitra said, her voice slicing through his words, "I don't have no jacket, and I haven't seen your ass today or any day since I got out. You got me confused with someone else. This is Danitra, remember? Danitra Peebles."

Hilton was dumbstruck by the resolve and levelheaded-ness in Danitra's voice. He could feel his pulse pounding in his fingertips as he held the telephone receiver.

"You there, Mr. James?" Danitra said, and he couldn't make a sound to answer. Danitra sighed again, and her voice changed. "Wait a minute . . . Is this J.T.? Nigger, if it is, I'm gonna—"

Hilton slammed down the receiver, breathing hard. He clutched his throat with his hand and glanced wild-eyed around the room. It was happening again, just like with Stu yesterday. What was happening to him?

Hilton shuffled through the hallway to the open door of Dede's bedroom. He stood a moment to allow his eyes to grow accustomed to the darkness and then made out Dede's sleeping face in the light from the patio. He stared at the leather reclining chair facing him, where her pad was abandoned in the seat. He glanced at his reflection in the bureau mirror. He walked to the bathroom and could see the white glow of his disposable Bic razor on the sink.

He shuddered, then remembered he must be cold because he was nearly nude and dripping with perspiration.

He walked to the closet and slowly pulled the door open,

triggering the dim light inside. He searched for the robe to match his silk pajamas. Then he paused and turned instead to the section reserved for his suits, which hung neatly in a row. He buried his hand behind his navy suit and felt the smooth fabric of an unseen jacket. He pulled it into the light.

His gray pinstriped suit. Jacket and slacks, on a hanger.

Hilton heard a faint snore from Dede and jumped, then he sank against the wall and closed his eyes, sobs tugging at his throat again. He sealed his mouth shut with his palm. He didn't dare look at the suit again. He had seen it. It was there.

The floor seemed to move beneath his feet. His brain began to play fragments of that Eliot poem he'd been forced to learn in high school. This is the way the world ends, he thought. This is the way the world ends. Not with a bang.

A whimper.

CHAPTER **17**

By the time Hilton reached the corner of Northeast Second Avenue and found the nondescript Cafeteria Borinquén with its faded facade and chipped paint, he was ravenous. Raul had apparently been waiting some time; he was already working on a plate of rice with pigeon peas and *pinchos*, pork roasted in small chunks on wooden sticks. He shrugged, seeing Hilton, and tapped his watch. "Sorry. If you had said one, I would have arrived at one. The food smelled too good," Raul said.

Hilton pulled out the wooden folding chair at Raul's table in the center of the busy cafe, beneath the whirring ceiling fan. The decor was jovial, with posters of Puerto Rico and cartoon images of the island's trademark frog, the *coquí*, blanketing the wood-paneled walls. The spastic cowbells from a salsa song danced from hidden speakers. "I got my east and west mixed up. What the hell is a Puerto Rican restaurant doing in Little Haiti?" Hilton asked.

"The great melting pot, no?" Raul said, absorbed in eating. He glanced up at him, stripping pork from its stick with his teeth and chewing quickly. "You look like hell."

"I love you, too," Hilton said, darting his eyes away. His stomach growled loudly. "Are there any fucking waiters in here, or do I have to go back there myself?"

Raul continued to gaze at him thoughtfully, then he raised his hand toward a lanky, dark-skinned man standing near the back. *"Oye, Pedro. Ven aquí, por favor, compadre."*

"Damn, the music's loud in here."

"Silence, you," Raul said, patting Hilton's hand as the man neared their table with a water glass, which he set down near Hilton. "Tell me what you like, and I'll translate for you."

"I don't know what food they have. He can't speak English? Jesus Christ."

Raul spoke rapid Spanish to the man, who nodded and replied.

"How about what I'm having? The *arroz con gandules*?"

"Yeah, whatever. Why aren't you drinking beer? They don't have beer?" Hilton asked.

"You know I don't drink during the workday. You don't either. Let's have coffee. *Dos cafés*, Pedro."

Hilton didn't answer, emptying his water glass in a series of long swallows. The ice clanked against the glass as he set it back down. He stared at the red-and-white checkerboard pattern on the tacky plastic tablecloth, drumming his fingers on the table.

"You're in a real mood today," Raul said.

Again, Hilton was silent. He wanted to launch right into everything, explaining that he was losing his mind somehow, but he'd lost his nerve after seeing his friend in person. He couldn't remember the words he'd chosen. The whole story sounded ridiculous, even to him. And what was the story, really?

The waiter brought a basket of warm flat bread, moist with melted butter, and Hilton dove into it hungrily while he felt Raul's eyes watching him. Raul reminded him of Dede sometimes, the way he probed without words and simply waited. Well, it would be a long wait today. Hilton didn't feel like talking.

"You might consider plastic surgery for the bags under your eyes," Raul said. "But I'm not certain it would help."

Hilton glared up at him. "That's not funny."

"It was no joke."

"Look, just lay off of me. I don't even know why I'm bothering with this."

"Bothering with what?"

"Trying to deal with you like a human being."

"Oh, I don't know . . . " Raul said gently, sipping from his half-empty water glass. "Sometimes that actually works. *Qué pasa*, eh? What's so important it couldn't wait until your party?"

Hilton set his jaw, staring at the bread basket while the waiter returned with tiny cups of Cuban-style coffee. Sullenly, Hilton bit into a second slice of bread. Raul reached into his linen jacket's front pocket and pulled out a business card, which he slid into Hilton's eyesight. Hilton read "Psychiatric Services" before he looked away.

"Get that away from me," he said.

"She's good. An M.D. I send her all of my former clients."

"I'm sure you do."

"Dede's been talking to me."

Hilton paused in midchew, glancing back up at Raul. The same probing eyes were there, trying to slip inside of him. "And?"

Raul shrugged. "And she's worried about you. She says you've been acting strangely. I, of course, said, 'How can you tell?'"

"You're an asshole."

Raul rested his chin on his palm, his gaze more serious. "She said something interesting: If she were still prone to jealousy, from the way you behave, she'd think you were having an affair." Hilton sighed, running his hand across the top of his head. The frenzied beats of the drums and blares from the salsa trumpets were making him feel fevered.

"So . . . are you?" Raul asked, not blinking.

Instead of turning away from his gaze, Hilton decided to face Raul. He leaned toward him. "You can't discuss this, Raul."

Raul nodded. "So you are, then. You're a prick if you are, I'll tell you that right now. As if you couldn't learn from me and my ex . . . You see how miserable I am, with no one."

"I'm not having an affair. But I did . . . "—he swallowed,

with considerable effort—"I did sleep with someone. A former client. At least, I think I did."

"Are you in denial, or do you have amnesia?"

"I know, I know. It sounds crazy. But I slept with this woman, and then she said she didn't remember. I mean, like it never happened. I don't think it did. And the jacket I left at her house was in my closet. It was like you and that Mets cap that time, remember? At Miami Arena?"

"You're making no fucking sense, Hilton. As usual."

"Some fucking doctor," Hilton shot back, stung.

"Your premise is wrong. I'm not your doctor."

"That's for damn sure. Just shut up and listen a minute. I think all of this has something to do with my dreams. I mean, things are happening to me and then I find out they never really happened. More than once. Like your Mets cap, and now this woman . . . I think maybe I just dreamed it. I never slept with her, I just thought I did. But Raul, it was so realistic. I was there. I can remember every detail, down to how she tasted."

"Do you mind? I'm eating."

Unexpectedly, Hilton slapped his palm down hard on the table, making his silverware jump up against his glass. Raul hesitated with his fork halfway to his mouth, surprised.

"Don't you get it?" Hilton said, his teeth gritted and his arms trembling at the elbows from anger and hunger combined.

Raul glanced around briefly to see if they were drawing stares, then rested his fork on his plate. He sighed. "No, Hilton . . . I don't get it. Explain it to me."

"There's something going on in my dreams I need to know about, because I don't think I'm really awake sometimes. Okay? It's like I could call you later and say, 'Thanks for lunch today,' and you would say 'What lunch?' I don't know what's real anymore. I'm afraid to sleep, man. I feel like I can't ever go back to exactly where I left, like I never know what I'll find."

For a long few seconds, Raul ate and didn't answer. The waiter brought a steaming plate of rice and beans to Hilton and set it in front of him with a smile and nod. Hilton didn't move to touch his food, waiting for Raul's assessment. He hated to feel so dependent on his friend, but Raul was all he had now. What you've described is very common, he might say. Nothing to worry about. A quick dose of hypnosis and you'll be fine, just like before.

Raul dabbed his mouth with his paper napkin. "Dede told me about the dreams. She hears you wake up at night, crying out."

"They're worse and worse. I only wish I could remember them."

"You approach dreams the way my brother does. Your dreams aren't *causing* your problem, they're a symptom. You can't view dreams as isolated entities controlling your life. Dreams are just that—dreams."

"Bullshit," Hilton said. "Live a day in my shoes, man, and then give me that crap. There's something in my dreams—I know it. If I could remember, I would understand. Maybe it goes back to Nana again."

"*Ay, Dios mío,*" Raul muttered, shaking his head. "Hocus-pocus. Is there a ghost in your dreams following you?"

"Maybe. Yes."

"You and my brother are quite a match. You know who you remind me of? A Haitian girl I treated more than a year ago. It was all the same thing, about dreams. Dreams and ghosts."

Hilton felt a sense of awakening in his lagging spirit. "Tell me about her."

"She was obsessed by her dreams, afraid to sleep. Just like you said just now. The stories she told . . . "

"Then she could remember them?"

"Unbelievable detail. I tell you, she was obsessed."

"What happened in her dreams?"

Raul sighed. "It's hard to remember now. They were nightmares. She was being chased, that sort of thing. Standard dreams. But you sounded just like her, talking about what's real and what isn't. She talked about that, too."

"What's her name?" Hilton blurted, anxious.

marguerite

"Never mind her name. I still have some ethics left."

"Where is she, then? What happened to her?"

"She quit therapy. She was a student. I know my brother talked to her for a project he's been working on at the university about near-death phenomenon."

"What does that have to do with her?"

"That's why her parents sent her to therapy. She fell from a fourth-floor balcony on spring break and nearly died. Very lucky, that one. Her dreams started after that."

Hilton felt a thudding boot in his chest. "Like Nana."

"Oh, stop with that already. What's like Nana?"

"That's when the dreams started, after I found her on the floor. She'd had an attack, remember? She was—"

"Everything is Nana with you. Listen to me, you're wasting your intellectual and emotional energy this way. What you need to do is call this doctor I recommended and keep your pants zipped up. You have to solve your problems with what's real before you can solve your dreams. Stop fucking around on your wife, and maybe your nightmares will go away. You disappoint me, *compadre*."

Hilton tasted his food but suddenly had no appetite. "I shouldn't have said anything to you."

"I hope at least you were safe."

"I'm crazy, not stupid."

"Don't piss it all away, I'm warning you. You have a self-destructive nature, and I see what you're doing. You don't deserve Dede, you're thinking. You don't deserve those bright children. So you work to destroy it. It's very, very foolish."

"Don't worry about it," Hilton said. "It won't happen again, and maybe it never happened at all."

"Hilton," Raul said in a somber tone, sliding the business card closer to him. "See her. Make an appointment. I do agree you need help. You have a severe sleeping disorder."

"I don't need her. I have you," Hilton said, his voice cracking unexpectedly as his words turned pleading.

"Don't you see? I cannot help you."

What did he have to tell Raul so he would understand? That he thought he had lost his mind? That he'd woken up the other night and nearly been compelled to put his shotgun in his mouth, that he'd come this close to blowing his brains out? Maybe that was what he needed to say, but he couldn't.

"You know who I'd rather talk to?" Hilton asked in a strained voice, staring at Raul. "Your brother and the Haitian girl."

"To chase dreams and ghosts?"

"Man, they're all I have left to chase," Hilton said.

CHAPTER 18

For one glistening pearl of a moment, everything was once again all right.

The dreadlock-wearing deejay stilled the sweaty bodies contorting to lively African high-life music with an abrupt switch to the soulful keyboard tease of Earth, Wind & Fire's "That's the Way of the World." Hilton, who stood talking to Curt near the front door, saw a faraway look creep across Dede's face as her eyes lighted on Hilton.

Without a word, Hilton handed Curt his beer can and walked up to Dede to slip his arms around her waist. As they swayed, she sang the song's lyrics softly near his ear and he closed his eyes, imagining that they were in the studio apartment he'd rented near the UM campus in grad school, with his posters of Funkadelic and George Clinton and the prickly sofa bed where she first spent the night with him. Her scent was the same, natural and wholly Dede. The voice in his ear was the same. He held her more tightly, as though he could physically meld them together.

This feeling was beyond desire; it was his being he clung to.

Hilton half expected to find them both transported back to UM when he opened his eyes. But he was afraid they would be right back in the same spot, so he didn't dare ruin it—not until the last of the song faded and the Afro-pop once again blared from the speakers.

No, they weren't back at UM. Dede's face was broader with the pounds the years had brought; her eyes were world-weary and sad. They were at a party in their own home with such tight security that each guest had been scrutinized at the door by Curt, who was wearing his uniform off-duty. The guard dog marched in the backyard, barking at the unfamiliar guests. Hilton's life with Dede wasn't at its beginning; he couldn't help feeling it was near its end.

"Thank you for the dance, Your Honor," he said spiritlessly, kissing her neck. Dede squeezed his forearm hard, her eyes still closed. He understood. She didn't want to let go either.

"Step up or move off, you loafers," came the accented, genteel voice of Dede's mother, who whirled next to them after grabbing Raul's hand for a dance.

Kessie was shorter and wore cornrows instead of an Afro, but in her youthful features she could have been Dede's twin. The most striking difference was the dark lines etched into Kessie's cheeks, ritualistic scars meant, in Ghana, to make her beautiful. She wore a regal white dress with a head wrap to match. Above the din of conversation her laugh filled the crowded room.

"You call that dancing? Just move natural," Kessie teased Raul. "There's plenty of our music in that island music you like, just as a cow's udder feeds the calf. Isn't that so?" Raul only laughed, mimicking Kessie's spirited two-step.

They'd invited sixty people, but it seemed that at least a hundred filled every corner of the house. Dede had been up until three in the morning preparing specialty dishes like goat meat and *fufu*, a mixture of plantains and cassava, and caterers provided the trays of curried chicken, pigeon peas and rice, and pork ribs. It was a combination of African, Caribbean, and good old soul food.

Many of the guests were the people they had seen at the candidates' reception last fall; politicians, lawyers, educators, artists. But there were more Africans, many from the organized Nigerian Ibo community in Miami, and also Ghanaians Dede's family knew. Hilton wished he could enjoy the United Nations fellowship assembled in his home, but he was too worried about intruders who might slip inside. Each time headlights lingered too long out front, casting a shifting glare against the curtains, Hilton's chest tightened with dread.

He felt a tug at his elbow as he glanced through the front picture window. "Hilton, sweetheart, we'll be going. It's a long drive back down south."

"You sure, Auntie?"

Hilton had never grown accustomed to calling the elementary school teacher and high school principal who adopted him Mom and Dad, and they had never insisted on it. He most often referred to the couple that had raised him merely as the Jameses, or C.J. and Auntie when he saw them in person.

The Jameses were at least seventy now, and they complemented each other well in their formal, unflappable demeanor. They'd taken him in without complaint and shown him every kindness, but at forty they hadn't been sure how to be parents again. Hilton's adoptive brother, a physician, had moved to New York for college long before Hilton moved in, and Hilton still barely knew him. He sometimes envied the warmth he saw when Dede interacted with her mother, who was younger and much more demonstrative. Hilton had set out, in many ways, to make certain the family he raised would be more close-knit than his own.

"It's late for us, child. Almost midnight," Auntie said, bundling herself in a bright red overcoat with a furlike collar. The temperature had dipped to the midfifties outside, a cool night for January in Miami.

Hilton's adoptive father, who was nearly bald and wore a moustache he enjoyed stroking, patted Hilton's arm. "Where are the babies? We're going to say good night."

"Supposed to be in bed, but I bet they're watching videos in Kaya's room. C.J., can you see well enough to drive?"

"You know you can't say anything to him," Auntie said, straining upward to kiss Hilton's bearded cheek. He saw a questioning flicker in her copper-colored eyes, but she would not ask him why he looked so weary or even mention the stalker she'd been told was threatening his family. The

Jameses firmly believed in respecting Hilton's privacy, as they always had. "Good night."

Hilton made his way aimlessly through all of the crowded rooms, pausing at huddles to overhear conversations about political empowerment or sports or the legal system. He checked to make sure both patio doors leading to the yard were locked, sampled a chicken wing, then weaved a path back to the front of the house.

"Man, these people ain't never going to leave, are they?" Curt asked him at the door.

"Sure doesn't look like it."

"That deejay needs to chill with that music." Curt whistled to the deejay, snapping him from his trance behind the turntables. He was playing Bob Marley's "Running Away," a hypnotic reggae beat. "Yo, man, bust that down. We got people trying to sleep up in Broward County."

The deejay gave Curt a thumbs-up sign and lowered the volume slightly. The couples on the dance floor groaned their disapproval, Kessie loudest of all.

Hilton sighed, nearly collapsing against the front door. What he would give to stretch out on the couch and close his eyes for just a few minutes, no matter how frustrating or futile. Hilton had been on his feet much of the day and could barely concentrate. The music's repetitive lyrics were a blur in his brain: "Why you can't find the place where you belong . . . running away, running away, running away . . . " Marley was singing to him.

"Curt, you can book if you want to. I know it's late."

"Forget it, man. I said I'd stay, so I'm here."

Hilton rubbed his face with his hands. "You got anything on Charles Ray Goode yet?"

"I'm working on it. Dede nailed him on aggravated battery, a domestic thing, but he never went to jail. He's ex-military, dishonorable discharge. My old girlfriend in D.C. is running his record for me. Takes me a few days to sweet-talk her."

"Ex-military. That's great goddamn news . . . "

"Bet he was a grunt, if he's like the guys I knew in the service. He can probably salute and peel potatoes, and that's it."

"He doesn't write like a grunt."

"Maybe Goode ain't the guy," Curt said. "I can't figure why he'd be so pissed off and he never did time."

"He's the guy," Hilton said, his voice muffled behind his hands. He fumbled to stand up straight.

"Why don't you go lie down somewhere?"

"Can't. There's a world-peace discussion group in my bedroom," Hilton said. "Lemme go mingle awhile."

Hilton's dazed wanderings through the house took him to the bar on the patio, where he grabbed another beer. Even with the patio door closed, he could hear vibrations from the music inside. Two dozen people were gathered around the pool, lost in conversation and washed in the patio light's green radiance that made them all look surreal to Hilton, as if they moved in slow motion. Standing near the screen, feet from the water, Hilton kept his eyes on the hibiscus hedges that grew against his back fence. A spy might be hiding there.

"Palm wine," said a deep voice close to his ear, startling him. A tall, heavy man draped in an African dress tunic and matching baggy pants stood behind him. He held his wine glass to Hilton's face in a toast. "I'm impressed. Authentic even down to the palm wine. I haven't had this since I went on holiday in London last fall."

His accent was a hybrid of English and Ghanaian. Hilton recognized him as one of Dede's cousins he had met before, a banker named Kofi with an unpronounceable surname. Hilton greeted him, trying to smile.

"I had no idea Dede was so traditional," Kofi said.

"Neither did I," Hilton muttered, wishing to be left alone.

"I met your daughter tonight. What a gracious child. Was she born early?"

Hilton scowled at him. "You mean premature? No. Why?"

Kofi sipped his wine. "I wondered why Dede chose to give her a born-to-die name."

dad-deeeeeee

Hilton nearly swooned in a rush of his senses, his eyes locked on the man's raven, sharp-featured face. He leaned against the patio's aluminum frame as his knees threatened to fold beneath him.

"A what?" he whispered.

A shadow flickered across Kofi's face as he sensed he may have tread somewhere he should not have. "Old superstitions," he said in a dismissive voice. "Rubbish. It doesn't matter."

In a mind-flash, Hilton remembered the confusion over naming his new daughter, how the Kiswahili name they'd originally chosen—Imani, meaning "faith"—was discarded when Dede voiced an unexpected objection. She'd crossed the name Imani from her birth certificate a day later and chosen Kaya, a name from Ghana. Kessie had insisted, Dede told him sheepishly. Kessie'd had a fit.

"No," Hilton said. "I'd like to know."

"Infant mortality is a problem in Africa," Kofi said. "That's where it's rooted. Many cultures have superstitions about children dying. You'd be surprised how prevalent they are. They have to do with spirits inhabiting the child and leaving the child to die, so we have traditional names meant to trick or implore the spirits, to keep the child alive. Symbolic names."

Hilton swallowed hard. Kessie had tried to name Jamil— he couldn't remember the name now—but Hilton had held fast with his son. He'd set his heart on an Arabic name for him, and his middle name was Hilton, naturally. He and Dede couldn't understand why Kessie fretted so, and the episode caused a two-month family rift.

What had Kessie known?

Perspiration tickled Hilton's scalp and armpits. "What," he asked in a frail voice, "does Kaya mean?"

Kofi rubbed his chin. "It's also pronounced Ka-YA, in my language. It roughly means 'Stay and don't go back.'"

☾

A half hour after the deejay packed and left, a trickle of guests remained in impassioned conversations. Hilton's shirt was unbuttoned to midchest, and his loosened tie dangled from his collar. He helped Dede and one of her girlfriends wrap the food in the kitchen, then he looked for Kessie. He found her in the family room in the midst of a debate about politics in Ghana. Without a word, he took her hand firmly and led her back to the deserted living room, where he sat down on the couch beneath the dim lamp. He gently tugged her until she was sitting on his lap and wrapped his arms around her middle. "Hilton, why are you kidnapping me? Let me up. I'm too heavy for you."

"No, Mama Kessie," he said, using his own nickname for her with his chin against her shoulder. "You're just the right size."

"Why do you look so bad?"

"Tired," he said.

"Go to sleep, then. Morning washes everything fresh."

He felt a fragile spell in this room, with the two of them alone. Many times Hilton had considered his mother-in-law as meddlesome and opinionated as any, if not more so, but now she seemed like an extension of himself. He felt like a blood relation to this African woman whose deep-scarred face suddenly looked exquisite framed between the masks hanging on the wall.

"Tell me what you need to say, Hilton. I'll answer you."

Slowly, he repeated his chance conversation with Kofi on the patio. She listened, nodding slightly, her face never changing except for the hint of a small, embarrassed smile. He stroked her hand. "You know what I want to ask you," he said.

She nodded yes, looking thoughtful. Her buttonlike brown eyes glistened in the lamplight. "And we have to talk about this thing from years ago right now? At two o'clock in the morning?"

"It'll help me sleep."

Kessie sighed, leaning more of her weight against him, letting go a bit. Her brow became furrowed, troubled. "Thirteen years. Who can believe it's been thirteen years since Kaya was born? A fat little girl-child."

"Fat and healthy."

"Oh, yes . . . and healthy."

"So why the name?" he asked. "Why Ka-YA?"

"I'll tell you this one time, but we won't speak of it again. And Dede is my daughter, but she mustn't hear this. All right?"

"All right."

Kessie took a deep breath and began in a soft, birdlike voice. "I've been a city girl most of my life, but not in the beginning. I still have many relatives in the village, far from Accra. You rarely hear English there. My five aunts, all of them are still there, my mother, and the rest. The bush, some would call it. I don't like that name. It's home to me.

"The village stays with you, even in the city. You are shaped by things you have seen and heard. I had a smaller brother once, for a short time. When he died, they said the spirits took him. My mother said she saw a spirit dance above his head an hour before his breathing stopped. A death spirit. She described its eyes, its stench, its touch. It took my brother before he lived at all. I, of course, was contrary and educated and Christian, and I never believed in spirits. I thought her mad with grief."

"But you believe now?"

"I believe in things I see."

Hilton closed his eyes, feeling an unexplained, intense pang of sadness, as though something he'd known forever was being translated for him in simple terms he couldn't ignore. He dreaded the sound of Kessie's voice. She seemed to sense it, touching his face. "I don't have to go on. Do you want the rest?"

With effort, he nodded yes.

"When Kaya was born, I befriended a nurse who agreed to let me hold her in the nursery. I stood a few feet before the glass window, and I could see my reflection there, and the reflection of the bundle in my arms. A movement in the glass caught my eye, so I looked up high. And I saw a colorless thing, an indescribable thing, dancing above her empty crib. I blinked my eyes and looked and looked, and I was sure of what I saw. A death spirit. So I told Dede she must change the child's name. I told her it was to honor my heritage, but it really was to help the baby flee."

"And Jamil?" Hilton asked, breathing painfully.

"I prayed I wouldn't ever see that thing again, and I never did. But I felt it, Hilton, from the first instant the second child was in my arms. Just like the first. I felt like mourning if I only touched them, as though what I held was less than a corpse. It was . . . nothing." Her voice was a guttural whisper.

those seedlings will choke soon enough

Abruptly, Kessie patted Hilton's knee. "But Mama Kessie was wrong, you see? So much for my superstitions. Kaya and Jamil both lived. We've managed to trick the spirits. Through prayer? Through resolve? I don't know how or why, but they are both still here, and here they'll stay. We won't speak of this again, as I said, because you'll think I'm a mad old bush woman."

"I could never think that about you," Hilton said, the image of the dancing spirit haunting his thoughts. Was that what he saw in his sleep? "Do you ever have dreams about them, Kessie?"

"Those children? No," she chuckled. "But from time to time I dream about you, Papa. You won't be flattered."

"What about me?"

"Once I dreamed I couldn't remember your face. I was talking to Dede about her husband, and then your face was gone from my mind. Your name, too. Poof. That's a funny dream, isn't it?"

Hilton didn't answer. Instead, he closed his eyes and rested his head fully against Kessie's warmth. He enjoyed a small relief in the midst of his trepidation. In some unknown way, he believed Kessie's story made him understand a little more why his life no longer fit exactly in place. He felt as though he'd laughed suddenly after a long, hard cry. Funny, he thought, but he'd never paused to realize how much he really loved Kessie. If Dede walked in and saw them now, Kessie on his lap, she wouldn't believe it. Mama Kessie. The name suited her, especially tonight.

"Someday I'll miss you, Kessie," he said.

She squeezed his knee and raised her hand to stroke his head. "Sleep, son," she said in a voice that sounded like Nana's.

CHAPTER 19

Antoinette's funeral.

Everything is as it was, the simple white casket beneath a gathering of flowers at the pew, a small congregation wearing black. Hilton stands near the back of the church, tightly clasping Kaya's hand. He glances down at her from time to time, and she smiles up at him, looking brave and sad. "Are you okay, Dad?" she asks. It's all the way it was that day.

Yet Hilton is anxious to leave this place. Small details are beginning to jar him, sliding out of place. The room is too bright, with a cloud of dust particles floating in the light gleaming through the stained-glass windows. Antoinette's casket was open, not closed as this one is. Kaya didn't wear bows in her hair to the funeral, did she? This isn't right.

The organist pounds out "Precious Lord, Take My Hand," and the mourners begin to sing. Hilton doesn't join them. This is his favorite spiritual, but no one played this for Antoinette. He glances around the church and notices that all of the pews are crammed tight, with more people standing in the back. Stu is here, as he was at Antoinette's funeral. But so is Raul. So is Curt, who wasn't there. Hilton also spots the mayor, Councilwoman Price, even Danitra standing teary-eyed in a clinging black dress.

"Whose funeral is this?" Hilton asks Kaya, but she is no longer standing beside him.

There are three caskets now, he sees. Three. One full-sized casket and two smaller ones, all matching in creamy rose.

A flash catches his eye as a photographer snaps a picture. He hadn't noticed all of the reporters until now, but they are a swarm at the front of the church with their blinding lights and video cameras from all of the news stations. Where are Kaya and Jamil? "... don't know how Dede made it ... She's up front, poor thing ... with her mother ... Eyes so empty ... can't even cry ... Shock, of course ... Can you imagine? ... At least they caught that man ... it's all over the national news ... "

He has to leave here. Faces stare past Hilton as he pushes through the crowd to try to escape through the church door, which he finds locked. He struggles with the knob until a cold, wrinkled hand seizes his. "Stop running, Hilton," Nana says. She looks angry. She is no longer beautiful or comforting in her loose-fitting, outdated clothes. He senses that she is not his friend.

"I won't stay here."

"You would rather go back to the highway? Or maybe to the beach? Where will you go? This is where you have chosen. There is nowhere else for you."

He peers at her shrunken, leathery face. Her lips are cracked and moistureless. This is not Nana at all, but the pale-faced man from the hearse window, wearing a white wig and Nana's dress. His breath smells dank and sour, of his bowels. "This isn't real," Hilton reminds himself out loud. "None of this is real."

The cold hand tightens its grip until it hurts and Hilton is certain his fingers will be ripped from their tendons. "Whatever you can touch is real," the man hisses in an icy voice that freezes Hilton's soul.

CHAPTER 20

"Bingo," Curt's voice crackled across the telephone.

"Bingo what?"

"Bingo on Charles Ray Goode," Curt said, nearly whooping. "The sister in D.C. came through, and you won't believe what she dug up. When can you get away?"

Hilton sat straight up, his heart flying. He held up his hand to Ahmad to signal he'd need a minute, so his assistant crossed his arms with a sigh and sat down in the chair in front of the desk. He looked irritated.

"I'm in a meeting, but fill me in. What'd you get?"

"You were right. He wasn't a grunt. He was ROTC, an officer recruited from an Ivy League in 1977. Discharged in 1985—and you'll never guess why."

"I've waited too long for guessing games, man."

"He was a munitions advisor for a fucking terrorist group called The Order, out of Seattle. More than one group, could be. White-hate Nazi stuff. Bunch of the leaders went to jail. You remember that radio talk-show guy who was killed? There was a movie about it a few years back. These guys killed him."

"I remember," Hilton said, his entire chest thudding.

"Anyway, it turns out Goode had ties to these guys, but the FBI couldn't prove anything. He's discharged anyway, and the whole thing is swept under the rug. Can you believe it? A fucking Green Beret officer."

"Jesus," Hilton said, full realization settling over him. He felt a leap in his stomach, nausea tickling his throat. This was the man after his family, a terrorist? "Lord Jesus."

"My major made me call the feds on it. I wanted to rush a search warrant and grab the guy myself, but the major's probably right. So we'll do it their way. They're moving today. You in?"

Hilton fumbled for a pen and held it gingerly. His right hand hurt like hell for some reason today, as though he'd slammed a door on his fingers. "Go."

Curt gave him the address of a trailer park in North Dade. Goode was still living with the woman he'd beaten, whose skull he had gashed with a crowbar. Federal officers planned to search his property at five-thirty, before nightfall, for explosives or the computer and printer used to write the threatening letters to Dede. With his record, and because of Florida's antistalking law, Curt said, they could send Goode's ass to jail. At least for a while.

"Man, I don't know how, but you knew," Curt finished, laughing. "Yo, you gotta give me six numbers for Lotto."

"You get this guy, Curt, and you can have anything you want."

((

Poinciana Haven, a few blocks east of Biscayne Boulevard near the county line, was home to several dozen neatly kept mobile homes equipped with carports, paved walkways, and elaborate gardens. This wasn't a roost for snowbirds; the residents here were settled, and many of them were elderly. Most of the population had come to gawk at the half dozen marked and unmarked police vehicles in front of the double-wide mobile home parked in lot 10G.

Goode and his girlfriend, who were still inside with FBI agents an hour after the convoy arrived, hadn't made an appearance to satisfy their curious neighbors. Two Metro-Dade officers stood in front of the trailer's open door to offer the stock answer that all the fuss was just routine. Just back off, said one who was losing his patience. Wasn't it about time for people to start cooking dinner?

"What happened to Charlie?" asked a resident arriving late, hobbling into the crowd with a cane.

"He musta' done something, Jack."

"Charlie? Can't be."

Hilton sat with Curt in his patrol car twenty yards from the trailer, nursing a lukewarm cup of coffee he'd picked up from McDonald's. His eyes were glued to the doorway. He'd seen Goode's silhouette for a brief second when he first opened his door at the FBI's announcement that they had a warrant, but Hilton was still bracing for his first good look. At least he'd know him then.

A flock of birds was squawking and quarreling from the lolling branches of a royal poinciana tree overhead. The more the sunlight faded, the more nervous Hilton felt. The Big Mac he'd wolfed down wasn't settling easily in his stomach. He'd taken a chance not telling Dede about Curt's news, hoping he'd be able to fill her in after Goode was already in custody. The unhappy alternative would be telling her the FBI suspected a neo-Nazi terrorist who was still free for lack of proof. The thought of it made Hilton rub his forehead with desperate frustration.

"Why haven't they brought him out yet?" Hilton asked.

"Easy, man. They're feds. By-the-book stuff, I guess."

A hoarse, angry shout suddenly emerged from the trailer: "So this is a game to you? . . . What, you thought it would be cute to go after a judge? It's not cute, Goode. It's stupid. . . . You hear me? Brainless and stupid. Because we're all over your ass now. You got that, Ivy League? Every time you take a piss, I'll have a report on my desk . . . "

Two federal officers in suits, an olive-skinned man and a woman Hilton recognized from earlier, walked out of the trailer with their pads in their hands and their eyes on the ground. The woman muttered something to the Metro-Dade officer as she passed. Hilton could see a shadow in the doorway cast by the lanky, blond-haired man Curt had told him was in charge of the investigation. He, apparently, was the one doing the shouting.

"They're leaving?" Hilton asked.

"I'll be damned." Curt opened his car door and climbed out. Hilton sat motionless, watching the doorway.

The shout rose again: "I said, bring your ass out here! . . . You too, miss . . . I've got somebody I want you to meet."

And there he was. Flanked by three FBI agents and a dark-haired woman wearing cutoffs and a bodysuit, there emerged Charles Ray Goode in jeans, muddy work boots, and a white undershirt. Just over six feet tall, Hilton judged. Light brown hair to his shoulders, strong jawline, clean-shaven. He ambled down the steps from the trailer door with his hands in his pockets, not appearing at all uncomfortable in the company of the Federal Bureau of Investigation. He looked almost bemused.

"What's going on, Charlie?" the old man with the cane called.

"Believe your own eyes, Jack," Goode called back. "It's official now. It's finally a crime to be a white man in the United States of America."

The blond agent pointed toward the car where Hilton sat and gave Goode a rough nudge. "Over there," he said.

Hilton quickly set his coffee down and opened his car door, wanting to be at full height when he faced Goode. As Goode sauntered toward him, their eyes met for the first time. His eyes were pale blue, nearly translucent, bewitching Hilton with the intensity of their hatred. Goode's face was innocuous, but his eyes spoke on their own.

he'd have almost thought of it himself

"I don't think you've had the honor of meeting this gentleman in person," the crew-cut blonde agent said to Goode when they stood before Hilton. "This is Hilton James. You remember. You've been threatening to kill his wife and children."

Goode nodded politely. "I'm afraid I don't know nothing about birthing no babies," he said nonsensically, still staring at Hilton dead-on. "I don't know what you're talking about, Miz Scaw-lett."

"You're a real smart-ass, aren't you?" the agent asked, his cheeks red. "That's useful. You're really going to crack up the other guys in your cell block at the federal pen."

"Believe what you want, officer."

The woman, too, stared at Hilton with poison, blaming him for disrupting her day and her life in front of the neighbors. She linked her arm around Goode's. Hilton, watching them, felt more numb than enraged. So here Goode was, close enough to touch. Curt walked to Hilton's side, probably to be sure he wouldn't spring at Goode. Curt would see those eyes, too, and know. Couldn't they arrest him for what was in his eyes?

"You look a little peaked, Mr. James," Goode observed in a sickly sweet voice. "I don't think you're getting enough sleep."

"Thanks for your concern."

"Don't push your luck, Goode," Curt said, bristling. "It's over. We got you. Let all that shit go, man. It ain't worth it."

"Again," Goode said, very deliberately, "I must repeat, I have no idea what any of you is talking about. And if there's nothing else here, I believe I may have some constitutional rights left." He smiled at Hilton, displaying rows of straight white teeth. "That okay with you, bro? Perhaps we'll meet another time."

"You know the way, motherfucker." The words leaped to Hilton's lips from a hidden wellspring. "Try me."

"You're real dumb for a smart man, Goode," the FBI agent said.

Ten minutes later, Goode and his girlfriend were back inside of their trailer with the door and thin white curtains closed. Most of the police cars, as well as the crowd, were gone. Only Curt, Hilton, and the blond agent remained in conference over the hood of Curt's car.

The agent shook Hilton's hand and introduced himself. He appeared to be in his late twenties but was older in his deportment. "Sorry to put you through that, but I was trying to unsettle him. It's not an easy job."

"I was hoping he'd spend the night in jail," Hilton said, rubbing his throbbing fingers. Goddammit. Had he fallen to the floor and crushed his hand while he slept last night? His fingers hadn't hurt the day before.   *whatever you can touch is real*

"Unfortunately, we came up dry here and at his workplace. He's doing drywall with his brother's firm, but they've got a shabby dot-matrix printer. No match. He doesn't even have a pocketknife here. I'm pretty sure Goode has been expecting us."

"He's smooth, all right," Curt said.

"He has a history with the FBI I can't discuss with you," the agent said, looking at Hilton earnestly, "but it's enough that we're going to keep him under surveillance. He has a shadow from now on, Mr. James. I can't promise you the same for your family, but we're going to see about getting some occasional surveillance at your home, too, especially at night."

Hilton explained the precautions he'd been taking after the more recent notes, and the agent nodded his approval. "Looks like you knew what you were up against," he said.

"I don't take chances with my family."

"Smart man."

They agreed on a time he and Dede would visit the local FBI office to make a formal statement and complaint, and the agent warned Hilton that his office had already gotten calls from the press. A story was likely in the next day's paper, he said.

"I'd better get on the phone with my wife and let her know what's going on before she sees it on TV," Hilton said. "Listen, I can tell her you all are going to get this guy, right?"

The agent exhaled, glancing back toward the trailer. "He's slippery, Mr. James. But whether or not we can ever charge him, I don't think you'll have to worry about any more threats."

"That's not good enough."

"Well, between his military record and his FBI file, I'm hoping we can pull up some evidence to link to those threats. The rest may be up to Mr. Goode."

Following the agent's gaze, Hilton noticed a shadow from where Charles Ray Goode stood behind his curtains in the trailer window, parting them slightly to gaze outside at the trio. His features were obscured in front of a lamp, but Hilton was almost certain he could see his eerie, empty eyes.

we've found someone to do our weeding

No, Hilton thought as a sharp breeze tinged with the scent of salt water tripped into his nostrils. The rest may be up to me.

CHAPTER 21

MIAMI—The FBI confirmed Monday that it is investigating death threats against newly elected circuit court judge Dede James, the county's only black woman criminal-court judge.

"There have been a series of threats delivered to Judge James in writing," said Miami FBI spokesman Lance Kinnebrew.

Although Kinnebrew refused to be specific, he did disclose that the threats have been racial in nature.

James, 37, won a close race last fall against former circuit court judge Phillip Reedman.

James spent 12 years as a prosecutor in the Dade state attorney's office, and is most recognized for her role in convicting the so-called Kendale Lakes Rapist in 1990.

Kinnebrew would not confirm or deny that the FBI has a suspect, but he said the threats are being taken seriously.

Bonita Dandridge, president of the civil rights group Miami Action Coalition, said she was disappointed and saddened.

"No matter what your accomplishments, there are always these reminders that racial hatred lives on," she said.

James lives near Coral Gables with her husband, Miami New Day Recovery Center director Hilton James, and their two children.

She could not be reached for comment.

CHAPTER **22**

Hilton is a boy again. His shoulders cannot reach the top of the barbed-wire fence as he walks on the gravel road. He is carrying a book called Spelling Primer *in his hand, slapping it against his thigh. Though the heat feels like midafternoon, a strange fog is settled everywhere, making it hard to see. His house is at the end of the street; he sees the pointed tip of the slanted roof poking through the mist.*

A strange man, a white man, is standing in the doorway with his arm leaning across the door frame. He wears jeans and a white T-shirt. He is waiting.

"Who are you?" Hilton calls out in his child's voice.

The fog breaks around the man's face, revealing his grin. Charles Ray.

"Get out of my dream," Hilton says.

"This is my *dream," Charles Ray says in a rasp that rakes Hilton's tiny spine, like ice water. Charles Ray nods his head toward the doorway. "You're late. Come on in. You know the way. Goddamn, it stinks in here. Something's burning."*

Hilton, nervous, walks past the three-wheeled red wagon sitting in the patch of grass he plays in. He trudges up the creaky wooden porch steps, keeping his eyes on Charles Ray's.

"Come on along, little niglet," Charles Ray coaxes, his grin trembling as though he can barely contain himself.

Hilton glares at him, then walks beneath Charles Ray's raised arm into the living room. He smells the sharp musk of Charles Ray's deodorant. Is this real, after all?

He is at home. Yes, this is home. Nana's pink robe is crum-

159

pled on the couch, covering the spot where the couch is frayed most badly. He walks across the woven straw mat on the floor and looks up at the wall, where he sees the portrait of Jesus. Next to it, taped to the same wall, he recognizes a fan from church with an image of Martin Luther King. He remembers this fan.

Nana has been writing hymns. On the table, he sees her handwritten sheet music with the heavy lines she has drawn for staffs, scattered with delicate-looking notes. This hymn, he reads from Nana's coarse script, is called "Glory Home."

"Glory Home!" He remembers this one. In his mind, he hears Nana's humming to follow the words he reads: *My Lord has made a bed for me . . . in my Glory Home . . .*

Charles Ray snatches the music from the table and scowls as he reads, shaking his head. "If there's one thing you all got, it's religion. You steal everything in sight on Earth, and you've got your eye on heaven, too."

"That's mine," Hilton says, but Charles Ray holds the pages above Hilton's head, out of his reach. Then he tosses the pages into the air and they vanish. Hilton gasps.

"Told you, boy. It's my dream," Charles Ray says. He pulls a pack of Marlboros out of his breast pocket, clamps a cigarette between his teeth, and slides it out of the pack. Then he finds his matches and strikes one, making a brilliant flame as he leans close to light it. Smoke floats upward, blending with the fog.

"You like it so far?" Charles Ray asks, tossing the burning match to the floor, where it quickly extinguishes against the wood. "The best part's coming next."

Hilton is shaking. He doesn't know why. His bare knees are trembling until he wants to sit down. It's thin smoke, not fog, that fills the room. And the burning smell all around them isn't coming from the match or the cigarette. It's from the kitchen.

"You know what?" Charles Ray says. "I've been cooling my heels here for quite a while, and I haven't seen that old bitch around. Now, what kind of a hostess is that? I wonder where she could be." He sniffs the air. "Well, I'll be damned. I believe somebody's cooking. Do you like your food well-done?"

Hilton runs past Charles Ray to the open kitchen doorway. Suddenly, everything is loud. A pot is boiling over on the stove, and the lid is clanking up and down like machinery. Smoke from a blackened frying pan is rising to the ceiling, and he can hear the hissing of burning meat.

Hilton covers his eyes, afraid to look at the floor, but then he peeks between his fingers. Nana is there in her flowered dress, her head wrapped in a white scarf, as though she curled up and decided to take a nap on the hard wood. Her face is damp, her lips drawn into a grimace. Her eyes are closed. Maybe she just fainted. It's so hot in here, of course she could faint.

Hilton kneels beside her. "Nana?" he asks.

He touches her arm but moves his hand away with a jolt. Her skin is cold. Dead-cold. Hilton screams, jumping to his feet.

He has to run. He has to get help.

Charles Ray blocks him in the doorway, still grinning. "I've got a joke for you: How do you spot a good nigger?"

Tears are running down Hilton's face. He cannot speak.

Charles Ray nudges the tip of his boot against Nana's calf, making her leg jump until the rubbery flesh falls back into place. "Here's one here," Charles Ray says. "She's dead. Get it? A good nigger? Think about it, boy. It'll come to you. You'll wake up at two in the morning laughing yourself silly."

"She's not dead," the Hilton-child sobs.

Charles Ray gazes at him with mock pity, his eyes wide as he nods up and down. He talks without moving the burning cigarette from his mouth, so his words sound slurred. "Oh, she's dead, all right. I'm sorry to be the one to break it to you. This is the way it's supposed to be. Just like it would have happened if the bitch hadn't fought so hard. She ain't fighting now, is she?"

Hilton stares down at Nana's frozen face.

Charles Ray sighs, his eyes searing down into Hilton's. "Now, if she's dead . . ." he begins, pulling the cigarette from his lips, "where does that leave you? Who's going to save you from drowning? Huh, boy? And who's going to spawn those *little niglets of yours? This changes things, doesn't it?"*

With a cry, Hilton lunges toward him, but he flies into thin air through the open doorway and stumbles across his feet to the floor, where his head knocks against the wood. Charles Ray is gone, just like the sheet music. Hilton's jaw is scraped and he feels dazed. He cannot see Charles Ray, but he hears his satisfied laugh all around him.

From nowhere, a lighted match falls in front of Hilton's nose. "Say good night, Gracie," Charles Ray's voice says.

In an instant, the match is a tower of flames.

CHAPTER 23

The grace period was over. The lines for battle were once again drawn in the James household. The shouting had begun the first night, when Dede demanded to know why she hadn't been told about Charles Ray Goode's history as soon as Hilton knew. "Instead, you're out playing cops and robbers like a young boy," she chastised while Kaya and Jamil listened in uncomfortable silence from the dinner table in the next room. "What were you thinking? When did you graduate from the police academy?"

That quickly deteriorated into complaints about his moodiness, rumors she'd heard that he was slacking off at work, questions about how he spent his time when he wasn't in bed with her at night. "How do I even know you're at home? Tell me that."

Hilton didn't fight back. Half of him didn't trust himself to control his anger, half couldn't blame her for the way she felt. He hadn't been a husband to her in so long, he couldn't remember the last time they'd made love. And there had been Danitra, whether their encounter had been real or an elaborate fantasy. He knew Dede could sense Danitra's intrusion in his silences.

That weekend, the accusations followed him around the house as he busied himself buffing the living room floor, clearing out the garage so both cars wouldn't be left vulnerable in the driveway, and polishing and loading the shotgun.

"Don't you touch that gun when I'm talking to you," Dede said. She cornered him in the doorway of the study, which he'd transformed into his bedroom and had become as cluttered as he felt. A mess. Both of their antique mahogany desks were buried beneath dirty clothes and piles of papers, and the room smelled musty. "It's unnatural, you and that gun. Put it down."

Hilton hesitated, rolling his eyes upward to look at her as he ran the cloth up and down the handsome black Remington's steel barrel. He answered for the first time that day. "Why? You think I'm going to shoot you?"

"God only knows what you would do. Look at you. You look like the devil, and act like him the rest of the time. Only a fool would be as sick as you and refuse to see a doctor."

Hilton had wearied of her voice too much to listen. "If I'm sick, you made me that way," he retorted. "Why do you think I'm doing all this? You think I like living in a goddamned prison with some psycho trying to kill us? What the fuck do you expect?"

And then the long silences followed, sometimes for hours. Kaya and Jamil weren't allowed to play outside or go to the mall or movies with their friends—period—so they were sulking. There wasn't anything good on TV, they said. It was hot, they said. Jamil ran down the street when he heard the ice-cream man's bell on Sunday and was greeted at the door by Hilton with a leather belt.

"But, Daddy, I said I was— "

"What did I tell you about leaving the house? Huh?" Hilton asked, thrashing Jamil's bottom with swift lashes through his denim jeans. Jamil, who hadn't earned a whipping in years, sobbed. "You go on and cry. Next time, goddammit, you'll listen to me."

New walls were erected throughout the house, walls of resentment, pain and doubt. Dede was beginning to sound like a broken record: Is all this really necessary? Didn't the FBI already have a tail on Goode? Do we really have to crawl on the ground to check the car for a bomb every time we drive to the store? Aren't you taking this too far?

Too far. As if there were such a thing.

No point in talking to her, trying to make her understand. No point in paying any attention to Kaya's and Jamil's immature complaints. The more they resisted, the more Hilton felt driven into his own thoughts, his own routines. No one greeted him when he came home from work in the evenings. Eyes darted away from him when he walked into a room.

Fine. He didn't need their fucking thanks. Goode was making them like this, and he'd be stopped soon enough. Goode's time would come.

A tense week passed after Hilton first met Goode and his eyes, and Hilton was certain they were both waiting for something. Then, sure enough, the time arrived. Goode finally came on a Friday.

Charlie had been restless in the front yard since nightfall, tugging against his chain and whimpering toward the sky. Hilton sat with him on the cool grass, rubbing the dog's sleek fur and massaging the graying hairs on his chin. Hilton watched the traffic passing on the busy thoroughfare three blocks east, a red haze from brake lights fighting their way in the last of the rush hour. His street was calm, silent. All of the neighbors were already inside, their lights and television sets on, and a circle of darkness surrounded Hilton from the peripheries of his security lights. Charlie whimpered again, then licked Hilton's ear in a rare display of affection. Hilton sensed suddenly that he should not be sitting outside without his gun, as good as naked. He must go inside.

He found Dede, Kaya, and Jamil playing Scrabble on the floor in the family room, a new favorite pastime since the children were restricted to the house. All three glanced up at him when he stood in the entranceway with his shotgun, but their attention returned quickly to the game. Jamil was arguing that he should be able to use the word *gonna*, and Dede and Kaya were holding fast. Although he was only eight, Jamil was an excellent speller; he wasn't allowed many breaks. Hilton gazed at them and listened to their banter, realizing that the three of them were a complete entity without him. This is the way they would look if he weren't here, and they would be all right. The thought was both sad and uplifting to him.

Silently, Hilton walked around their circle and closed the blinds across the sliding glass door. How many times had he told them someone could see them through the patio door if they left the light on inside and the blinds wide open?

"It's still your go, Jamil. Try again," Dede said in a too-cheerful voice, ignoring Hilton's presence. He left them.

Hours later, after the children were in bed and Dede had closed herself up in her bedroom, Hilton returned to the family room, turned off the light, and sat in a white wicker chair to stare out at the patio through the glass. He watched the bright shimmering from the pool's water waving across his lap, then grasped the gun tightly beside him and trained his eyes outside.

He could tell he would have trouble staying awake tonight. He hadn't slept much at all the past four nights because he'd been so shaken by a dream after meeting Goode. His catnaps at work had been cut short, and coffee seared through his stomach when he tried to drink it. His stomach was so raw that even Cokes blistered his insides.

To occupy his mind, Hilton studied each plant and item of furniture on the patio and tried to remember when they first brought them home. That god-awful mock Greek statue had been from Dede's father, so it stayed for sentimental reasons. The oversized raft floating in the pool was one of Jamil's Christmas presents. The black Art Deco bar counter was from a garage sale on Old Cutler Road, Dede's favorite scenic drive.

"Dad?"

Hilton jumped, clutching the gun, until his brain processed the voice as Kaya's. She stood in the family room entrance in a robe, her hair mussed. "You know better than to walk up behind me like that. What are you doing up?" His voice was hard.

Kaya didn't speak, shuffling into the room to sit on the floor at his feet. Up close, he could see her face in the odd patio light. She looked so young to him.

"Did you hear me? What time is it?"

"It's almost midnight. I can't sleep," she said. She hadn't gazed at him this closely, like a daughter, in a long time.

Her gaze melted his irritation. He relaxed in the chair. "What's wrong? This maniac out there got you scared?"

She shook her head. "I had a weird dream."

Hilton mumbled empathetically and sighed. "I hope you're not having nightmares too."

"Sort of. She was sitting right in my room with me, on my bed. She said I have to watch out for Ray Charles."

"Who said that?"

"Antoinette," Kaya said, pronouncing her name softly.

Ray Charles. Hilton straightened in the chair to try to see Kaya more clearly. She was looking up at him like a moonbeam. Everything in the room vanished except her face.

"What else did she say?"

"Lots of stuff. She just talked and talked. She said she had to look for me a long time because she found places where there's no such thing as Kaya James. No such thing, she kept saying. She says I wasn't supposed to be born."

Unreality threatened to wash over Hilton and sweep his consciousness aside, but he anchored his thoughts on Kaya's face and the sound of her whispered voice spoken without emotion. He ignored the familiar quickening in his chest.

"Did that scare you?" he asked her.

"A little, but she said other things to make me feel better."

"Like?"

Kaya smiled as though telling a girlish secret, wrapping her arms around her bent knees on the floor. "Well, she said I'm going to grow up to be a famous doctor—as long as I look out for Ray Charles. Isn't he that blind singer?"

"Maybe she said Charles Ray."

Kaya's mouth dropped open. "That's right," she gasped. "She said Charles Ray. How did you know?"

"Because Charles Ray is the name of the man who wants to hurt us," Hilton said, matching her matter-of-fact tone. Although they had described him in detail, he and Dede

167

hadn't seen a reason to tell Kaya and Jamil the man's name, but it seemed natural now. He told Kaya about how they found Charles Ray and how he'd seen him at the trailer park with his smile, his eyes. The disclosure affected Kaya, because she was quiet for some time. All traces of fun left her face, and she turned her gaze toward the patio's glass door. She began to rub her arms as though she were cold. "Dad," she started slowly, "do you think my dream was real?"

"Dreams can't be real, at least I don't believe they can. My grandmother, Nana, used to say she had dreams that came true, but I don't know. You probably heard us talking about Charles Ray Goode and incorporated him in your dream." Hilton didn't even believe himself as he spoke, but the words sounded reassuring.

"What's a tea cell?" Kaya asked suddenly.

"Why?"

"Because Antoinette said I'm going to discover a way to make people more tea cells. She said she wouldn't have died if somebody knew how to do that."

The feeling of submersion came again, and Hilton could no longer ignore the powerful beating of his heart. He tried to make his voice sound steady for Kaya. "I know that people with the HIV virus are worried about their T cells. It has something to do with the immune system. Kaya, what else did Antoinette tell you?"

Kaya exhaled, looking thoughtful as she searched her memory. "It's all fuzzy now. She talked a lot."

"Just try," he said.

"I remember she kept talking about doorways. She said she couldn't find me in all of the doorways. She said stuff about you, too. She said you're going to doorways you're not supposed to, and that's why I wasn't supposed to be born. Jamil either."

do you think you can keep dying forever?

"I don't know what that means."

Kaya snapped her fingers: "Oh, I remember something weird she said now. She said one time you went through a doorway, and you woke up and saw something in your closet."

"What did I see?"

"She said you saw your jacket in your closet," Kaya said, remembering clearly. "A gray jacket. And then you knew the truth. What truth?"

Hilton began to blink suddenly, and he realized he was near tears as he heard the shadows of his tryst with Danitra from the mouth of his daughter. He'd run out of rationalizations and explanations now, and he'd known for some time that they no longer applied to any portion of his life. The room felt frozen in time.

"I don't know, honey," he said in a helpless voice. "I don't know what I'm supposed to know. I really don't."

"Antoinette told me to tell you to rest."

"She did?"

Kaya nodded. "Uh huh. She said everything will be all right if you just rest and stop fighting. She promised, Daddy."

Daddy. For the first time, Hilton saw the raw pain in Kaya's face as she gazed at him. Of course she must miss her daddy, the daddy she knew only a short time ago. How could she understand what was happening to him when he didn't understand himself?

"Are you and Mom getting a divorce?" Kaya's voice was tight.

Hilton swallowed hard and wiped his dry lips. "I don't have an answer for that, hon," he said. "Was that in your dream?"

Kaya shook her head. "No. That's from when I'm awake."

He struggled to find a way to explain it all to her. "Funny things happen when people are under strain, Kaya. It doesn't mean your mom and I don't love each other. We're all having a hard time now. That's why sometimes I get upset. Your mom, too."

"Don't you think Antoinette is right and it'll be better if you get some rest? She said if you stop fighting, you'll be able to sleep from now on. Forever, she said."

stop fighting, hilton. it's wrong to fight.

"I will," Hilton said, reaching to smooth Kaya's hair back. "I promise, when I can, I will."

"Cross your heart?" Kaya asked.

Hilton opened his mouth but couldn't bring himself to utter the vow that lighted naturally on his tongue: hope to die.

☾

The glowing hand on the wall clock was creeping past 3:20 A.M., and Hilton still sat in the wicker chair in front of the patio door. *He scans the patio once more and decides to stretch out, take a look at the front of the house and check on Charlie. When he stands, he sees a man with a shotgun blocking the doorway in the darkness. He is Hilton's height and size.*

"Get out of my way," Hilton says to him.

The man folds his arms across his chest, still holding the gun. "Not this time," the man says in Hilton's own voice.

Another voice speaks up from the pass-through kitchen counter, where a man is munching on potato chips. "You've run out of doorways," the eating man says. He, too, is a Hilton figure, the one with the horribly mangled face. His flesh looks scorched.

"Sleeping on the job," scolds the Hilton figure with the gun. Hilton glances behind him and sees himself asleep in the wicker chair, his gun leaning on the wall in front of him. His chin is resting against his chest. Hilton can't move to shake himself.

"Forget it," says the mangled Hilton figure, reaching for another handful of potato chips. "It's too late now. He's here."

"He's been here for some time."

"Just let it all be over. It's not as hard as you think."

"Everybody has to let go sometime."

Hilton clasps his hands together in front of his face to implore them. "Leave Dede alone."

"Of course. Dede belongs here."

"And Kaya and Jamil?"

Neither Hilton figure answers. The armed one standing in the doorway hangs his head, exhaling a deep breath that circles the air until it lingers beneath Hilton's nostrils with the scent of the dead. Its coolness allures Hilton, makes him sleepy.

"What about Kaya and Jamil?" Hilton asks, his energy fading.

"What's done is done is done," says the Hilton figure from the counter. "It's time for all of us to rest."

Hilton sees a movement on the patio, which is clouded in a green early-morning fog. Kaya and Jamil are out there, clasping the hands of a lanky girl in a hospital gown. Their backs are facing them, and they are walking toward the swimming pool, where steam is rising from the glowing green water. The tall girl turns around to smile at Hilton over her shoulder. Antoinette.

"No!" Hilton screams, breaking free from the death spell. He pounds on the glass door, shouting their names with all of his resolve. His voice shreds the air and time in countless hidden worlds.

A low, focused barking outside awoke Hilton. He jumped from his chair and reached for his gun, but it was no longer against the wall where he'd left it. He felt a stifling panic until he spotted the gun's glimmer at the family room entrance, lying across the floor. He paused for a split second before running to grab it. Who had moved his gun? He glanced up at the clock. It wasn't quite 3:15. The dead of night, and Charlie was barking at someone.

It must be him.

The only light on in the house was in the hallway between the family room and living room, and Hilton switched it off. He knew every nuance of his home's floor plan from his weeks of sleepless sentry duty, so he stole his way from room to room to glance out of the windows at the rustling hedges and serene sidewalks. Charlie's barking was less tentative now, and he could hear him yanking hard against the chain. Hilton could go outside and let Charlie loose, he realized, but he thought better of it.

No. That would only chase him away. He didn't want that.

Back in the family room, Hilton flicked off the patio's green floodlights with the switch next to the sliding glass door. He ran his hand across the gun's barrel until he felt the chamber, and he cycled the first shotgun plug into place behind the gun's hammer with a loud, heavy clacking that echoed throughout the room. Hilton's heart was leaping in circles, but his hands were steady. Painstakingly, he unlocked the glass door and gently eased it open on its track until he felt the night air on the patio. The backyard was cast in light from the solar lamp, but the patio itself was hidden in darkness. He heard the pool's water lapping gently, unseen. Hilton padded across the tiles to the pool's edge and walked around it until he'd reached the corner closest to the yard and the shed. He poised the gun against the screen to shoot.

Hilton heard a sound from the fence that could be a cat or a squirrel, and his gun's nozzle snapped toward the spot in an instant as his breathing grew heavier. The son of a bitch was really here. Right outside of his property. Walking right into a twelve-gauge, just like that.

"Come on out, you prick," Hilton whispered. Nervous perspiration dripped into his right eyelid, but he sealed it shut and didn't move despite the painful sting. He waited.

There. A crunch on the gravel from his neighbor's yard, fifteen yards from his shed, thirty yards from where Hilton stood. Charlie's barking grew louder, more frenzied. Charlie knew, too, even from the front yard. Maybe Charlie could smell him in the air. A whipping breeze shimmied through the leaves overhead.

"Come on," Hilton breathed.

Hilton heard feet whistling through his neighbor's grass. He was running along the fence, hidden behind the hedges. Goddammit. Why was he running? Hilton followed the sound with the shotgun, straining to see anything, any glimpse that could serve as a target. His prayer was answered when he saw a flash of pale skin; maybe his neck, maybe his arm or his face.

Hilton squeezed the trigger and the gun pumped, its nozzle exploding and the butt kicking his chin so hard that he took two steps back. Glass shattered in the darkness. Hilton cycled and fired twice more, ripping the screen apart with singed gaps, tracking the hidden flesh he'd seen. He was breathing in gasps by now, but he stood perfectly still. Waiting. For one perfect second he heard silence, and he dared to believe he'd hit his mark.

Then his senses were rushed with Charlie's hysteria, joining the chorus of alarmed dogs up and down the street. He heard one of his children crying and Dede screaming his name. He was still frozen with the gun raised as he watched his neighbors' bedroom lights flick on with nearly synchronized swiftness.

Hilton was startled by a sudden lick of warm water against his leg. Who— He whirled around, and his foot plunged into the deep end of his pool before his mind even registered that he'd backed against its concrete edge. He cried out, flinging the shotgun away as he toppled, arms flailing, into the water.

you come back here, boy   you hear me?

He was submerged. Everything was silent, dark, and peaceful. Hilton felt the water gathering at his nose, but he remembered to keep his mouth closed. His eyes were also squeezed shut to keep out the chlorine. He didn't move. Don't panic, he thought. Hold your breath. Float to the top. Just climb out.

look, hil ton

In the din of water rushing his ears, Hilton thought he heard a whisper of a voice calling him. He opened his eyes and realized he was close enough to the bottom to see the black tile letters splayed in front of him, larger than life. The letters seemed to be glowing, waving. He stared hard to make sure he wasn't hallucinating; instead of the loving tribute to the previous owner's wife, the oversized letters now spelled *D-I-E*.

That instant, Hilton choked on the water fighting for possession of his mouth. To his amazement, the water tasted bitterly of salt.

Now he was panicked, swimming furiously. His chest and lungs hurt as the water seemed to crush him. He craned his neck and stroked toward the faint light from the solar lamp shining across the surface, but something was wrong. His clothes felt like pure lead pulling him to the pool's bottom. His swimming strokes seemed useless, and the depth had grown to far more than eight feet. The harder he stroked, the farther the surface yawned up away from him, a canyon of water growing, growing until he could barely make out the light or the rounded corner of concrete above where he should have been able to hoist himself out easily.

This couldn't be happening. This was worse than his dreams. Drowning. Lord Jesus, he was drowning.

The water was growing colder, making him shiver uncontrollably and swallow more of the salt that was stinging tears from his eyes. No, he wasn't on his patio. He could plainly see the specks of plankton and algae floating all around him, could feel the sand particles brushing against his face. He believed he heard a man laughing somewhere below, from the depths drawing him further and further. Charles Ray's laugh.

He gasped, drawing more of the water into his lungs. The tightness in his chest was going away. Instead of burning the way he remembered when he was a boy, the water was soothing him now. He felt an urge to suck it in like a drunkard in need of wine. He remained motionless, floating downward in a lazy spiral as the light above grew to a faraway glimmer, like a star.

Then, as before, a solid, massive arm wrapped around his middle. He felt himself being pulled upward, swept past the floating algae in a beating rush that left him dizzy. In an instant, his head popped above the surface and the thick air wrapped around him, feeding his starving lungs. He began to cough violently, thrashing to reach the edge of the pool.

"Thank you," he tried to gasp but couldn't because he could barely breathe. Oh, Jesus, thank you.   *thank you*
nana

Dede ran to the pool's edge and kneeled, screaming. He'd never seen such a wild look in her eyes. "Are you shot?" she asked inexplicably, reaching to grab his soaked, clinging shirt. "Are you shot?"

When his coughing fit subsided, he saw the shotgun he'd thrown against the patio tile and heard the barking and commotion all around him. For the first time, he remembered Charles Ray in the bushes.

He'd missed. Charles Ray had been there, right there, but now he was gone. It would be a waste of time to search his neighbor's hedges with a flashlight for what might be left of him. Hilton knew this, just as he'd known Charles Ray was there at all. The knowing was the hardest part.

PART **THREE**

. . . Man, why should thought of death cause you to weep,
Since death is but an endless, dreamless sleep.

—James Weldon Johnson,
 "Blessed Sleep"

CHAPTER 24

"Hil, come here. Let's talk," Curt said, beckoning.

Flaggingly, Hilton pulled himself from beneath Dede's arm on the living room sofa and followed his uniformed friend into the hallway. He hated to leave her warmth; he was wearing dry clothes but still felt soaked and chilly. The sky was dipped in 5:00 A.M. velvet, and Hilton's household was bustling. Kaya and Jamil were watching a *Terminator* video at a soft volume, too giddy to sleep, and the front door was open so the Miami police officers still gathered outside could walk in and out with ease.

Dede had served coffee earlier, and now she sat on the sofa with a dazed face, her eyes red. Occasionally, their neighbor's hoarse voice rose to a near-shout as he spoke to the officers outside. ". . . and he's going to pay for it, god-dammit, that's all I know. I don't care if he's Jesse Jackson."

Hilton heard the man's voice floating inside the house just before Curt closed the door to the master bedroom. Hilton had never been introduced to his gruff neighbor whose son had called Jamil a nigger, but now he knew his name all too well. He'd been hearing it all night.

Curt paced before Hilton with a sigh, his hands clenched behind his neck as he stared up at the ceiling.

"He was out there, Curt," Hilton said.

Curt stopped, staring at Hilton straight in the face, and Hilton could see the anger tugging at his jowls. "Man, stop it. You act like you don't know what the hell's going on here. Don't you get it? You've got to wake up."

"I know it looks bad . . . "

"Looks bad?" Curt repeated, laughing ruefully. "Do you understand you almost took a ride tonight? Huh? We just spent an hour talking that redneck son of a bitch out of pressing charges against you. Illegal discharge of a firearm. Reckless endangerment. Hell, he thinks you did it on purpose. Are you starting to get the picture now? Or didn't you go back there and take a look at the hole you blew in his bedroom window, two feet above his head?"

"I know. The shot went wild." His eyes were low.

Curt was shouting by now. "Man, you can't fire a weapon like that! If I'd known you were that crazy, I never would have let you get a gun. And I thought for damn sure you knew you can't fire at somebody you think's in the bushes, and he ain't even on your property. It's supposed to be self-defense, not big-game hunting."

"It's him or us, Curt."

Curt paused, stepping closer to Hilton to probe his eyes. He looked as though he couldn't believe what he'd just heard. "You're really gone, aren't you?"

"What the fuck is so crazy about shooting at a terrorist sneaking behind your yard?"

"Because he wasn't even here, goddammit!" Curt shouted back. "No way in hell you can shoot three shotgun slugs within thirty feet and you won't blow somebody apart. No way. There ain't no such thing as missing with a shotgun like that."

Hilton exhaled, struggling to reason with his friend. "Curt . . . He's ex-military. The first shot goes wild, he hits the ground. The next two don't get near him. Then he books."

"And he drives all the way the hell back up to North Dade in time for his FBI tail to wake him up from dead sleep?"

"It was forty minutes before anybody from the FBI even scratched their ass, and you know it. At least."

Annoyed, Curt waved his hand in dismissal and turned away from him. "Hilton, you're scaring the hell out of me.

You told me yourself you never even saw a face clearly. Didn't even *see* him."

"It was him. Charlie knew. He was barking like—"

"Oh, man, shut up," Curt cut him off. "I can't listen to this. If you'd hit somebody, maybe Charlie could testify at your goddamn murder trial to corroborate your story. 'Cause that's where your ass would have been, in a goddamn jail cell."

Hilton didn't answer, sitting on the edge of the unmade bed where Dede had been roused from sleep in a fit when she heard the gunfire. She'd hugged Hilton, clinging to him, when she finally found him on the patio, but her own questions would come later when the shock finally gave way. Slowly, Curt's words began to sink into Hilton's consciousness. It was all spinning out of control.

"We both know it doesn't make sense," Hilton said dully, unable to meet Curt's eyes, "but I know what really happened."

Curt shook his head, looking at Hilton askance, then walked toward the door. "You need to rap with God tonight and thank sweet Jesus all you hit was that dude's window and walls," Curt said.

"All right, man. I'm sorry."

"Sorry don't cut it," Curt said, more gently, opening the door. "Just get yourself together, Hil. Get yourself straight."

Hilton heard the echo of Dede's voice through the open doorway as Curt walked back out to the living room. "Is everything going to be okay with him?"

"Yeah. Don't sweat it, Dede. It's all taken care of."

"I'm sorry, Curt."

He shushed her. "I don't want to hear that now. He did what he thought he had to do, that's all."

It would all be so different, Hilton thought, if only his first shot had been sure. Then what was left of Goode would be a harmless, bloody heap on the grass. He might have spent some time in jail, like Curt said, but at least his waking nightmare would be over. Would he have another chance?

Still sitting on the bed, Hilton heard Curt and a couple of the other officers say good-bye, then the front door closed and someone latched the locks into place. Dede told Kaya and Jamil to try to go back to sleep. Hilton leaped up, feeling the need to say a proper good night.

"There's Daddy," Jamil said, wide awake and grinning. He ran to Hilton's side, his beating apparently finally forgotten.

Though Hilton was rejoicing inside, he couldn't alter his face to match. He rested his hand on Jamil's shoulder, risking a glance at Dede's eyes; they were confused and helpless. Kaya's eyes were less confused, but she still regarded Hilton as though he were a new specimen in strange lighting.

"Your mom's right. Get back in bed. I'll try to be quiet if I want to take another swim. Or get more target practice."

"Ha, ha," Kaya said, smiling a little. She stood up and walked to Hilton, tiptoeing to kiss his cheek. "Later, Dad."

"You'll get him next time, Daddy," Jamil said, jabbing Hilton's kidneys the way he used to during their Great Tickle-Offs, vicious tickling battles from long ago. Hilton didn't jab back. He could only blink and nod, noticing how his own children were being so patronizing and cautious with him. And God only knew what was going through Dede's mind.

He would have to wait to find out. Dede hugged him, squeezing hard. "You scared the life out of me," she whispered, brushing her fingertip along his hairline. He felt grainy particles rain against his face. "Your hair is full of sand or something."

"I know," Hilton said, clasping her hand. "Thank you for pulling me out of the pool."

Dede gazed at him with questions but didn't speak. Hilton knew she hadn't been the one whose arm carried him from death. Did she know what he'd meant? Did she understand, too?

"You need some sleep," Dede said instead, walking toward the master bedroom. She left the door ajar, but only slightly.

Hilton didn't know whether or not he was welcome to follow her, but he didn't. Instead, he crept back out to the patio.

Very carefully, while his family slept and a pink daylight began to dawn, he watched the swimming pool drain until it was empty.

CHAPTER 25

MIAMI—Gunfire roared through a quiet street skirting Coral Gables Friday morning from an unlikely gunman: Hilton James, director of the Miami New Day Recovery Center.

His alleged target: a suspect in the mysterious racial threats mailed to his wife, circuit court judge Dede James.

James, 38, was questioned but not charged after the 3:30 A.M. shooting incident. Police say James fired three shotgun rounds into the backyard of his neighbor Martin Leary.

One of the rounds flew through Leary's bedroom window and lodged two feet above his bed, where he and his wife were sleeping. Two other rounds blasted holes in his wall outside, police say.

James, who did not return repeated phone calls, told police he'd sighted a man he believed was responsible for the spate of death threats against Dede James since last fall.

But police say there was no sign of any intruder. No one was injured in the shooting.

"He could have killed somebody," said Leary, 35, a Miami diving instructor. "Just because somebody's threatening you doesn't give you the right to randomly shoot up the neighborhood. If you ask me, the guy's a nut."

CHAPTER **26**

GO AHEAD . . . MAKE MY DAY!!!

The bold banner, printed across several sheets of green-striped office computer paper, was taped to Hilton's doorway Monday morning. Hilton felt his secretary's eyes following him as he walked up to it, but then Wanda busied herself on the telephone. Hilton reached up, pulled the banner down, and crumpled it with both hands. His anger was leaden against his temples, giving him a headache twice as bad as the one he'd woken up with.

He slammed his fist on Wanda's desk and left the large ball of paper next to her coffee mug. "Staff meeting—now," he said, not looking at her as he walked past.

So they thought it was funny. He'd show them fucking funny.

Within ten minutes the staff was assembled in the conference room. When the dozen seats around the table were filled, stragglers found chairs in the back or remained standing. The room was conspicuously free of conversation as the counselors and administrators gazed at Hilton. Their arms were crossed, their eyes hard to read.

"Someone in here is a Clint Eastwood fan," Hilton began, "and decided to abuse the center's office equipment and resources to try to make a joke. I don't happen to think it's goddamn funny."

Hilton saw people whispering amongst themselves, asking what he meant. Those who knew wouldn't answer in front of Hilton, shushing their coworkers with promises to fill them

185

in later. Hilton went on. "None of you is going to think it's funny in a minute, you hear? It's nine-thirty now, and no one is leaving this room until I know who did it. Just like in elementary school. When you act like goddamn children, that's how you'll be treated."

"What'd I miss?" Stu asked loudly in a lighthearted tone, walking in late.

"You missed somebody who thinks it's a big laugh when a racist threatens to kill a bunch of niggers," Hilton snapped.

Stu looked surprised, and Hilton felt the discomfort level rise in the room among his racially mixed staff. Ahmad cleared his throat, glancing at two white counselors who seemed taken aback.

"I don't think it's about that, Mr. James," Ahmad said.

"I didn't ask you what you think it's about. I know what it's about, young brother. I know what's up. You're so brave when nobody's looking, why don't you show your face now and explain why it's funny when somebody wants to kill an uppity nigger's children?" Hilton asked. The more he spoke, the more infuriated he felt. His fingers were trembling. His staff watched him, their faces solemn.

"Oh, so it ain't funny now, is it? Where's the big joke now? Who's laughing now? Huh? Why don't you say in front of my face what you've been saying behind my back? 'I wonder what's wrong with Mr. James. I wonder why Mr. James sleeps so much. I wonder why he's so upset somebody wants to kill his family.' Where's all that now? Huh?" His voice cracked as he raised it.

The silence in the room was dreadful, and the faces staring back at Hilton ranged from pale to confused to indignant.

"It was probably someone from night or weekend shift, Mr. James," Ahmad said finally. "I don't think it's fair to keep everyone away from their work when it might not be one of us."

Insolent, know-it-all son of a bitch. All of the frustrations and fury bottled up inside of Hilton gave way. He stood up, a rasping sound rising in his throat that emerged as a strangled shout. When he tried to walk away, his foot caught in his chair leg and knocked the chair to the floor with a sharp crack of wood. Hearing gasps and murmurs, Hilton stormed out of the room.

He spent the day in his office with his door firmly closed, and he didn't emerge even when he got hungry in the late afternoon. No one dared disturb him except Stu, who knocked once to inquire about him, but Hilton said he was fine and asked Stu if he had any rounds to make. Wanda apparently wasn't putting any of his calls through, and Hilton ignored the occasional flashing on his private line. Dede, no doubt.

As hours passed and Hilton tried to concentrate on paperwork, his mind replayed the scene in the backyard with Charles Ray Goode. He'd heard the footsteps, seen the flesh, and fired. How did he go wrong? He'd been startled when the gun kicked, so maybe that was when his aim slipped. He should have been using buckshot. He would have sprayed Goode if he'd been using buckshot, no matter where he was hiding.

The fucking FBI was useless, letting him slip out like that.

Everyone was fucking useless. Everyone.

At ten minutes to five, Hilton wondered where the day had gone. He couldn't remember whether he'd slept at all, but he was certain he hadn't dreamed. That, at least, was something to be happy about. He rubbed his face, dreading the return home to the tension that waited for him there. Dede had curbed her shouting, apparently somewhat afraid of him now, but she hadn't softened her cutting gazes.

Hilton would rather be anywhere but there.

He began to wander through the center's hallways, where a custodian was mopping. Most of the clients were in the cafeteria, so the rooms were empty except for a few people either sleeping or watching television. Arriving night-shift staffers gazed at Hilton only briefly before averting their eyes; apparently, word of his morning outburst had spread. Fuck them, too.

The ribbon-cutting for the new wing was scheduled for Friday, and the work was finished except for sweeping and touch-up painting. Hilton found himself in the darkened, deserted enclave at the mouth of a long hallway. Light streamed from beneath a door at the opposite end. No one was supposed to be in there yet.

"Mr. James?" Ahmad's voice. Hilton whirled around, and his assistant stepped back slightly. "Just so you'll know, your friend with Metro Police brought in a blind homeless man this afternoon. He found the old guy wandering on I-95, about to get hit. We gave him lunch and a bed until we hear back from a shelter. He wanted to sleep."

"This isn't Camillus House. You know we can't—"

Ahmad shrugged, not letting him finish. "I know. I made the call on this one, and I'm sorry if it's wrong. I felt bad for him. I know someone at a shelter who promised to pick him up by six. I figured that's what you would have done."

Nice kiss-ass line. Annoyed but too tired to argue, Hilton dismissed Ahmad and faced the empty hallway once more. As he stared at the rows of closed doors on each side, he was seized by a déjà vu that made his stomach feel queasy. Must be the stench of the fresh turpentine and plaster, Hilton decided. His shoes echoed against the dusty floor as he walked through the dark wing he'd helped to create from nothing.

Each door had a two-foot vertical window above the door-knob; Hilton glanced through each one into darkness and tried each knob. Locked. He'd left his keys in his desk drawer, and he wanted to look at the beds and check out the view from the windows his new clients would have when they arrived. Another one locked. Damn.

For some reason, his heart's pace was growing more rapid. The longer he walked through the hallway and the more doors he tried, the more uneasy and sick to his stomach he felt. He also felt more determined to find a door that would yield and let him in.

The old man. Hilton hadn't wanted to disturb him, but it

was the only door left. And it was sure to be unlocked.

Each room slept four, and the paint inside was a cheery peach color so the clients would feel relaxed. Although the mattresses were bare, Hilton saw an old man in several layers of tatters sprawled across the bed closest to the door. His nightstand light was on, and Hilton found a laminated Social Security card there, apparently the man's only possession. Antonio Guspacci, it said.

He was older than Hilton expected, at least eighty. The man's lips were crusted and his patchy white beard unkempt and filthy. His wrinkled face was sun-reddened and probably needed some skin treatment. He lay on the bed unnaturally, with one leg twisted behind him and a wrist dangling over the mattress's edge. Hilton wondered suddenly if the man was dead.

But no. Beneath the man's coffee-stained down vest, Hilton could see his chest rising and falling with bottomless breaths. The next time he looked at the man's face, the clouded eyes were wide open as though they were staring right back at Hilton. Hilton's joints felt chilled.

"Somebody's there," the man stated. His voice was ancient.

Hilton sat in the chair next to the bed. "Yes sir, Mr. Guspacci. My name is Mr. James, and I'm the director of this center. The police found you—"

The man's gnarled hand dropped on top of Hilton's. His fingers were cold. Hilton wondered, angrily, why no one had brought the old man a blanket for his nap.

"You're a traveler, too," the man wheezed, smiling suddenly. Most of his teeth were gone, and the remaining ones were brown, eaten with decay. "Come closer."

Hilton leaned over to oblige him. The man smelled as though he hadn't bathed in some time, but Hilton was accustomed to that smell. The man's cold, rough fingers played with Hilton's facial features, painting a picture of him in his mind. His smile faded slightly. "You're so young," he said, distressed. "Why so young?"

Ahmad should have called the county mental hospital,

Hilton realized, but so many of the homeless were mentally ill that the old man's ramblings didn't surprise him. He tried to bring him back to the time and place they shared: "What do you remember about the expressway? What were you doing on I-95?"

"Do you have a family?" the old man asked.

Hilton nodded, forgetting the man couldn't see him.

Tears sprang to the man's sightless eyes and rolled down the crevices across his face until they were lost in his beard. "Of course you do. But not me. There's no one here, no one for me. That's why I don't understand. There's no reason I should be traveling still. Maybe I'm only meant to talk to you."

His speech, though halting, was so refined and articulate that Hilton wondered what kind of life the man led before his circumstances struck him down so. He was probably educated. Hilton didn't know which was harder for him to accept, homeless children or the homeless aged.

Again, the man's hand rested on Hilton's. "I finished at Bucknell in Pennsylvania. That's where I met Carol. I taught there some time. But leukemia took our child, and then grief took Carol years later. So I know what it is to bury a child. I belong to that most unnatural fellowship. Old folks like me shouldn't be burying our children every day like we are. But our fellowship grows. When the old have buried all the young, that's when the world dies."

The old man's voice grew hushed and reverent, as though he were reading from a sacred text. "Can you hear your continent's weeping? I hear it, a chorus of elders. But this is a plague from man, not from God. Evil is arrogant, just as in the days when it breathed through the slave traders, and then the Nazis. It is still strong today, but that arrogance can be ours to use against it. It's like the Bible says: 'And a little child shall lead them.' Which child, we don't know." He paused, his ruined eyes still locked on Hilton—"Or do we?"

Hilton didn't speak, his mind sifting through the man's mutterings for the shrouded logic. He spoke with such wisdom and confidence, Hilton wanted to accept every word.

But he was lost, and he suddenly felt foolish for trying to understand.

The man went on, a spell broken: "I had a good life once. But I'm no fighter. I'm not stuck on this world, not like you."

"Stuck how?" Hilton asked, trying to be conversational.

"You know what I mean. Stuck. Clinging. I'm not that way."

Hilton suddenly felt more than a little edgy under the man's grip. He remembered something C.J. often said: a fool may be crazy for ranting, but you're a bigger fool for listening. He pulled his hand free and patted the man's cold knuckle. "I think I'd better get you a blanket so you won't freeze."

"I hope I'm finished traveling. I'm ready to sleep."

"Where are you traveling to?" Hilton asked, half smiling.

"To here," the man said matter-of-factly. "With you."

O-kay, Hilton thought, raising his eyebrows. Time to excuse himself. The old man definitely wasn't making a lick of sense.

"Don't worry, you'll understand," the old man said, as though eavesdropping on Hilton's thoughts. "When you're traveling, it only seems like dreams. Worse than dreams. But they're not. They're real. They're journeys. All journeys make you tired."

"Go to sleep," Hilton said softly, close to his ear, then he stood and walked toward the door. He heard a chuckling behind him, and he saw the old man's wide, toothless grin again as he began to laugh like an old friend.

"He sure wasn't expecting what you had waiting for him. Was he, Hilton?" the old man called, his voice nearly buried in phlegm.

"What?" Hilton asked, a split second before he remembered he'd never told the old man his first name.

The man laughed merrily until he coughed. "He wasn't expecting you to have a gun," he said.

Hilton stood paralyzed while the old man's words ruptured his reason. He gazed at the man hard, his throat swollen with his breath arrested there. The old man was still chuckling to himself with his eyes closed. Hilton's mind rang with his words.

After a few helpless seconds, Hilton breathed. Simple enough. The old guy must have heard something about the shooting incident from a staffer during the day. That was all. It might not explain everything, but it would have to do.

On his way to the supply room in the main annex, Hilton ran into Stu, who was walking toward him with a briefcase and his coat folded over his arm. Stu smiled warmly, seeing him. "Welcome to the world of the living," Stu said.

Hilton put his hand on Stu's shoulder, a gesture of reconciliation also meant to halt any questions. "Stu, before you split for the day, there's a Baker Act in the last room in the new wing. He's a real old guy, blind. Would you mind giving him a quick look before you leave? He may have a bad cold."

"Sure thing. I'll go right now."

Wanda had gone home when Hilton returned to his office, but a note from her waited on his desk: "Don't let it get to you. Believe it or not, we're your friends." Hilton smiled, reading it. He recalled his tantrum earlier that day with a sense of shame. He must have scared the daylights out of his staff. The thought of the banner still made him angry, but he'd overreacted. He'd have to convene another meeting tomorrow morning to apologize.

Another wasted day. Hilton began to pack his briefcase with papers he knew he'd never look at once he got home. But hope springs eternal, he thought to himself.

He didn't realize Stu was standing in the office with him, so he gave a start when he heard the doctor's calm voice. "Hil, I just told Ahmad to get an ambulance here."

"He's that bad?"

"He's dead." He said it carefully, gauging Hilton's response.

Hilton let his leather briefcase flap shut. "Jesus."

"Can I ask who brought him here? He's not a client."

"I think Curt brought him, until a shelter could come get him. He's homeless." Hilton felt a bit unhinged, and he dreaded the task of filling out a police report. Just what he needed.

Stu sighed. "Not much chance of finding his family, I guess."

"He doesn't have any family. He told me it's just him."

Stu gazed at Hilton over the top of his reading glasses. "He told you that when?"

"I'd just left his room when I saw you, Stu. I was talking to the guy. That's why I figured he had a cold, because his voice was so bad and he was coughing. But I didn't think—"

Stu slowly pulled out Hilton's chair and sat down, his face glum and thoughtful. He pulled his reading glasses off.

"What?" Hilton asked.

Stu wrapped his hands around his glasses, staring straight ahead toward Hilton's desk. "Hil . . . I'm no M.E., but the corpse in that room is in early rigor mortis. He's cold and stiff. He's been dead at least a couple of hours, probably longer."

i hope i'm finished traveling

Hilton's hand began to tingle where the old man had touched him with his icy fingers. He couldn't speak as the tingle began to course through his entire frame, holding him motionless. He should have known that touch, just like Nana's. Tears came from nowhere, breaking the spell, and Hilton quickly wiped his eyes. He turned away from Stu. "He went to Bucknell. He said his wife's name was Carol. His kid died of leukemia," Hilton said hoarsely, feeling a flood of grief, as though he'd lost someone dear to him.

Stu's voice was unsteady but firm. "You need a leave, Hil. I mean it. You need time away from here."

Hilton sniffed, gazing at his skin where the old man's pale fingers had found him. "He was a traveler, he said. Like me."

"Are you hearing me, Hil?" Stu asked, sounding alarmed.

Hilton could only nod.

193

At first, a week away from Miami New Day helped repair Hilton's disposition and peace of mind. With nothing else to do, he began to obsessively clean the house, starting with his sanctuary in the den and making his way to the kitchen, the bathrooms, the floors, and then outside to scrub the empty pool with bleach, prune the trees, and mow the grass. He walked Charlie several times a day, covering two miles with each outing, then drove to pick up Kaya and Jamil at their schools in the afternoon. For dinner, his steaks and pastas became the house staples. Hilton was the model of industry.

Anything to keep busy. Anything to ward off sleep.

Kaya and Jamil were visibly pleased with seeing so much more of Hilton during his "vacation," as he'd explained it. The divorce fears ran deeply, apparently, so they were possessive of his attention. After school, instead of heading to their rooms to do their homework, they lingered with him. Kaya would ask him to help her run lines for the musical she was rehearsing and to coach her maturing singing voice, which was thin as a wisp but lovely.

"Yo, Daddy, want to go to the park and shoot hoops?" Jamil asked one afternoon, and Hilton obliged. His son was small but strong and had an accurate shot when he was close enough to the towering net. They played shirtless at a park a short drive away, and Hilton pushed himself so hard that he was breathing in gulps and felt slicing pains in his side. "You give up, Daddy?" Jamil asked, grinning as he dribbled the ball in a circle around him.

"That's it for today. I'm too old for this, chump."

"You're not even forty yet."

"I'm aging in dog years," Hilton gasped.

"Then you'd be . . . more than two hundred."

Hilton laughed, wrapping his arm around Jamil's head as they headed off the court. The laughter felt good to his battered spirit. "You did that in your head, huh? You can do our taxes."

"Unh-uh. I'm gonna be a ballplayer."

"And what happens when you get injured?"

"Then I'll be a judge, like Mom."

After Hilton showered and realized he still had an hour before he should start cooking dinner if he wanted it to be hot when Dede got home, the living room couch looked too inviting to ignore. He crawled across the cushions and enjoyed the fiery luminosity of the near-dusk sunlight flooding the living room through the open curtains. There his mind wandered to Dede; unless it was his imagination, life with her felt better. He'd seen an occasional smile spring across her face, she was willing to share the frustrations she felt after a month on the bench, and she even slipped into unselfconscious conversation with him when she allowed herself to forget how strained life had become for them. One night, they'd talked for an hour about which Spike Lee film was the most didactic and why, as they would have months before.

Even Charles Ray Goode, strangely, seemed far away. He hadn't sent any more notes, just as the FBI had predicted, and Hilton was freed of the nagging sense that Goode was nearby.

On the couch, Hilton ached to rest, but as usual his insides stiffened involuntarily when he feared sleep might come. He'd forgotten what it felt like to surrender to the comfort of tranquility. Even his eyes hurt because they were overtired.

Hilton felt a bump against the back of the couch.

"Sorry, Daddy," Jamil said, bounding toward the birdcage to feed Abbott and Costello, who flitted their wings, cooed, and whistled. Jamil shook the box of seed into their trough loudly. He was wearing a fading Disney World T-shirt from the family's trip last spring, a shirt he wore nearly every day after school.

"No problem. I'm awake," Hilton mumbled.

"Costello's such a pig. See? He eats so fast. That's why he's fat. *He sure wasn't expecting what you had waiting for him.*"

Hilton sits up, bewildered. He tries to make out Jamil's blurred figure in the torrent of bright light. "What did you say?" Hilton asks. "Jamil?"

"Daddy?" The voice is distant, suddenly, winding away from him in every direction. Hilton doesn't know where to turn to pursue him, and his limbs feel weighted down. He is still sitting on the couch, so he tries to stand. He can barely see in the blaze, which waves around him like searchlights, but he pushes toward what he believes is Jamil's room.

"I'm in here, Daddy."

Hilton stands in Jamil's doorway but stops when he feels something soft beneath his bare foot. When he squats down to the floor to see what it is, he finds a duckling with its neck twisted, its eyes wide and startled at the cruel suddenness of death.

"Here, Daddy. Come here."

Hilton props his hand against Jamil's wall to steady himself so he can stand, but his palm slides away and he nearly falls. The wall feels as though it is splattered with thick syrup. Hilton brings his palm to his nose and his head jerks back at the strong, acrid scent. Blood. Blood everywhere. When he takes a step into the room, his foot slips on warm blood.

"Get out of here, Jamil!" Hilton screams, fighting for his balance. Next, his foot glides across something small that feels fleshy, like a limb. His toes curl tight. He is afraid to look at what is there. "Jamil!"

"I'll huff and I'll puff," says a voice that resembles Jamil's at first, but then it sounds gravelly, like a monster's: "And I'll blow your house down."

The floor has collapsed from beneath Hilton, the walls have folded until there is nothing but solid light suspending him as he flails his arms. This isn't real, he tells himself. This is just a dream. I'll wake up and it'll all be over. I'll wake up.

He looks at his palm, and the blood is still smeared there, seeping beneath his fingernails. He knows the blood is Jamil's, and his chest feels crushed with sorrow. This is real. The blood is real. What's done is done is—

"Jamil!" he wails one last time.

Hilton hears a pattering child's voice somewhere beyond his reach, beyond his comprehension, like a hundred-year-old memory.

Hilton awoke with an unsung cry in his throat, thrusting his hands to the floor in time to prevent himself from falling off of the couch. The sunlight from the windows was blinding, and he blinked into the light feeling panic. He was alone in the living room. He must have been sleeping, his mind reassured him eagerly. A dream, yet again.

He felt a sharp bump against the back of the couch, which made him snap to sitting. Jamil scooted from behind him, clasping an orange box of Hartz birdseed. "Sorry, Daddy," Jamil said.

"No problem. I'm—" Hilton started to answer, but sat motionless as Jamil opened the door to the birdcage and began to shake the food into the trough. The seed rained against the tin.

Jamil giggled. "Look, Daddy. Costello's a pig. He eats too fast. That's why he's so fat."

Panic clutched Hilton again, and he felt the blood draining from his face and neck. Jamil was standing against the light in the window, wearing his too-big Miami Heat jersey that reached his knees, and the sun darted beneath his arm in a brilliant shaft when Jamil raised it to latch the cage closed. "Just watch him, Daddy." Then Jamil stood motionless, silent in the cast of light. Hilton's heart was thrashing as the room around him felt as though it were swerving, careening between planes. He'd just lived this moment once before.

This wasn't a dream, was it? Had dreams finally taken his life hostage?

Hilton realized that his son was staring at him, spell-bound. "What's wrong, Daddy?"

"Come here," Hilton ordered him. The sound of his own voice, the firm resonance against the walls, encouraged him. He spoke again, sounding more harsh than he intended. "Come here, Jamil."

"What did I do?"

The child felt like less than a corpse in her arms, Kessie had told him on this exact spot on the couch. Like nothing. Hilton held out his arms to Jamil, as though he would hug him. "You didn't do anything. Come here. Let me touch you."

"What for?" Jamil took an uncertain step forward.

"Right now," Hilton said, angry.

Jamil cocked his head slightly to the side but walked to the spot between Hilton's knees so Hilton could look at his face. They were eye to eye, and Hilton peered into the deep brown of his son's irises. Jamil's eyes.

Hilton ran his fingers across the smooth fabric of Jamil's black jersey. "When did you put this on?" Hilton whispered.

"After we played basketball." Jamil looked nervous, still suspecting he'd done something he would be whipped for.

"Where's your Mickey Mouse shirt?"

"Mom put it in the wash last night."

Hilton took the box of birdseed from Jamil's fingers and shook it; it was half full. "How many times did you feed Abbott and Costello today?" Hilton asked, still barely audible.

"A little before school, and just now," Jamil said, a whine creeping into his voice. "Like I'm s'posed to, right?"

Hilton allowed the birdseed box to fall to the floor, and he suddenly clamped his palms across Jamil's cheeks so he could study the tawny face that was his in miniature at the nose and forehead, but Dede's at the mouth and eyes. Less than a corpse. Hilton's fingers were trembling slightly, and he tightened his grip.

"What's wrong?" Jamil asked, his lips pushed into a pucker.

It has to make sense somehow, Hilton thought. The Mickey Mouse shirt, the jersey, the remarks about Costello being fat. He struggled to find the sense of it, searching every possibility in his mind. He was still groggy, as he felt more and more often, so maybe he was dreaming after all. If not, the possibilities were more than his thoughts could endure. He'd already endured so much. "Are you real, Jamil?" Hilton implored him. "Is this real?"

Frightened tears flooded Jamil's eyes. He gently tried to pull his face away, but Hilton held on. The tears flowed across Jamil's cheeks, dampening Hilton's fingers, and Hilton saw Jamil's face changing shades, turning darker. Real tears.

"You're . . . scaring . . . me . . . Daddy," Jamil said in a strangled voice. His brown face was staining with bright red.

Terrified. The kid was terrified of him.

Instantly, Hilton released him. His palms had left pale prints on Jamil's face, which filled with color once he was free; Hilton didn't realize he'd been holding him so tightly. Hilton's breathing quickened as he saw their exchange through Jamil's eyes. Jesus, Jamil didn't understand. He couldn't possibly understand.

Hilton grabbed Jamil and pulled him close in a hug. "I'm sorry, Jamil," he said tenderly. "Don't be afraid. Daddy's okay. Everything's okay. Daddy's sorry."

He heard Jamil sob in his ear, so he patted his back and tried to quiet him. He didn't want Kaya to hear him crying from her room. He couldn't explain to her what had happened either. Jamil hugged Hilton back, clinging hard.

"You okay?" Hilton asked, and he felt Jamil's head nod against his shoulder. "Hush up, then. Go on to your room and clean up your face. I'm sorry."

Once Jamil scampered out of the room, Hilton curled into the fetal position on the couch and stared at the countless tiny balls of many-colored seed scattered on the shining wooden floorboards.

☾

The last two strips of seasoned sirloin were sizzling in the pan on the stove, and Hilton stirred the rice once more to make sure it wasn't sticking before checking the temperature of the fresh green beans simmering with almonds on the rear burner. Perfect timing. Time to tell Kaya and Jamil to set the table.

He would never have the chance.

Hilton hadn't even realized Dede was home because he didn't hear her unlock the front door, nor had he heard her voice in the house, but when he glanced away from the stove he saw her sitting at the kitchen table, resting her forehead against her hands as she stared at the Formica tabletop. Her face was stricken with melancholy. Had there been another note?

"Baby?" he prompted.

Dede looked at him. Her red eyes were free of tears. "I understood about the gun, Hilton, I really did," she said. "You may not think so, but I've been trying so hard. Even after that day you were cleaning the gun and you asked if I was afraid you would shoot me, and I realized I was. I've lived with it, being afraid. I've lived with the gunfire in the backyard, the compulsive security, even when a voice in my head was telling me, 'No, Dede, something's not right. Something's terribly wrong.'"

"What are you talking about?" Hilton asked, concerned by the look on her face. He'd never seen it there before, even in their worst days together.

Dede went on without answering, barely leaving a pause. "But I told myself, fooling myself, that I could cope as long as you never hit me. As long as you never hurt the children."

Suddenly, Hilton understood her despaired expression, the reason for the hastily recited speech. He felt stunned. I can explain about Jamil, his mind said, but he couldn't bring any words to his lips. In the moment of silence, he heard sizzling and realized the beef was getting too brown. He turned around to flip the steaks.

"You have to go," Dede said in a phantom's voice.

Mechanically, Hilton poked the two-pronged fork into one steak to flip it, then the other. Smoke floated into his eyes.

"I've asked you to get help," Dede went on, "but you've ignored me. I can't help you, Hilton. I don't know how. I wish I did, but I don't. So now I'm left holding on to the one truth I know: I can't let you stay here to do whatever you did to Jamil today, or worse. I can't allow it. No fit mother would."

"Do I get to testify on my own behalf, Your Honor?" he asked without looking at her, his voice sharp with sarcasm.

"His jaw is still hurting him!" Dede screamed at him, losing the composure she'd no doubt been mustering since she'd seen Jamil. "He'll barely say a word to me or Kaya. There's no excuse! I want you out, Hilton, and I want you out tonight."

The rage that had visited Hilton at Miami New Day reappeared, and he flung the pan from the stovetop with his palm, burning his fingers, until the metal clattered to the floor and spilled hot grease and food two feet from Dede's feet. She cried out, leaping out of her chair. Dede backed away from Hilton, her eyes wide, and took refuge on the other side of the pass-through counter.

She raised an unsteady finger at him. "You see? Just look."

"This is my house," Hilton said, "and you need me here, you ungrateful bitch. You need me here. Kaya and Jamil need me here."

"You need to go to a hospital, Hilton," Dede said, her face wrenching with suppressed tears. "Please go. I'm afraid of you. He's afraid of you."

"Afraid?" Hilton roared, taking a step toward her. "What the fuck is there to be afraid of? I've given him his life. He wouldn't even be here if it wasn't for me. Don't you get it? They weren't even supposed to be born!"

Dede began to sob, shaking her head as she backed from Hilton. "Get out!" she shouted.

Hilton lashed at her with a fierce flurry of obscenities he'd been holding back since the days, weeks before, when her insensitivity first began to infuriate him. He heard words flying from his mouth he'd never spoken, that he'd never consciously thought. Dede shrank from him, crying, until she was backed against the wall in the family room.

Suddenly, her eyes darted away from him to the family room entrance. "No. Go to your room," Dede choked.

Kaya was there. Her face was splotchy and damp with tears, and all of her limbs were trembling. "Why are you doing this?" she shrieked at Hilton with a rage in her eyes that robbed them of their youth.

Hilton felt dizzy under their stares, by the suddenness of the moment's turn against him. He took a lurching step toward Kaya, who ran away from him into Dede's waiting arms. "Stop it, Hilton," Dede pleaded, clinging to Kaya. "Please stop. Please."

I wasn't going to hurt her, Hilton thought, wounded to his soul. Jesus. Why would I try to hurt her? He gave them both a baleful look, then he stumbled out of the family room through the hallway, grabbing his wallet and car keys from the table in the foyer. He could barely breathe, they'd hurt him so much with their fear. All of them.

Standing near the front door, he stared down the hallway at Jamil's closed room and fought not to go there, sit on Jamil's bed and try to fix everything. He could barely comprehend the idea that he was not free to go to his son's room, that in Dede's state she might actually call the police.

Hilton took one last glance at his serene living room, then fumbled with the doorknob to face the darkening skies outside.

CHAPTER 28

Screaming, Hilton finds himself flung inside a dance of bright, hungry flames. When he moves, the hissing fire licks at his face and bare chest. He bats at the blaze as though it is a cloud of marsh mosquitoes, spittle running down his chin.

Then he sees her.

She is thin, tall, with an angular neck and her chin held high as she stands motionless in the wall of fire, which does not seem to touch her. She is a young woman Hilton has never seen before, but instantly he divines everything about her: she speaks French and Creole, she was born in Port-au-Prince, her name is Marguerite. She is beautiful and dark, and he longs to hug her like a sister. He wants to take her hand and run.

How is it she doesn't writhe in the heat or feel the pain? The girl lowers her chin until her large brown eyes are staring at Hilton dead-on. She is weary, he sees. She is too tired even to scream.

"Your last death," she says in a fractured whisper, "will come in a burst of flames. It's not so difficult. Just watch."

Then, slowly, she clasps her hands in front of her chest and begins to kneel. The flames seize her; first stripping away her shoulder-length hair, then feeding off of her dress and her flesh until she is so charred she begins to wither before him. Her eyes watch him, unblinking in the sockets of her bubbling skull.

"Come, Hilton," she says.

CHAPTER 29

"*La reina*, Celia Cruz," the radio announcer kept saying between salsa sets, and Hilton tried to invoke his sopho-more-year Spanish to remember what the word meant. He passed five minutes drumming his fingers against his temple until it hit him: the queen. Relief washed through him like an elixir. The smallest victories were so important to him.

Raul hadn't moved his Biscayne Boulevard office, though the neighborhood around it had grown more shabby in the years since Hilton last visited. He had plush carpeting now and central air conditioning instead of fans, but he was in the same building, playing the same Spanish-language radio station. Hilton flipped through the issues of *Cosmopolitan* in Spanish and *Psychology Today* on the magazine rack, simply waiting, as he had been for nearly two hours. All of the pages were a blur to him. The seats around him were empty, and he was alone except for Raul's receptionist.

The door to Raul's office opened, and a middle-aged woman wearing a black dress and veil, mourning clothes, walked out. Her face was nearly covered in liver spots. She seemed to take a long gaze at Hilton, then she said a few friendly words to the receptionist in Spanish, pausing to con-firm her next appointment. Already, Hilton was on his feet.

"One moment, sir," the receptionist said to him, looking annoyed. She didn't know Hilton, and he'd been hounding her all morning. She finished her conversation with the woman in black, pointedly taking her time, then punched her speaker phone to buzz Raul on his intercom.

"Dr. Puerta, there's a man here—"

"It's lunchtime, Mercedes," Raul's voice came back.

The receptionist shrugged at Hilton. "I know. He wants to—"

"It's me, Raul," Hilton said, leaning over into the speaker.

"Hilton?" the voice crackled back. In an instant, Raul was standing in front of him, holding tightly to Hilton's forearms as though he would kiss him, his expression overjoyed but cautious. "I've been trying to find you for three days. Come in."

"Where's the funeral?" Hilton asked, following Raul into his office, which now had walnut bookshelves stacked across the walls and gave the room an air of dignity that had been absent before. Hilton felt as though Raul were someone entirely different now; not the therapist he'd known, not the friend he'd been so at ease with.

"Mrs. Sanchez? She's a widow. We're doing grief-resolution therapy. You shouldn't make fun. Grief is a monster many people lose their lives to."

"Letting go . . . " Hilton mumbled.

"Exactly."

"Believe me, I'm in no position to poke fun at anyone," Hilton said dourly. He refused the coffee Raul offered him from the espresso machine on his desk and watched while Raul poured the thick, dark liquid into a nearly thimble-sized plastic cup for himself. As much as Raul tried to hide it, Hilton could see Raul was disturbed by his looks, and he couldn't blame him. With his beard growing untrimmed and the swollen discoloration beneath his eyes, Hilton had barely recognized himself that morning when he caught a glimpse of his reflection in the mirror. He'd been living at the Holiday Inn on South Dixie Highway, ten minutes from his home.

"So, *compadre* . . . how are you?" Raul asked.

"If you were looking for me, you must have some idea."

Raul acknowledged him with a sheepish smile. "I tried to call you at home over the weekend, and I spoke to Dede at length. I'm very sorry, Hilton."

Hilton blinked, staring out of the window at the vagrants and underdressed women passing outside. No one had offered him condolences until now because he'd avoided his friends, including Curt, and Raul's words stung him anew with their finality. Then anger replaced his sadness. "I'm sure she told you I've turned into Jack Nicholson from *The Shining*."

Raul hesitated. "Dede is in a lot of pain."

"She can join the fucking club."

"Tell me what happened, exactly."

"If I do, you'll take her side."

"Look at me, Hilton," Raul said, and Hilton gazed back at his friend's soft eyes. "You know me better than that. Since when do I take sides? She's very eager to find solutions. She said she's willing to start counseling if you—"

"If I what? Commit myself to Bellevue?"

"It's not like you to close your mind so, Hilton," Raul said. Not fucking like him. It also wasn't like him to carry on conversations with corpses. Between the look on Raul's face and the ridiculous understatement he'd just made, Hilton couldn't help laughing. He sank into his chair until he was slouching, the laughter was so deep and quenching.

Raul wasn't smiling. "Why didn't you call me?"

Hilton's laughter stopped abruptly. "Because I needed a therapist," Hilton said, glaring.

Raul lowered his eyes. "Touché. I deserved that, so I'll accept your hostility. But I had no idea of the extent of this, Hilton. If I had, I would have behaved much differently. Whatever you need me for, I'm here for you now."

Finally. Those were the words he'd craved to hear. "If I am cracking up, it's because of my dreams. Hypnotize me. I need to remember, Raul."

Raul sighed, distressed. He tasted his coffee in silence. "If not, I walk. It's that simple," Hilton said.

"Yes, yes," Raul said. "All right. I can see you intend to make my work more uncomfortable than it is already. You want me to be your therapist, yet you diagnose yourself and offer your own treatment. You realize you've never been able to recollect the dreams under hypnosis before."

"I realize that. Let's go. I don't care how long it takes."

Raul began to fumble with the cassette player he used to record his hypnosis sessions, and he pulled a small glistening boom box from under his desk. "You need to be relaxed."

"I am relaxed. As relaxed as I'm going to be, wired on caffeine and sugar and getting no goddamn sleep."

"Sit all the way back in your chair, and put your feet flat on the floor," Raul said. He flipped on gliding, futuristic-sounding music at a barely audible level. "Allow your eyes to close."

Relax. For an hour, they had little success. It's not working, Hilton kept saying, but Raul pressed on with a patience that softened Hilton's mood. Raul told Hilton to imagine himself at the top of a steep mountain, and with each step down he felt ten times more relaxed. Together, they breathed deeply. In and out, in and out. Bit by bit, Hilton felt himself letting go.

"Did you dream last night, Hilton?"

"Yes."

"Tell me what happened in the dream."

Complete silence, Hilton would hear on Raul's recording when they listened to the tape an hour later. Hilton couldn't remember much of the session, and he couldn't understand why his friend looked so shaken, why his fingers were unsteady as he pressed the button to fast-forward the tape. He was almost afraid to find out, as he'd felt afraid to hear the answer to the question he'd asked Kessie that night.

"We didn't have much luck with the dreams," Raul explained as the tape whirred on its spools, "but there's something very important I want you to hear, from when your trance state was deepest." Raul pressed the PLAY button, and Hilton heard the conversational drone of his own voice in midsentence:

HILTON:	—journeys. All journeys make you tired.
RAUL:	What kind of journeys? Where do you go?
HILTON:	To here.
RAUL:	To this room with me?
HILTON:	To here. Wherever I am is here. Here is wherever I'm safe. Where they can't follow me.
RAUL:	Who is following you?
HILTON:	All of them.
RAUL:	Who are they?
HILTON:	The others. The ones who are gone. They're angry with me.
RAUL:	Angry why?
HILTON:	Because I have the gift of flight. Because I can always find doorways, like Nana could. They envy me. They want me gone.
RAUL:	Gone from where?
HILTON:	No one is meant to live in the between. They thought the hearse would take care of it, but I fled again. Now it's nearly time for another birthday. I've stolen thirty birthdays from them. That's why they've sent him.
RAUL:	Who?
HILTON:	Charles Ray. He isn't a traveler, but they talk to him when he sleeps.
RAUL:	Tell me about your dreams, Hilton.
HILTON:	I already told you. They're not dreams. There's no such thing as dreams.

Raul turned the tape off, his eyes weighing heavily on Hilton.

Hilton didn't move, the words from the cassette still ringing in his ears with their utter lack of sense, spoken from his own lips.

"So what the hell is that supposed to mean?" Hilton asked.

"You tell me."

Hilton squirmed, uncomfortable under Raul's desperate eyes. "It's a lot of horseshit. One thing sounds familiar, something a blind man at Miami New Day told me about dreams being journeys. Give me a break. I was under hypnosis."

"Hilton," Raul said, leaning closer to his face, "being under hypnosis wouldn't make you say such things. Hypnosis is the road to the unconscious mind. What you were saying about 'the others, the between,' that's coming from you. Do you understand? I don't plant what grows there, I merely harvest it."

"Play that again," Hilton said, and they listened to the exchange in silence. By the time the tape finished the second time, Hilton's heart was pounding and his palms were damp. Was he really crazy, after all?

Raul's voice had never been so firm: "Tell me the truth, Hilton. Are you taking large amounts of cocaine?"

"Go fuck yourself," Hilton snapped.

Raul sighed, wiping perspiration from his forehead with a handkerchief. "I'll tell you why I ask. You're my friend, Hilton, and therefore I have to be honest with you," he said, as though it were difficult to speak. "I'm very concerned about what I've just heard. It's paranoid and delusional. Sometimes that's the effect of too much cocaine, or amphetamines. You've constructed an entire fantasy world in your mind, and I suspect that sometimes it has spilled into your consciousness. That would explain some of your erratic behavior, the episode with Jamil. We need to give this closer attention."

The others. The between. What the hell could it mean?

"I'm not going to a hospital," Hilton said, his mouth dry.

"You have a severe sleeping disorder. That much is clear," Raul said. Again, he rubbed his forehead nervously. "But I think there's something else that may or may not be related, something more serious. And we can control it with treatment. Medication."

"What?"

Raul paused a long time before speaking. "Schizophrenia."

Hilton didn't answer. His eyes felt glassy. He could barely grasp Raul's words as he began to explain what schizophrenia was, how it altered the sufferer's perception and reality, his thought processes. If the schizophrenia was latent, Raul said, it might have been triggered by his stress since the death threats began. Or, he said, it may be genetic.

As Raul spoke, Hilton recalled the string of strange occurrences plaguing him for months. Danitra. The dead man at Miami New Day. Reliving the moment with Jamil at the birdcage.

"Hilton, have you seriously considered suicide recently?"

Hilton looked at his lap. He could only nod. When he looked back at Raul, his friend was frozen with his finger thoughtfully poised beneath his nose. He looked as lost as Hilton felt, with nowhere to go.

"Schizophrenia does not mean you'll be committed. You're very lucid right now. It's an illness, that's all. Don't think your life will necessarily be significantly changed forever." His voice was hollow.

"Then why do you look like you just buried your best friend?"

Raul smiled and nodded, deftly wiping the corner of his eye. "Because, Hilton, I blame myself for not seeing it. Now you understand why I don't like to befriend my patients. A good friend is not necessarily a good therapist. I have failed you. You never see what's closest to you. I tell my clients that all the time."

"So I remember," Hilton said, and cleared his throat. Schizophrenia. Hilton wondered if the genetic predispositions Raul had mentioned might explain some of Nana's oddities, the way she'd forgotten things and talked about things that never happened. Hilton remembered, with a pang, that he'd never known the psychological histories of his parents. He'd never known them at all. "Say you're right about this. Can it . . . can it be cured?"

"Many cases, properly treated, are entirely controlled."

"And how many end up total nutcases?"

Raul shrugged, uneasy. "Hilton . . . "

"Tell me, Raul."

"A very small percentage remain severely impaired. You should focus on healing, Hilton, not fear. I realize you must be—"

Hilton was shaking his head furiously. "No. I don't believe it. I know it makes sense to you, but not to me. It's something else. A whole lot of tests and treatments aren't going to change what's happening to me. The answer is in my dreams, probably even on that tape. I know it, Raul. I know it."

Raul ignored him, scribbling notes on his pad. "We're going to begin regular appointments so I can assess you, including a CAT scan. I'm going to bring in an M.D. I work with."

Hilton was breathing more rapidly, exasperated. There were no answers for him in Raul's world of science and logic. He needed someone who could help him see his dreams, or to understand them. "Raul, you mentioned another girl who had dreams like mine. A Haitian girl. Where is she?"

"I don't know, Hilton. My brother spoke to her last, at the university." He sounded distracted, still taking notes.

"Is he still there?"

Raul nodded wearily. "I wish you wouldn't torture yourself with this useless exercise. My brother would only confuse you. He has very strange beliefs."

"What's his name, Raul?"

Raul met Hilton's eyes, looking at him as though he'd never seen such a pitiable case. "If I tell you, do you promise to come back to begin your treatments?"

"If my way doesn't work, I'll try it your way."

Raul ripped a piece of paper out of his notebook and began to write in block letters. "He's a graduate psych student at UM, but he spends most of his time on Miami Beach. His name is Andres."

"Andres Puerta . . . "

"Don't be shocked by him."

"Shocked how?"

"We're very different, the two of us. I'll leave it at that."
Hilton took the paper with Andres Puerta's name and telephone number as though he were grasping the key to the
fortress of his nightmares. He stood up, buoyed by a new
energy.

"I hope you won't be disappointed, Hilton."

Hilton grinned, memorizing the seven digits. "I won't be."

CHAPTER 30

When he opens his eyes, he sees her sitting at the foot of his bed watching a game show. She is wearing the dress he remembers from the day he found her on the floor, a thin housedress with a pattern of linked daisies. Her straight white hair is tied behind her in a braid that winds down her back. They are in his hotel room, but the room is bigger than it was before, and all four walls box them in with door after door. Closed doors, all around.

"I knew you'd never leave me, Nana," he says.

She doesn't turn around to look at him, shaking her head. "You've done swum out too far. It pains me to watch. All over again. Again and again."

"Thank you for the night at the pool," he says, stroking the braid. "My savior. Again."

She makes a sound, a half laugh. "I've done got attached to them now. To her."

"Who?" Hilton asks.

"My great-grands. The girl. If you'd gone, they would have followed you. He'd have seen to that. And just when I was starting to see things. Things to come, just maybe. If only—"

"Look at me, Nana."

She shakes her head, more firmly. "You don't want to see me like this, child."

"Yes I do. Look at me."

Slowly, she shifts on the bed until she has turned her body to face him. What remains of her brittle flesh is cleaved to her skull, with nothing but holes where her eyes and nose should

213

be. Her lips are gone, exposing her teeth in a wide, maniacal death grin. He is afraid, but he forces himself to remain still. He extends his trembling hand to touch her flesh, which feels like dust. It is dust, he discovers; black particles remain on his fingers when he pulls them away.

"Help me save them, Nana," Hilton says.

"You know they have no time that belongs to them. They came to be from what you stole. Breaks my heart to say it, but . . ."

Hilton hangs his head, the world's sorrows weighing against his chest so he can hardly breathe. "I have nowhere left to go. I know that. I just want to fix it like you did for me, Nana. I want to fix it so they're all right. All of them. You know what love is, Nana. You know what it can do."

Nana sighs, expelling the irresistible smell from inside her, the scent that nearly compels him to close his eyes and sleep. He shakes his head to clear the smell away. "I didn't really fix it, child," she says. "I tried to. I only thought I did."

"But you did. You fixed it. Show me how."

Nana stands, extending the grubby bones of her fingers for him to hold. He takes her hand, clinging to the frailness, and she surveys the room until she faces a door that stands where his room's window used to be. "Here," she says. "I'll show you."

When they walk through, they are standing on the curving sidewalk in front of his yard. It is late afternoon, and the shadowed street is deserted. Charlie is in the backyard barking, standing against the fence on his hind legs. Charlie knows something is wrong. Charlie smells something he is trained to detect in the air all around them, tormenting his keen senses.

"This is the day," Hilton says, shattered, knowing.

"Yes. This is the day."

He searches the familiar surroundings hungrily for clues. The driveway is empty. There is a light on in the living room. Some sort of banner is strung across the picture window inside, but Hilton can't make out the letters from where he stands with Nana. Charlie's barking is frenzied.

"Will it be soon?" Hilton asks.

Nana nods, her revolting grin rocking up and down.

"Show me what to do, Nana," he begs. "You fought and stayed not only for me, but for them too. You know you did."

Nana does not answer, but Hilton follows her gaze to the aluminum garbage can standing in the grass by the curb, just outside of the coral wall. It is covered tightly. Yes, the answer is here, he realizes. This is what's meant to be. He releases Nana's hand and steps toward the can.

"Once you open it, there's no more doorways," Nana says. "Can't be no more. No more running, Hilton."

Hilton gazes at the garbage can and studies the ridges running up and down the light-colored metal. He takes a deep breath and grasps the cold handle. "Thank you, Nana," he says, and lifts it.

CHAPTER 31

For two days, Hilton's calls to Andres Puerta were unanswered. He called him virtually every two hours, from early morning until after eleven, always finding the same answering machine with a message against strange, synthesized music: "This is Andres. If it's fate, we'll catch up to each other. Leave a message." When he called Raul to ask him why his brother never called back, Raul said it was unusual. Maybe he was out of town or staying at a friend's. I don't keep up with Andres's friends, Raul said.

While he waited, Hilton kept his mind occupied with routine.

Bit by bit, his cramped economy room on the ground floor of the Holiday Inn was taking on aspects of the home he'd left behind. Each night just before midnight, he parked his Corolla beneath the dangling brown aerial roots of the huge weeping fig tree across the street from his house, just out of Charlie's eyesight. From there, he simply watched and waited. He saw the glow of the television set that stayed on late in the living room, where presumably Dede was up by herself watching CNN. Occasionally, he saw the light in Kaya's room on as she finished her homework. Usually, the house was dark except for the security lights. Although Curt had personally impounded his shotgun, and Hilton knew he wasn't much use at his post except as an extra pair of eyes, at least he felt more in control being there. Just in case.

At daybreak, after Dede turned off the floodlights, Hilton drove his car around the corner to get his breakfast at

Dunkin' Donuts. When he returned after eight, Dede's Audi was gone and he knew the house was empty. That was when he went inside, day by day, and retrieved the things he needed; clothes, his shaving kit, shoes, books. One day, he brought a big stuffed pink elephant for Kaya and an NBA All-Star basketball for Jamil and left the gifts on their beds. "I'll see you soon. I love you. Daddy." He fought not to call them after school each day. He wasn't ready. He needed his answers first, and only then could he be a father and husband to his family again.

Each afternoon, Hilton returned to the hotel room to watch TV or read for a few hours, waiting in vain for his telephone to ring, then he headed up to North Dade by five o'clock.

That was when Charles Ray came home from work.

Hilton spotted Goode's FBI tail right away; a navy blue Dodge Aries K car that sidled up soon after Goode arrived in his white Jeep each day. Hilton didn't recognize the agent, a dark-haired man who couldn't be more stereotypical in his white dress shirt and sunglasses. Hilton discovered that he could park on a strip of grass outside of the trailer park's gate and still watch Goode through the fence. The agent, not hiding his presence, usually parked just inside the gate in the visitor's parking lot. Goode apparently did part-time work as the park's maintenance man, because he often emerged bare-chested with a shovel or a hammer.

Every other day at five-thirty, Goode crossed the street to buy Marlboros from the Circle K, walking within feet of the agent's car. If Goode ever noticed either of them, he didn't show it. He strolled as casually as he had the day Hilton met him, hands in his pockets, his eyes looking nowhere in particular.

Hilton wasn't sure why he wanted to watch Goode. He did enjoy the knowledge that as long as Goode was in his sight, he couldn't be prowling near his house after his family, but a part of him also believed he might learn something from him. He watched Goode's trailer until about eleven, then drove back toward his house to begin his surveillance there.

The third day after his visit to Raul, the front desk told Hilton he finally had a message. His heart danced until he glanced at the number, which he didn't recognize. The name on the paper was simply Stan. Must be a mistake, he thought, but he dialed anyway. Stan might have some news about Andres Puerta.

"Sunshine Gun Shop," a man's voice answered. The shop's name sounded familiar. Of course. He'd bought his shotgun there just after New Year's, when Dede received the threat at her office, but that was more than two months ago. How could the shop find him? Even Dede and Raul didn't know where he was.

"Is Stan there?" Hilton asked, uncertain.

"You got him."

Hilton explained who he was, that he'd received a message at his hotel. "Oh, yeah, Mr. James. Just calling to remind you that your waiting period is over. Everything's checked out. Come pick her up whenever you're ready."

Jesus. Hilton didn't speak for a moment, searching his mind for a recollection. Involuntarily, his breathing was already more shallow. "Pick up . . . "

"We've got your Colt forty-five. Paid for, ready to roll."

At the shop, two miles south on South Dixie Highway, Stan showed Hilton where he'd billed the gun to his American Express card and signed for it. Hilton searched his wallet and found his own copy of the receipt, dated the week before, two days after he moved out. His own signature. He'd bought the gun somewhere, somehow. He remembered entertaining the idea of getting a new gun after Curt took his shotgun, but he'd never gone through with it—as far as he knew. But then again, he had. Here he was.

The nickel-plated military-style revolver looked huge to Hilton, and it sat heavy and foreign in his hand. He felt like a sleepwalker during the transaction, as though he'd snap awake at any moment. Stan asked him if he remembered how he'd shown him to load the clip. Remind me, Hilton said.

That was how Hilton came to have a loaded gun tucked in his denim-jacket pocket the next time he made the drive to North Dade to park in front of Charles Ray Goode's trailer park. Whenever his mind began to dwell on the impossibility of a purchase he couldn't even remember, he forced himself to think about other things. There were too many other incidents that needed explanations. What's done is done is done, he told himself. Someone used to tell him that all the time, a long time ago.

It was Goode's cigarette day, Hilton remembered. At 5:30 exactly Goode jogged down his trailer's steps and walked through Poinciana Haven's front gate, looking neither right nor left. He waited at Biscayne for a pause in the traffic flow, then he crossed the street and disappeared inside the Circle K.

On impulse, Hilton jumped out of his car. He glanced back at the Aries K to see if the agent had seen Goode, but he couldn't tell. The agent's face was buried in his newspaper. Fucking useless. No wonder Goode had been able to slip away that night, and who knew how many other times before and since.

Without realizing it, Hilton slid his hand inside of his pocket until it was wrapped around the cold butt of the gun. He was alarmed by his actions as he waited for an empty schoolbus to speed past him so he could cross the street. No wonder people testified in court they'd had no control, that they were moved by something larger. Maybe he really was schizophrenic, like Raul said. What was he doing stalking his stalker with a gun he had no recollection of buying? I'll just watch him, he vowed. That's all.

Goode must have decided to stock up on more than Marlboros, because he wasn't standing in the line at the front counter to ask for cigarettes. A young black woman in a red-and-white Circle K uniform manned the register, ringing up an old man's six-packs of beer and lottery tickets. Hilton glanced up at the security mirror at the rear of the store and saw the red from Goode's plaid shirt. He was standing at the magazine rack.

Hilton stole to the row beside Goode's, standing purposely close to the shelves, and pretended to scan the canned goods as he edged toward the back of the store. Just like the night in the backyard, his heart was shaking his frame with the intensity of its pumping. His palm felt clammy against the gun, so he let go of the steel to wipe his hand on his jeans. The next time he glanced up at the mirror, Goode's reflection was gone.

"I don't know about you, but I can't eat vegetables from a can," a voice said next to him. "I like things natural, simple. That's best."

Goode was running his fingers along the cans' labels, not looking at Hilton. Goode's sharp jawline needed a shave today, and his clothes smelled of cigarette smoke. He and Hilton were the same height, roughly the same build. Beside him, Hilton felt strangely at ease. Today he had the advantage. He felt a swell of power taking the place of his fear.

"Useless, ain't he?" Goode went on. "I call him Goober. Sometimes I wake him up to let him know when I'm going to work. I think he'd sleep all day, otherwise. He and a second man switch off. You're a better tail than both of them put together."

"I guess my stakes are higher," Hilton said.

Goode smiled at him, sizing him up. Hilton felt swallowed by his eyes again, which seemed kind but glistened with something else beyond the pale, pale blue.

"Ironic, isn't it?" Goode said. "Someone is paying Goober a salary to protect you from me. But in the end, it turns out he's really only protecting me from you. Except at night, of course. You leave at night. I don't blame you. Goober sleeps, so that's when I like to roam. But you know that already, don't you? Good thing you have shitty aim."

Validation, for the first time. Hilton had allowed himself to believe he really might have only imagined Goode was in the yard that night, but now he knew. Finally, in all the haze and confusion, a truth he could seize. "How do you know I'm not wearing a wire?" Hilton asked.

Goode didn't even glance back his way, lifting a can of creamed corn to read the back label. "Because you're not smart enough for that. You're a lone wolf now. You're sick of the system's way, and so you've come up with your own way. Chances are, you've bought yourself a little number, maybe a thirty-eight, maybe a forty-five, and you sit there with it in your glove compartment waiting for the right moment. You already missed once, and you're itching for your chance. You might have even brought it into the store with you right now. In your pocket, maybe? I see the bulge."

His heart's thumping was jouncing Hilton's brain by now. This was bigger than a fanatic's death threats, he began to realize as he listened to Goode read his thoughts. This was bigger. It was part of something he wasn't allowing himself to understand.

Hilton could barely speak. "Maybe. Maybe not."

Goode laughed, carefully replacing the can of corn and picking up another. "I learned a lot from some pals of mine who were in 'Nam, and I never forgot what they told me. You know, it was mostly niggers they sent over there. And my buddies had to live with them, fight with them. They said you never scrap with a nigger. You know why? They don't have anything to lose. They can beat your ass. I never under-estimate a nigger. Never."

"You did once," Hilton said.

Goode glanced at him over his shoulder and shrugged. "That? Yeah, I ate some dirt that night. That's what I get for deviating from simplicity. I didn't trust myself. I was trying to think of a way maybe I could fuck your wife first, have some fun. I wanted to play with the little niglets. I even dropped by Kessie's place to see them after school."

Hilton's face changed abruptly, and he lost his sense of grounding. The upper hand he'd felt with Goode vanished as his face grew hot. Goode smiled, watching him. "I asked her if she needed someone to cut her grass. She said to come back next week. You niggers sure have some names, don't you? Did I pronounce that right? Kessie Campbell. That was the name on her light bill. What tribe is that name from?"

Hilton slid his trembling fingers back inside of his jacket pocket, once again finding the gun.

"Uh-oh. Pissed him off now," Goode said, amused, noticing Hilton's movement. "I've got to admit, I admire you. You've gone through a lot of trouble to piss on my parade. It's almost sad, in a remote way, because we both know I'm going to win."

"What makes you so sure?" Hilton asked, his fingers grasping the butt. He carefully slid his index fingertip across the trigger, and he felt his molars clamp together tightly. *Now*, his mind screamed. Get it over with now.

Goode grinned at him, a beyond-human grin that chilled him. "I saw it in a dream," he said, speaking slowly to emphasize his words. "You know how I'm going to do it, and you know when. That's a fact. And when the time comes, it'll be so simple it'll blow your mind. Literally. You think you can change fate? Then shoot me. Do it."

I'll show you fate, you son of a bitch, Hilton thought as his chest heaved. He yanked his hand from his pocket, snagging the gun against his jacket's lining. He struggled to free it, hearing a jangling from the Circle K's front door. "Excuse me," came the old man's voice. Someone else must have entered the store as the old man left, Hilton realized.

"Too late," Goode said, still grinning. "That'll be Goober. He's wondering what's taking me so long, if I slipped out back like I did once before. I don't suppose you're up to shooting it out with the FBI, are you?"

The agent, still wearing his sunglasses, strolled casually past their aisle, glancing at Goode and making brief eye contact with Hilton, who quickly shoved his hand as far back into his pocket as it would go. Hilton couldn't tell from the agent's face whether or not he even recognized him as the man Goode was threatening. Apparently, the agent hadn't seen the flash of metal from the gun.

"That's a real shame, bro," Goode said. "You were so close. Things just aren't working your way, are they?"

"I can still shoot you."

"I know. That's the beauty of it," Goode said, dropping a can of black-eyed peas into Hilton's free palm. "You can. But you won't. That's what I said about fate. Personally, I like it a hell of a lot more when it's on my side."

Goode turned his back to Hilton and walked away. He didn't glance back, and it wouldn't have mattered if he had. Hilton saw Kaya's face in his mind, imagining her horror if her father were shot dead by the FBI in a convenience store. This was not the way. This was not the time. There might not ever be a time.

Hilton heard his murderer ask the cashier for two packs of Marlboros, calm and easy as could be.

CHAPTER **32**

Kessie's voice raised a half octave in surprise when she recognized Hilton on the telephone. "Dede just left here with your children," she said. "She still calls me crying at night."

Maybe she shouldn't have thrown me out of my own goddamn house, Hilton thought, but he suppressed his anger when he remembered his reason for calling. "I want you to listen to me, Mama Kessie."

"I won't pass messages. Don't put me in the middle."

"A white man came by your house, about six feet tall with light brown hair. He might have needed a shave. Do you know the one?"

"A white man?" Kessie was silent a moment. "There was a lawn man . . . Hilton, what are you saying to me?"

When Hilton told her about his conversation with Charles Ray Goode, she became nearly hysterical. How did he find us? Did he follow us from the children's schools? I live here alone, she cried. Hilton did his best to assure her that Goode probably would not be back, that he had an FBI tail and couldn't simply come and go as he pleased. He'd already complained to the agent, so the visit was a fluke, Hilton said. Just please be more careful. He wants to scare us.

"Hilton, please go back home," Kessie said. "See a doctor, do what you have to do, but you must go back to your family as long as that man is out there."

"I will, Mama Kessie," he promised.

As soon as Hilton hung up his phone, his red message light was glowing for the first time since he'd lived in the hotel. He didn't even have to check to see who it was.

Finally, Andres Puerta was home.

Andres sounded much younger than Hilton expected, with an easygoing and jovial tone that contrasted with Raul's deliberate thoughtfulness. He had hardly any trace of an accent. Andres explained he'd been out of town at a terminal caregivers' conference upstate, or he would have called sooner. The more Andres spoke, the more certain Hilton felt that he'd reached the right person. His stomach was tight, nervous.

"So you want to know about Marguerite Chastain?"

"Yes. Raul mentioned her," Hilton said. "Is she—"

"We need to meet in person," Andres interrupted. "How about lunch tomorrow on the beach? Do you know the News Cafe?"

Tomorrow was an eternity. Hilton would feel the maddeningly slow passing of each hour until then without the luxury of sleep, but he agreed nonetheless. Noon. The News Cafe on Ocean Drive.

"Will you bring Marguerite with you?" Hilton asked.

"I can't do that," Andres said. "I'll explain tomorrow."

(

Their scheduled meeting was the last day of February, which found South Beach thronging with northern and European tourists and modeling-production trucks despite a noontime chill that prompted Hilton to wear his jacket over his shorts and T-shirt. The sun flamed against the restored Art Deco architecture up and down Ocean Drive, enlivening the paints of lime green, salmon, peach, and pale yellow that distinguished the strip. To the east, where the beach stretched to the shoreline, the ocean was dyed turquoise, balancing sailboats and more-distant cruise ships.

hilton, you get back here, boy

The scene from his sidewalk table at the News Cafe was at

once breathtaking and unnerving to Hilton. He rarely came here. In his regimented existence between his hotel room, his home street, and Goode's trailer park, he'd forgotten that he lived in a region that inspired photographers and drew the snow-weary with its charms. As he studied the bohemian and self-consciously hip people passing by, he realized that much had changed since his last visit to South Beach. A different place had sprung up while his back was turned. The world had gone on without him.

Hilton had been waiting since eleven, working on his second glass of iced tea despite complaints from his stomach, and he was tired of scanning faces for Hispanic men who looked like Raul. He had no idea what Andres looked like, and he had been fidgeting since his yellow Timex sports watch flashed noon ten minutes before. It was after five o'clock in London, after six in Madrid. No matter what the time zone, Andres was late.

He'd seen the chestnut-colored young man in a tank top and black biker shorts survey the cafe twice, but he'd dismissed him. When Hilton noticed the man peering at him from behind rose-tinted granny glasses, he glanced away quickly, thinking the man was one of the locals checking him out. The next thing he knew, the man was standing over his table with a woven knapsack slung over his shoulder. He smelled of cologne, and his dark hair was gelled down flat across his scalp.

Get lost, Hilton thought. Instead, he said, "Can I help you?"

"Excuse me, but are you Hilton James?" the man asked in a clear, deep voice Hilton recognized from the telephone.

Hilton leaped up, smiling apologetically, and shook the young man's hand. He couldn't be much older than twenty-five. He looked like a model, not a graduate psychology student. "Andres? Yes, it's me. I'm sorry. I thought you would look . . . more like your brother."

"We have the same smile," Andres said, taking his seat, and smiled to prove it. The similarity of their teeth was uncanny, although their complexions and facial structures couldn't be more different. Puerto Rican families, Hilton decided, must be as varied in appearance as some blacks. "See?"

"So you do."

A waiter who'd been hovering near Hilton's table since his arrival, waiting for a more significant order, returned to ask what they would be eating. Andres ordered a salad-and-bread plate without glancing at the menu. Hilton noticed, with discomfort, an extended eye contact between Andres and the waiter. Hilton ordered a smoked turkey sandwich, keeping his eyes straight ahead. Yes, he recalled, Raul had said something once about his brother being gay, but he'd forgotten the remark before now. Hilton didn't have any gay friends, although Dede did, and he knew he suffered from the same mild form of homophobia most of his men friends did. Still, if Andres could help him, Hilton didn't care if he was gay, a Jesuit priest, or a bigamist.

As soon as the waiter was gone, Hilton launched into his story. "Raul wasn't sure I should see you. He thinks I'm schizophrenic. But I think it's something else. I have a problem with bad dreams."

Andres nodded with recognition. "Like Marguerite."

"He never told me her name, just bits of her story. He said I reminded him of a Haitian girl with nightmares."

"She was a vision. She had the most lovely face," Andres said dreamily, sipping his ice water. "I always told her I'd marry her, but she never believed me. I knew her a year ago, while I was still an undergrad. Her family moved up to central Florida after a few months. She dropped out of school, her dreams were so bad."

Hilton felt disappointed, but he began to recount the nightmares he'd suffered from since he was an orphaned eight-year-old pulled from the salt water at Virginia Key Beach. He discussed his therapy with Raul, the dreams' five-year disappearance, and their reappearance when the threatening notes began. He tried to remember all of the unusual circumstances that followed, even confessing his infidelity, then described his encounter with the blind man, with Jamil, and how he'd found himself owning a handgun. Finally, he told him about finding Nana on the kitchen floor. How she'd had bad dreams, too.

By the time he finished, Andres had eaten his salad and was leaning back in his seat with his arms folded, absorbing every word Hilton spoke. His eyes were nearly unblinking. Hilton's throat was parched from speaking. He slurped down the rest of his tea, which was barely cold and diluted from melted ice.

"Raul was right to send you to me," Andres said quietly, opening his knapsack to pull out a notebook. "At first, I thought your hopes might have been raised for nothing. But I believe I can help you find perspective."

There. He'd sounded exactly like his brother then. "I was hoping you'd say that."

"Although I'm completely shocked. My brother has never taken my work very seriously." Andres parted his lips, hesitating. "How much do you know about what I do?"

"Nothing."

"Then let me explain," Andres said, sighing. "I started college pretty late because I spent three years nursing my best friend until he died of AIDS. That got me pretty closely acquainted with death, more closely than I wanted to be. But after visiting him so long at the hospice, I decided I wanted to work at one as a therapist, helping people deal with death and dying. We don't know enough about it, and we don't *want* to know even though we all have to face it someday."

Hilton nodded. The tightening he'd felt in his stomach earlier began growing into a small churn. He remembered to begin eating, though he knew the feeling gnawing at him wasn't hunger.

"What I discovered, even with Bryan, is that everybody has different superstitions about death. He was Cuban, and his mother believed in Santería—in Chango, the war god; and in Hermano José, the ghost of the old black slave who talks to the Cuban soothsayers. It's all the religion the Africans took with them to Cuba. So I've been interviewing people about their beliefs, gathering everything I can on death culture and near-death experiences. I've heard some freaky stories, believe me. But I'm a student, not a practitioner. This place is too thick with spirits for me, with the Cubans and their *santeros* and the Haitians with their vodun. I only observe, and listen. So, I learn.

"You say you're afraid of your dreams? Listen, dreams are where we face our mortality, so it's natural to be afraid. Why else do we have the superstition that if you die in your dream, you die in real life? Marguerite understood the relationship between the two like few others. That's why she came to me. She heard about my near-death research from a friend, and she wanted to talk to someone who would believe her."

Hilton tried, but he couldn't continue eating. The food in his mouth tasted like paste against his dry tongue. He pushed his plate away from him. From the beach, Hilton heard the sudden rhythmic pounding of several drums. He turned to see four old men on folding chairs in a sandy strip of grass, their hands flying across congas in an impromptu session. One man sang a short chorus in Spanish across the beat, and the others repeated in unison, a call and response. Hilton realized they were singing an old song.

"What did Marguerite tell you?" Hilton asked.

"She told me about her dreams," Andres said. "They were so clear to her, she woke up screaming and couldn't be convinced they weren't real. She dreamed of voices tormenting her with what she called death spells. She'd fallen from a balcony before the dreams started, and her heart stopped beating in surgery, but she recovered. In her dreams, the voices told her she'd died in that fall, on the operating table. She saw her funeral. She saw her own dead body rotting. She said she met her twins in her dreams. She had many twins, she said. They always chased her."

how many times do you think you can die?

Hilton fidgeted, wishing he had something more to drink. "May I?" he asked, touching Andres's half-emptied water

229

glass. Andres nodded, so Hilton swallowed the cool liquid down. He felt too warm suddenly, even at their shaded spot under the cafe's awning, so he pulled his jacket off and arranged it on the back of his chair.

"Does it sound familiar?" Andres asked, watching him, poised to take notes.

"I never remember my dreams," Hilton said. The drums on the beach grew more frantic as the old men's voices blended with the rhythm. "I must be suppressing them."

"Marguerite didn't. Because of her dreams, she was obsessed with death. She was convinced she would die soon, that she'd died already. Every time she heard an ambulance siren, she turned her head."

"That sounds familiar," Hilton said hoarsely.

"Her family tried therapy with Raul before she met me, but it didn't work. Finally, they got desperate and took her to a *houngan*, a voodoo priest. That was a big step. They were a very conservative family, not superstitious at all." He paused. "The *houngan* told Marguerite she was the walking dead."

Listening, Hilton rubbed his face and sighed, leaning back in the padded folding chair. Andres watched his discomfort. "Hearing this bothers you," he observed.

Hilton nodded.

"Do you know why?"

"Not a clue," Hilton whispered. From habit, his fingertips crept to the carotid artery on his neck and monitored the blood swimming through his veins in rapid spasms. "My pulse is up."

"Maybe we should do this another day," Andres said.

Hilton shook his head. "No. Go on. I've been waiting a long time to hear this, I think."

Andres took off his sunglasses and rested them on the table. "Marguerite came to see me that day, and I'll never forget it. She was wrecked. That was when she decided to drop out of school, and her family moved upstate about a month later. The *houngan* told her she walked between life, death, and the gods. She was unnatural, he said. She was between."

"I said something like that under hypnosis to Raul, about the between," Hilton said. "I didn't know what it meant. No one is supposed to live there, I said, or something."

Andres began to scribble notes, his face unchanged. "What else did you say?"

"I talked about being chased by some 'others' who are 'gone.' I said I'd stolen thirty birthdays, and they'd sent someone to get me. There's a terrorist threatening my family."

"In your dreams?" Andres asked, confused.

"No. In real life. The guy has an FBI file for terrorist activities. When I was under hypnosis, I said the 'others' were talking to him in his sleep." Andres made a thoughtful sound, still writing, so Hilton searched his memory for other clues. "I called myself a traveler. I said something about finding doorways."

Suddenly, Andres's eyes were on him. Now the young man's tanned face was visibly captivated. The pupils of his light brown eyes were dilated, huge. "Yes. Marguerite always talked about doorways. That's the whole thing, we decided."

Hilton felt an unbearable urge to run, and his stomach heaved as though he would vomit. A part of him refused to stay, refused to learn. He quickly excused himself and searched for the men's room inside of the cafe, passing the newsstand and bookshelves of paperbacks that gave the popular cafe its name. He felt the eyes of the other patrons on him as he stumbled toward the rear, past the kitchen. Once in the bathroom, he leaned over the toilet bowl and wondered if he would faint. His head throbbed in sync with his wild heartbeat.

James, J-A-M-E-S. Hilton, H-I-L-T-O-N, like the hotel
is this one slice and dice or on ice?

These are just stories, he told himself. They don't mean anything. Get some control. Maybe these are your dreams, after all, and knowing them will help you conquer them.

231

Knowing will help you conquer. After three minutes, the heaving from his abdomen stopped and he felt steady enough to return to the table.

Two fresh glasses of water were waiting for him. Andres smiled at him gently, like Raul would. "Are you okay?"

Hilton nodded, taking his seat. "I need you to go on," he said. "You were telling me about the doorways."

Andres folded his hands, apparently searching for words. "This is the part that's hardest for me to explain, Hilton. One day, Marguerite came to me and asked me why I shaved my moustache. Well, I never *had* a moustache. But she described every word of a conversation she said we'd had the week before, when I was growing a moustache—and she knew personal things, mind you, things about Bryan I would never discuss. And the conversation she referred to never happened."

"Was it a dream?"

"That's what I thought, but she said it wasn't a dream. She insisted. She said she'd had enough dreams to tell the difference. Every time she dreamed and woke up, she said, she felt as though things had shifted out of place. Not big things, but small things here and there. Once, her clothes were different. Another time, she'd written three pages on a paper she knew she hadn't started. But that thing with me and my moustache was the biggest difference. It reminds me of you and some of the things you said, like that woman you slept with. And waking up to find your son feeding the bird again. Marguerite said that when she dreamed, she walked through different doorways. She had to choose a new one each time. What she found when she woke up depended on the doorway."

"Traveling . . ." Hilton murmured, remembering the old man at Miami New Day. He felt as though someone were brushing a feather's tip against the back of his neck.

"It's like Marguerite walked between natural worlds and spirit worlds. From what she said, if there's more than one doorway to a spirit, maybe there's more than one natural world. More than one reality. Say Marguerite really did die in that fall, in one version of reality. Her spirit fled to another doorway, to another version. And everything was fine until she slept. Then her dreams were like a bridge between the worlds, and she always had to run because she knew she was supposed to be dead."

"But which version is real?" Hilton asked. "The one where you have a moustache or not?"

"Maybe all of them are real. Maybe none of them," Andres said. "I believe that wherever the spirit rests is that moment's reality."

"You said you've talked to other people with near-death experiences. Do they all say the same thing?"

"No. That's why I agree with Marguerite's *houngan*, that it must be unnatural. Most people die and go to wherever the beyond is, or they live to tell what they saw or felt while their hearts were stopped and then go on normally. But some people, like Marguerite, die and refuse to go. So they run away. They find the other doorways. Maybe it's a special gift. Maybe it happens for a special reason. I think I know Marguerite's reason."

"What?"

Andres's face grew reflective, sad. He stared at the table a moment before speaking. "Three months after Marguerite moved upstate, her aunt's house caught fire. Marguerite pulled out her three young cousins and saved them. Everyone said she got confused and ran into the burning house a fourth time. She never came out."

"So Marguerite is dead," Hilton said, feeling desolate suddenly, left alone by this stranger he'd intended to seek out as his shepherd. He could almost picture her face in the flames, her eyes, arms reaching . . .

"Yes. My own theory is that she walked back into the fire on purpose. I think she decided to finally stop fighting. Maybe saving them was why she'd stayed behind all along, cheating death. Those children would have died if she hadn't been there. In this reality we know, anyway."

Stop fighting. Who had told him that? Hilton remembered hearing the words from Kaya, but he didn't know when or why. Maybe it was when she told him about her dream the night he fired his shotgun. Yes, it was. The dream when Antoinette told her she wasn't supposed to be born. And why wasn't she supposed to be born? Why not? Because she really had no father?

Hilton shuddered. He rubbed his hand along the back of his neck, which now felt feverish. He swallowed against the bitter-tasting bile tickling the back of his throat. "From my point of view, there's a big problem with this theory of yours," he said.

"I know," Andres said, looking away from his eyes.

"I'm not dead." He said it uncertainly at first, but he felt a strength from the sound of the words. The chorus of old men's voices was louder, laced inside their steady drumbeats. "I'm not dead. I've never died. I've never had a near-death experience."

Andres looked out toward the water. "You said something about stealing thirty birthdays. What about when you nearly drowned?"

"I know what you're thinking, man, but it wasn't like that. Maybe I passed out for a few seconds, but that's all. I never stopped breathing. My heart never stopped beating. I didn't see flashing lights and all that crap you probably hear about."

Andres didn't smile. "Are you sure?"

"I'm sure. I'm sure I'm alive. It's not like Marguerite. Maybe that's what happened to Nana and that's why she had the dreams. I think Nana died that day I found her. I really do. And then she saved me, just like Marguerite saved her cousins. I can see your point, I see the similarities, but . . . " He faltered. His eyes felt glazed as he followed Andres's stare to the waters, where the choppy waves foamed white.

"Why do you think you have the dreams?" Andres asked in a gentle monotone.

"I don't know why. They went away once, after my therapy. Then they came back last year."

"When?"

Hilton sighed. "I told you. They started again right after my wife's election, when the death threats started. I think it was the night . . . "

"The night what?"

The car. The hearse. A too-pale man's face and sunglasses peering at him, peculiar, through the back curtains. "I bumped my head on the windshield. We nearly had an accident. That's when they started again."

Abruptly, the drumming on the beach stopped. Hilton heard the old men laugh, bragging and joking in Spanish. He hadn't realized before now that his face and armpits were itching with perspiration, even in the cool air. "I didn't die," Hilton said firmly. "I'm not Marguerite."

Andres smiled at him, although Hilton could catch a glimpse of the sadness concealed in his face. "I'm glad to hear it. I like you," Raul's brother said.

The strained voice of one of the old men rose in the breeze, and the drums exploded once more in an ancient dance.

CHAPTER **33**

Just before he began to doze in his car parked beneath the tree across from his house, Hilton heard a tapping at his passenger-side window. He bit his tongue, nearly drawing blood, and whirled his head around to try to make out the shape in the darkness. Instinctively, he reached for the glove compartment and the gun he'd hidden there. "Hilton?" Dede's voice called softly.

Hilton slammed the glove compartment shut. He reached over to unlock the door, finally seeing the sheen of Dede's robe in the dark. When she climbed into the car beside him, he smelled the musk of her bath oil on her skin. He looked away from her, toward Charlie pacing the backyard behind the fence.

"You come here every night?" Dede asked after a silence.

Hilton nodded, rubbing his nose.

Dede didn't sound like herself. She was uncertain of her words, and her voice was artificially cheery. Hilton wondered if she was waiting for him to apologize. That would be so simple, but he couldn't. He remembered her face screaming at him, the distrust in her eyes, and his mouth remained clamped.

"You are a man who loves his family," Dede said. "I never doubted that. Even through all the mess I didn't understand, I knew it was only your way of showing it."

Hilton couldn't answer.

"Raul called me," Dede said, and Hilton blinked. She reached for his fingers and clasped them hard. Hilton squeezed back. Through his open window he heard the trilling of crickets around them, and he felt as though the entire city slept except for them. Dede sighed. "You know what I was thinking about? When Daddy got sick. It was worst right near the end, when he was fed up with everyone and everything and nobody could tell him anything. You remember how it was, with Mom frantic and me losing my mind, too."

"I remember," Hilton said. Lionel Campbell's colon cancer had gone too long undetected, and he died three months after his diagnosis, living hardly a day without intense pain. Hilton remembered feeling acutely relieved when the ordeal was over. Not relieved for Dede, Kessie, or himself; relieved for Dede's father. "I think that was the hardest thing for her. It was bad enough losing him at all, but she'd lost him already to this other man, this bitter man who'd forgotten how to smile and who'd throw his plate on the floor when he didn't want to eat. She'd just cry and cry, Hilton. And I'd hold her hand, just like this, and say, 'He's sick, Mom. You can't blame people for being sick.'" Dede's voice splintered at the end.

Raul must have told her, he realized. So much for doctor-patient confidentiality. But Hilton couldn't blame Raul; he'd known them both for years, and he was right to do it. Hilton would have wanted the same if the situation had been reversed.

"I haven't forgotten how to smile," Hilton said. "I haven't forgotten a thing I've ever said or done with you. I know you were wearing a white sundress the day we met. That part of me isn't gone now, and it never will be."

Dede leaned to him and kissed him tenderly on the mouth, rubbing her hands across his head. He wrapped both arms around her, burying his face in her bosom until her smell swallowed him and shut out his other senses. Here, like this, he thought, he could sleep safely, without dreams.

CHAPTER 34

The phone rang early the next morning, a Sunday. Dede was in the shower, so Hilton reached across the bed they had shared for the first time all year to pick up the receiver. He felt renewed after a long-awaited night of rest. He'd really slept this time.

"Hilton? Damn, it's you. Didn't know you were back, man," came Curt's excited voice.

"In the flesh. Whassup?"

Curt paused, and Hilton wondered what Dede had told him, if anything. "You all right, partner?" Curt asked.

"I'm all right. We got it under control."

Jamil's head peeked through the bedroom doorway tentatively. He was wearing his GI Joe pajamas, fresh from sleep. Both he and Kaya had gotten up the night before when Hilton made his reappearance, wrestling him to the floor with hugs. Now Jamil was checking to make sure he was still there. He grinned at Hilton and vanished after Hilton waved. That kid was handsome, Hilton thought. He sure would be a heartbreaker someday if he ever—

Grows up. What a strange thought to have, Hilton realized.

"Well, I was calling to give Dede the good news, but guess I'll just pass it to you," Curt said. "I gotta give you credit. I didn't know what to think when the FBI told me you'd been up at Goode's place, but you must have done something right."

"What do you mean?"

"He told his probation officer he wants to move up to

Pensacola. He's got a job lined up and everything. The FBI's so glad to get rid of him, they're helping pay his expenses, if you can believe that. They've been shadowing his ass like a motherfucker. I guess he figures the heat will ease up once he's gone, and he's probably right. Goode and his girl'll be gone by Monday."

"You're shitting me," Hilton said, stunned. This was too easy, too simple. He waited for the punch line.

"You scared that SOB straight out of town. Guess it's an early Christmas present for you, man."

"More like an early birthday present," Hilton said. Goode was leaving, and his thirty-ninth birthday was in ten days. Last night, he'd heard Kaya and Jamil whispering about a surprise party they could plan now that he was back at home. They were so anxious for things to be back to normal, they were beside themselves.

"Y'all just try to hang on and rest a little easier. I think it's over, man. You need to just work on keeping things together, you know what I'm saying?"

"I know," Hilton said, feeling a surge of warmth for his friend. "Man, I don't know what to say. You've really been here for us. I don't know what we would have done without your big ass hanging around here drinking up our coffee."

Curt laughed heartily. "You better watch out. I think Dede's got a thing for me. It's the uniform, I'm telling you."

"Well, maybe I better get one."

"Maybe you better. Hey, let's see the Heat sometime this month. We should hook up with Raul. Boys' night out."

Hilton paused. Between the therapy plan he'd mapped out with Dede that morning, making arrangements to go back to work, figuring out the financial mess he'd made by purchasing such an expensive security system, and living in a hotel for so long, he knew there was no time. He wouldn't be able to see the Heat with Curt.

"That's a date," Hilton said, a lie.

"Bless you, man," Curt said. "I'll catch you later."

Goode was leaving. It was true, Hilton's sixth sense told

him. After hanging up, Hilton felt a glow that made him giddy. He leaped out of bed and crept across the bathroom tiles to surprise Dede behind the shower curtain, where she was lathered and looked luscious. She screamed with laughter when he wrapped his arms around her, as the water pelted splotched patterns across his pajamas. He kissed her neck.

"Not again. You'll wear me out, Hil," Dede said.

"Goode is leaving town. I just heard from Curt."

Her face grew bright, girlish. "Are we free again?"

"Absolutely free," he said, kissing her again. "Absolutely."

Kaya cooked pancakes for breakfast, and Dede suggested they should eat on the patio and enjoy the Florida living they rarely appreciated from the confines of their central air conditioning. Between the sweet smell of frying batter wafting from the house and the comforting sight of the nursery of plants growing around them as they ate, Hilton fought off the dreamlike sensation he'd felt so many times before.

Everyone was trying so hard, that was part of it. Kaya and Jamil sat fully dressed with their hair combed, which wasn't like them on a Sunday morning. Dede was going out of her way to be pleasant, often meeting Hilton's eyes to smile at him. They all wanted this to work, to remain like this. They were all trying to forget that he'd just returned after spending nearly two weeks away. They were trying to pretend away the shouting and the fear that had been in the house, on this very patio. The scorched holes in the patio screen from Hilton's shotgun blasts still flapped in the morning breeze, but no one looked that way.

"Daddy, what you have, what's it called again?" Jamil asked suddenly, his mouth nearly full. Kaya gave him a disdainful look from across the table.

Hilton chuckled, pouring swirls of thick syrup on top of his pancake stack. He hadn't been prepared to spell out everything to Kaya and Jamil just yet, but as usual children didn't leave much leeway for planning. Cooties, he could say. But instead of giving a smart-ass answer, he decided to look Jamil right in the eye. "It's called schizophrenia."

"What's that?" Jamil persisted.

"Oh, God, Jamil," Kaya murmured. "Will you be quiet?"

"We'll talk about this later, Jamil," Dede said.

"No, it's all right," Hilton said, patting Dede's wrist. "It's a sickness in my head that makes me act funny sometimes when I don't want to. But I can go to a doctor and get better."

Jamil smiled, satisfied. "So you can't die from it?"

"No. I won't die from it. Once I start taking medicine, it'll be just like it's gone." Hilton felt as though he were explaining his condition to himself as much as to Jamil, since this was his first conscious admission that Raul was probably right about what had been troubling him for these past few months.

After his meeting with Andres Puerta, Hilton had locked himself in his hotel room and sat in darkness for two days, his curtains drawn, racked with tears. He was harrowed by images of a thin, dark, beautiful girl on her knees, flailing her arms against an assault of bright flames with a silent scream. And yet, for some reason, she did not run.

In that room Hilton remembered clearly, for the first time since the near-accident, how he'd stared at a pale man with sunglasses in the back of the hearse while he still felt dizzy from the blow to his head. And then the man was gone.

He reached for the Gideon Bible in his hotel drawer, but his hands trembled when he tried to flip the stiff pages to John 3:16. Whosoever believeth in Him, whosoever believeth in Him, his mind repeated.

Shall have everlasting life. Everlasting life.

Did he believe? Did he believe enough to let go, to kneel in front of the fire as Marguerite Chastain had done? His mind's biblical chant was replaced by a new one. No. No. No. No.

He found himself dialing Raul's number. It was after midnight. He felt such despair, he thought he would leap from the hotel's rooftop if no one answered Raul's phone.

"Where are you?" Raul asked, concerned by Hilton's voice.

"At my hotel."

"Where are you staying? I'm coming there now."

Hilton didn't answer, making a sound that resembled a whimper. He realized that he was petrified in a way he had never felt, as helpless as a child. His own intellect and psyche had betrayed him, leaving him unable to function.

"You're confused, Hilton. I understand that," came his friend's patient voice. "You're an intelligent man whose mind is playing horrible tricks on him. You don't know how to reconcile what's going through your head with what you know to be truth, or what you thought you knew. You may feel as though some other force is controlling your life. It's a bad feeling, isn't it?"

"Yes," Hilton choked.

"The truth hasn't changed, Hilton. Your mind has changed. This is normal in schizophrenia's early stages, this confusion. You know something is wrong. You only have to accept it."

"I . . . I'm not sure . . . "

"You're not sure of what?" Raul asked, and Hilton didn't answer. "Did you talk to my brother?"

"Yes."

"And what did he say to you?"

New tears sprang to Hilton's eyes. "That maybe I'm dead."

There was a long pause, followed by a flurry of curses in Spanish as Raul lost his cool. He struggled to calm his voice, remembering Hilton on the phone. "Hilton, listen to me. I don't know what nonsense Andres has filled your head with, but I warned you not to see him. I'm giving you a simple, concise, physiological reason your perceptions and behavior have changed. You reject all that for a theory that you're some sort of living ghost? That is preferable to you?"

Right then, to Hilton, his alternatives became clear. There were none. At once, he felt his breath flowing with ease through his lungs. "No," he said. "I know I'm not dead."

"Well, thank goodness one of you has some sense," Raul said. "Come back to my office as soon as possible. My doctor friend and I will assess you, and I'll explain every step to you. For now, I think you should go home. Go to your wife and children. I have a feeling you'll be more than welcome there now."

No wonder Raul had that feeling, Hilton thought, since he had told Dede everything about his visit and the preliminary diagnosis. When Hilton first walked into Dede's bedroom the night she pulled him from the car, he found a half dozen library books on mental illness lying across the bed and pages of scrawled notes and charts on her legal pad. She'd even found a support group for spouses of schizophrenics, circling the newspaper listing with a red pen.

Now, at breakfast, it was clear she'd even explained some of his condition to Kaya and Jamil. They had all set out to make this a family struggle, not merely his own. Watching their faces as they wolfed down the pancakes, Hilton felt transfixed by his love for them. As though she knew what he was thinking, Dede playfully rested her hand on Hilton's thigh. Kaya, seeing the blurred shape of Dede's hand through the glass-top table, smiled a secret smile. Hilton decided he would get better, not for himself, but for them. Everything he had done or would do in his life was for these three. Forever.

CHAPTER 35

The white street sign flaking with rust says Douglass Road.

Hilton doesn't know how long he has been walking, but his bare feet trudge along a sinuous dirt path in a haze of darkness. Cool, thick fog envelops everything around him, holding the dreary scene still. The fog is hard to breathe, but Hilton forces the thick air into his lungs and walks on. On his left he sees a barbed wire fence hanging in disrepair along a string of crooked wooden posts. Beyond that, it is hard to see.

The endless stretch of overgrown grass could be a meadow, could be farmland, could be a cemetery. Yes, a cemetery. As he strains to peer through the darkness, he sees tombstones and upright crosses dotting the field. The same sight meets him when he looks to his right, as far as his vision can reach. This is a village of the dead, and he walks alone.

He hears the loud chugging of a motor. In the distance ahead, two white pinpricks sweep before him as a vehicle meanders along the twisted path, closer and closer until Hilton can no longer see past the lights' rigorous gleaming.

The lights stop within feet of Hilton, casting him as a silhouette in the night. Hilton steps aside slightly and can make out the shape of the huge vehicle, an antiquated black hearse with white curtains in the windows. He cannot see the driver.

"Would you like a ride?" a man's friendly voice calls.

Hilton shakes his head. He pats the ice-cold hood of the hearse and walks around it until he finds the path again.

Loose stones hurt his feet, but he presses on. He isn't sure where he is going, but he knows he will be there soon.

"Happy birthday, Hilton," Charles Ray calls after him, and Hilton hears his voice chuckling over the struggling motor as the hearse drives into the dead night.

CHAPTER **36**

"Well, my goodness gracious, if this isn't the biggest surprise," Auntie said, beaming, as she opened the screen door to the painted porch where Hilton had spent hours reading Superman comics when he was young, Richard Wright when he was older.

"Who's that? Lucius and them?" C.J.'s voice called from inside.

"No, Carl, it's Hilton."

C.J. chuckled sarcastically. "Hilton? Hilton who?"

Auntie extended her cheek for the customary peck, but Hilton instead reached to hug her warmly in the doorway, holding her close to him. Auntie was startled at first, but then her frame shuddered as she relaxed and rubbed his back, laughing. "Welcome home, sweetheart."

Home. Exiled in his hotel room for all of those days, Hilton had kept his thoughts anchored to home, to Kaya and Jamil and Dede, nourishing himself with memories of before. Before the threats. Before the return of the dreams. But after he was welcomed back and resumed his cleaning routine while Dede worked and Kaya and Jamil were in school, Hilton still felt in himself an overpowering longing to go home, somewhere else.

He thought of the two-bedroom house in Richmond Heights, with its old Florida-style jalousie windows and painted aluminum shutters, where he'd lived with Auntie and C.J. until he was eighteen. He'd never moved back, even for a night, after he left home for college. C.J. had lost part of his roof to Hurricane Andrew, but Hilton barely noticed the difference now, except that the house was repainted white instead of the bright aqua blue it had been for as long as Hilton could remember.

"Well, shut the screen before you let all the mosquitoes in," C.J. said crankily.

"There are hardly any durn mosquitoes out here in March," said Auntie, giving Hilton a last pat before she pulled him inside.

C.J. sat in his old blue recliner, watching a soap opera Hilton didn't recognize on their color console TV. "You just missed a big lunch Lorraine fixed an hour ago, baked chicken and—"

Hilton leaned over to kiss C.J.'s bald forehead, an unusual gesture for him with his adoptive father. "I ate already. Sorry to just barge in without calling."

"Shoot, we aren't doing anything here except watching the stories," Auntie said, clearing newspapers from a chair for him.

"Foolishness," C.J. muttered.

"Oh, just listen to him. And he's the worst one at twelve-thirty, talking about where's 'The Young and the Restless'?"

"Just keep on fibbing. It'll come back to haunt you one day."

Hilton smiled, listening to them. They were both older now than Nana must have been when she died. They'd never seemed old to him, but they were. Auntie was thinner than ever, with drawn cheeks, and she walked delicately, bracing for pains. Because of a heart condition, C.J. had long ago given up golf and jogging in favor of his recliner, and he was more humorless than ever. Hilton didn't visit them often enough, but each visit since they'd retired was much the same. Food, habitual quarrels, and television. And a pointed reminder that both of them might not live much longer, and then he would lose what little grounding he still had in his past.

"I've got some pound cake in the back, Hilton."

Hilton knew there was no point in trying to turn down Auntie's offering. "That sounds great. Homemade, I hope."

Auntie scowled at him. "As opposed to what? What other kind of cake do I ever have in this house?"

With Auntie in the kitchen, C.J.'s attention returned to the television's argument between a blond woman and a man with a moustache. Hilton wandered the cluttered living room, surveying the watercolor paintings of black family scenes and framed photographs on the walls. Unlike Dede, Auntie was a pack rat who crammed every space in her house with some object or another, and she was constantly rearranging. She had a large collection of mammy dolls and darkie memorabilia from the 1930s and 1940s, watermelon-eating and big-lipped reminders of the times she'd grown up in. Better for me to collect it than those other folks, she always said.

Hilton was surprised to see on the wall a framed, fading black-and-white picture he'd left on his bureau when he moved, a photograph of Nana with black hair streaked with white hanging past her shoulders. It must have been taken when she was middle-aged. She looked very different in the photo from when Hilton had known her because she was so heavy, and her dark face so smooth, but Hilton felt a familiar quiver as he gazed at her eyes. Nana.

"When did you put this up?" Hilton asked Auntie when she handed him a plate with a huge slice of yellow cake.

"Months ago, Hilton. You just never saw it. I got tired of letting it sit up in the room. Take it with you if you want."

Yes, he wanted to, more badly than he'd realized before Auntie offered. It was a crime he'd left it here all of these years with so little thought. This photograph was the only memento he'd taken with him from her little house in Belle Glade when C.J. and Auntie drove him up to gather his clothes after she died. He'd left behind her hymns, her books, everything. He'd thoughtlessly abandoned any chance he might have had to know her.

Carefully, Hilton lifted the photo's frame from the nail on the wall, admiring his grandmother's face. Her nose was African, broad and flat, and the Seminole jutted in her sharp cheekbones. She was a warrior, to the last.

"I miss her," Hilton said unexpectedly.

"'Course you do," Auntie said.

Hilton sat and ate, the photo in his lap, while C.J. and Auntie watched television and threw out bits of news from the neighborhood—whose children had married, whose children were on drugs or had AIDS. Neither said a word about Hilton's separation from Dede, nor did they ask him why he wasn't at work in the middle of a Tuesday afternoon. That was their way. They'd treated him like a man since the day he first walked through their door, and they believed a man's business was his own.

But Hilton wanted them to know everything. He told them about Goode's sudden disappearance, and they expressed their relief. Hilton wanted to tell them about his marriage problems, what Raul had told him, and why he wouldn't be back to work for at least a few more weeks. But the story was so long, and the silence had become so ingrained, Hilton had no idea where to begin.

And though they were both educated, could they really understand the idea of his schizophrenia without fastening ignorant stereotypes to the illness? C.J.'s sister was certifiably senile, and C.J. had a tendency to talk about her mercilessly. Hilton didn't know if it was a defense mechanism because of his own fears of aging or a genuine lack of empathy. Guess what, C.J., Hilton could say, I'm crazy too.

Without prompting, C.J. raised the remote control and zapped the television set mute as the soap opera's ending credits rolled across the screen. "That woman was something else," he said.

"Who?" Auntie and Hilton asked in unison.

"Hilton's Grandma Kelly. I don't know if I ever met her outright. I can't recall. The Belle Glade Kellys could be standoffish and didn't always come to the reunions."

"No more standoffish than the Miami Jameses," Auntie said.

C.J. ignored her, shifting in his seat until he was facing Hilton. "I met her for sure the time she brought you to

Virginia Key, but only in passing. She was setting up a table of desserts, and she was introduced with a whole bunch of other folks I hadn't seen. She must have been, say, in her sixties, close to seventy."

"Sure didn't look it," Auntie said, coaxing her Siamese cat to jump into her lap. She scratched the cat's chin.

C.J. was chuckling suddenly, hiding his mouth behind his palm. "I don't know what you're laughing at, Carl," Auntie said. "There's not a thing funny I can remember about that day."

C.J. nodded his agreement, swallowing the last of his chuckles. Hilton left his half-eaten cake on the coffee table beside his chair, listening. He remembered Nana had brought cake with coconut icing that day, but little else. His memories of the beach were vague, more recollections of emotions rather than of occurrences. C.J. was about to tell a story, perhaps a story Hilton hadn't heard before. C.J. wasn't a storyteller, so this would be a rare moment. This, Hilton realized, was why he had come.

"I'm sorry to laugh," C.J. said, "but Hilton, I was just remembering the sight of your Grandma Kelly running across the beach that day."

"That's enough, Carl," Auntie warned.

"No, go on, C.J.," Hilton said. "I want to hear."

C.J. mopped his glistening brow with his forearm. Their house wasn't air-conditioned, and the breeze trickling through the open windows wasn't quite comfortable on a March midafternoon when Miami's truer climate was reappearing after a winter respite.

"She was a giant, maybe six foot tall. She was running like I'd never seen a woman run, like she was possessed, almost. I can see her now, panting, saying, 'My boy's going to drown!' And we all looked at each other, because we couldn't see anyone in the water at all. Not a soul. Truth be told, we were all chasing after that old coot so she wouldn't drown herself. We thought maybe she was sanctified, wanted to baptize herself right there."

"You ought to be ashamed," Auntie said, cross.

"I know it," C.J. said, laughing. "But I'm just telling the truth, now. That's what we thought. Next thing we know, she's ripping at her clothes, pulling her dress off. We just knew she'd lost her mind then."

"I wish you would listen to yourself—" Auntie said.

C.J. held up his hand, his face turning serious. His eyes drifted away from them as he began to remember. "Even with all of us chasing her, and I mean grown men in full pursuit, we couldn't catch that half-naked woman before she hit the water. And we thought she was fast before? Now, that woman could swim. We still talk about that, don't we, Lorraine? Like a streak, like an Olympian. I tell you, I've never seen a thing like it, and I never will again. It was almost like she was riding on the water instead of swimming." *hillll-ton* . . .

> *where you goin', mrs. kelly?*
> *you get back here, boy   do you hear me?*

Listening to C.J., Hilton was almost convinced he could taste the traces of the bitter salt water that had filled his mouth that day. He felt disquieted, as he had felt listening to Andres Puerta at the cafe with the ocean mocking behind him.

C.J. went on, his gray eyebrows furrowed. "I used to swim in school, so I was the closest behind her. Must have been five, six men in the water. Yeah, it was six, because Matt Coombs was there and had no business there because he could hardly walk up a flight of steps. Somebody had to pull him out of that undertow, too."

"What about Nana?" Hilton asked, edging forward in his chair.

"I was swimming right up behind your Grandma Kelly, and suddenly I could see you, Hilton. You weren't anything but a brown spot beneath the water—good thing the sun was bright that day, and the water was clear. She was right up on you too, dove down like a fish and brought you back up again before I could get within five feet of her.

251

"I'll never forget the look on her face: she was past tired, so tired she looked like it hurt. That Indian hair of hers was wet and stringy, all wrapped around her face. But to look at her mouth, you could see nothing but contentment. I can't fix exactly how to put it right, like she was saying, 'There. That's done.' Like it was the answer to everything."

nana?
nana won't leave you, hilton. go back now.
it's not time for you yet

As C.J. described Nana's face, Hilton was sure he could see it, blurred through the water that stung his eyes mercilessly when Nana's strong arms lifted him back into the air. He could almost remember hearing shouts all around him. He could almost remember talking to Nana. Had he talked to her? What had she said? Hilton sat rigid as C.J. continued.

"Now, I could feel that current stirring when she handed you over to me—and you were heavy, boy—but before I could open my mouth to warn her, she was gone. Somebody said they saw her head sink below the water, as serene as could be, but I was close enough to touch her and I never saw a thing. Not a damn thing. Somebody started yelling about the undertow then—I think it was Matt Coombs, if I remember right—and we all had to swim like hell to get clear. That current was something else that day."

"He still won't go to the beach," Auntie said.

"Damn right. Me or anyone else who was there, just ask them. Matt's dead now, but when I see your Uncle Rick or Lucius to this day, all I have to say is, 'You remember that day at Virginia Key?' And they all groan like they're still fighting it. Grown men." His expression grew distant, and he turned his eyes back to Hilton, looking pensive. "This is going to sound funny, but it's like it wanted you, boy. The water wanted you. That's the only way I can put it. It was like we were fighting all of nature to bring you back."

Hilton blinked rapidly and cleared his throat. He'd heard

enough, he decided. "That's something else . . . " he muttered, ready to change the subject.

"More like a miracle," Auntie said.

C.J. shook his head. "And it's a good thing Lucius got his medic training in Korea," he said.

"How so?" Hilton asked.

"He's the one who got you breathing again."

go back, hilton

At once, Hilton's lungs felt empty. No sound came from his mouth when he tried to speak at first, so he had to breathe deeply to form his words. "What do you mean?"

Auntie began to fret. "Well, we didn't think we ought to . . . "

"Guess we never told you about that part," C.J. said matter-of-factly. "When I laid you down on the beach, Lucius leaned over your chest and said you weren't breathing. No heartbeat, either. Lord, you should have seen our faces fall. We were still in a fit over losing your Grandma Kelly in the water, but nobody expected to lose the little boy."

a tiny coffin like that
you never know what the boy could'a been, could'a done
  go back, hilton

"A miracle, like I said," Auntie sighed, shaking her head.

"But Lucius knew what to do. He sat you up and pumped the water out, breathed some air into you, and the next thing we knew you were coughing and coughing, asking for your grandma. 'Don't leave me here, Nana,' you said."

"Broke our hearts."

"We decided right then and there you'd be coming home with us. We didn't even talk it over. And with our boy grown and off to college, neither of us ever thought we'd ever have another child in the house. We just—"

"We just knew," Auntie finished, smiling at Hilton. "We knew there was a plan for you."

CHAPTER **37**

To keep the peace with Dede, Hilton dutifully showed up for his appointments with Raul and met with Laura Ming, a Chinese-American doctor Raul was bent on sending him to. But as he met with them with his legs crossed, answering their questions about his moods and thoughts in a cooperative drone, his mind was unanchored.

He no longer looked forward to seeing Raul the way he had before, and he rarely joked with him now. Raul had been right; he couldn't be his therapist as well as his friend. Raul, as a trained healer determined to find a treatment, had lost his blithe edge with Hilton. The idea of asking Raul to schedule a Heat game with him seemed out of the question, out of line. Hilton always left Raul's office feeling empty and dissatisfied. And sad.

"So we can expect to see you Monday, the thirteenth?" Raul asked at the close of their third meeting Friday, as Hilton stood to find the door. Hilton's eyes had rarely left his watch, which had passed the hour into languid increments.

"Fine," Hilton said, sighing.

"Is something wrong?"

Hilton shook his head. What could he say? That the treatment was useless? That he'd decided his condition, even the whispers of voices he'd occasionally begun to hear just within his consciousness, had nothing to do with schizophrenia?

"It gets better, Hilton. It takes time," Raul said.

Hilton nodded and waved a silent good-bye to Raul, closing the door behind him. But once he was in the reception area and he saw his car parked at the meter through the glass doors, he paused. That wasn't a proper way to say good-bye.

Hilton knocked twice and opened the door again, finding Raul finishing his notes. "Back for more?"

Hilton realized he didn't know what he had come back to say. In his discomfort, he had to force himself to keep his eyes focused on Raul instead of glancing purposelessly around his office. "I just . . . uh . . . " He wanted to hug his friend. He fumbled, then shrugged. "I just wanted to say thanks."

Raul rested his pen, puzzled at first, then he smiled. "Not necessary. You'd do the same for me."

"Don't be so sure," Hilton joked, although he felt anything but jovial. Again, an interminable pause. "Okay. Well. I'll see you on Monday."

"And by the way, Hilton," Raul said as Hilton turned to leave. "Isn't Sunday the big day? *Feliz cumpleaños.*"

The phrase sounded familiar. "What does that mean?"

"Happy birthday."

Hilton stared back at Raul over his shoulder. The words barely registered, as though Raul had uttered them in a different language again. He hadn't forgotten about his birthday, not with Kaya and Jamil so excited about the supposedly surprise family dinner they were planning, along with gifts and a skit show. Yet the wish from Raul's lips sounded ironic. Why was the day's approach something he should be happy about?

"We're getting old, my friend," Raul went on.

Again, a joke emerged from habit. "Speak for yourself, man."

Instead of driving home, Hilton tooled north on Biscayne Boulevard until he reached the gates to Poinciana Haven, where he could see the mobile home Charles Ray Goode had left behind with a FOR SALE sign in the window. He'd left his curtains hanging inside, but that was about all, Hilton saw when he stood on a cement block to peer between them. He halfway expected to find Charles Ray still standing there, staring back at him.

But no. Just a tabletop piled with fast food wrappers, and empty cabinets hanging open. He was really gone, just as Curt had verified through the FBI and his new probation officer upstate. For now, they were making him check in daily. That simple.

Hilton made it back to Coral Gables just in time to pick up Kaya and Jamil from their schools. In another couple of weeks, the family had decided, Kaya and Jamil would be allowed to take the bus or ride home with friends the way they had before Goode entered their lives. For now, while Hilton was on leave, he enjoyed picking them up—not as a safety measure, but just to do it. Parked in front of their schools, he felt buoyant each time the crowd of children cleared and he saw his own bounding up to the car with breathless stories or complaints from the school day.

Kaya didn't like her algebra teacher. Jamil was sick of the bully bothering him at lunch, picking at his food.

"He plays too much. I could beat him up," Jamil said.

"Don't let me catch you fighting," Hilton warned.

Jamil sighed. "But it's his fault. He's the one who starts it. If he won't leave me alone and I hit him, why should I get in trouble? That's not fair."

"You're not supposed to fight. Period. A lot of people think black children are aggressive, so you have to be smarter than that. Eyes are always watching you, Jamil. Remember that."

His son had lost the argument with Kaya over who would sit up front, so Hilton glanced at Jamil's dubious face in the rearview mirror. How many black boys Jamil's age would one day end up staring down the barrel of a police officer's gun because of a quick assumption, or fear? That could happen to his hotheaded son, if he wasn't careful. That could happen soon.

"You got that? Promise me you'll remember that, okay?"

"I'll remember."

"I said to promise."

"Cross my heart, Daddy," Jamil said. "Hope to die."

（

The reading light was on in Kaya's room, so Hilton knocked on her door, which was ajar. Since it was nearly midnight, Kaya was already in bed beneath her sheets, but she was enthralled in a teen paperback picturing two laughing blond girls on the cover. She barely glanced up at Hilton as her eyes devoured the words.

"Why are you up so late?" he asked her, sitting cross-legged on her carpeted floor.

"I just want to finish this chapter," she said.

He hadn't had a chance to really talk to Kaya since he'd been back. He'd found himself wanting to apologize about the scene when he left the house, but she had never stopped her cheerful chatter long enough to give him a chance. They'd danced around each other for days, occasionally catching the other in thoughtful gazes, but they hadn't sat down to share their feelings. And it didn't look like she planned to give him an opportunity tonight, either.

Kaya had big, pretty brown eyes like her mother's. Long lashes. She was wearing a bright pink nightshirt, which framed her face perfectly, softly. Her hair was tied behind her head in a ponytail, so she looked older to him than she usually did with her braids on either side. She might not look much different as a young woman in her twenties, her thirties. She would be taller, but she wouldn't look very different at all.

Kaya's eyes gazed up at him from behind the book. She smiled. "What are you looking at?"

"You, that's all. My little girl."

"Please don't start that, Dad."

Hilton saw a gleam of silver on Kaya's nightstand beneath her brass banker's light, so he reached up to touch it. It was a pin, a winged staff with twin serpents entwined around it. The medical insignia.

"Where'd you get this?"

Kaya sat up in her bed, closing the book. "Oh, my science teacher gave me that. He said I'm so advanced, I could be in a tenth-grade science class. I told him I'm going to be a doctor. That's a pin from a real doctor. It's his son's."

Hilton studied the tiny pin in his palm. Mr. Bonetti. He remembered the man from the parent-teacher conferences last fall. He was a good man, kind and smart. He was the sort of man Kaya could keep in touch with for advice and encouragement for years even after she left middle school. Maybe.

"I told him about my dream that time," Kaya said suddenly.

"Which dream?"

"You know the one. I told him I met a girl who died of AIDS and I dreamed about her. And how she said I'm going to do something with T cells."

"What did he say?"

"He just laughed," Kaya said, shrugging. "He said he doesn't believe in ghosts."

They both fell silent, and Hilton became aware of the silence all throughout the house. He realized that he and Kaya both believed in ghosts, at least for tonight. Hilton closed his fingers tightly around the pin.

"You can keep that if you want to," Kaya said. "Then you can give it back to me when I finish medical school."

"That's a bargain," Hilton said softly, stroking her head. Hilton could see the corners of Kaya's mouth drooping with adult worries that had been absent in her face six months ago. She stared at the floor, biting her lip. It was time to talk, at last. "How long will you be here, Dad?"

"A long time, I hope."

"Is that crazy guy really gone?"

"As far as I know. I think so. Why?"

Kaya shook her head, silent. Then she sighed and met Hilton's eyes. "I don't know. I just don't feel like he's really gone. I feel like everything is going to be different from now on."

"Everything will be different, for a while," Hilton said.

"Nothing will be like it was before, will it?" Kaya asked stubbornly, looking unhappy. "It won't be like before."

Hilton paused to think. He knew she was right. Nothing would ever again be exactly the same for the James family. Some of it was lost forever, like Kaya's baby teeth and his own peaceful nights. But he felt an overpowering sense that what lay ahead for Kaya, just possibly, was too wonderful for him to even imagine.

He took his daughter's hand. "That's the whole trouble with this world," he said. "Everything always becomes different, in the end. But different doesn't mean bad, just different. You know?"

Kaya nodded, and Hilton saw a pool of tears in her eyes. She blinked and wiped them away. "I just don't want you to leave again," she said.

He squeezed her hand, his throat aching. "I know," he said. "I'm trying hard to fix everything, but I can't make promises about the future. Nobody can. You know that, right?" Kaya nodded. "Now stop that crying, or you'll have me doing it."

Kaya laughed halfheartedly. "I thought men aren't supposed to cry," she said.

"Men do a lot of things they're not supposed to."

"I love you, Dad," Kaya whispered.

The silence in the house screamed at him. He remembered the first time she'd spoken those words to him, at eighteen months old, still in diapers. A part of him knew a circle was closing around them. The first time. The last time.

"I know, Pumpkin. I love you, too."

CHAPTER 38

Hilton's birthday, a Sunday, dawned with a bright sun fighting its way through thick cloud cover, signaling another day of sporadic south Florida rainstorms. Hilton lay awake beside Dede for a long time before she stirred, gazing at the photograph of Nana he'd propped up on the bureau. The photo gave him some peace, but all night he hadn't slept or dreamed. He'd been waiting for morning, for this day to begin.

Already, it wasn't what he had expected. After all of the talk about stealing birthdays with Raul and Andres, he'd believed he would wake up to find every inner sensor rife with unpleasant premonitions. He felt good, though, except for his fatigue and a slight disappointment in the glum rain clouds outside. He was thirty-nine years old today, in good physical health, in his wife's bed. So far, so good.

"I'm supposed to pretend I've forgotten all about your birthday," Dede told him sleepily when she woke up, kissing the tip of his nose. "I'm a bad actress. I can't do it. Happy birthday."

"I won't tell."

She furrowed her brow, concerned. "Did you sleep?"

"Some," he lied. "I just woke up early. I saw the sun rise." She nestled her back against him, and he wrapped his arm around her middle with his chin resting gently against her neck. "No more dreams?" she asked hopefully.

"No more dreams."

By the time they came out of the bedroom, Kaya and Jamil

were sitting in front of the television set, balancing cereal bowls in their laps. As he'd been warned, they simply mumbled good morning without a word about his birthday. Kaya was completely straightfaced, but Jamil had the giggles.

"You might as well know," Dede said quietly while they brewed coffee alone in the kitchen. "I've been instructed to send you on a long errand this afternoon to get you out of the house. Which errand do you prefer?"

"Jesus, just not the grocery store—please."

"I do need to go, but that wouldn't take long enough, anyway." Now Hilton felt slightly uneasy. "I don't have to stay away all day, do I?"

"Three or four hours," she said, handing him his mug. "Please, Hil. You don't know how they've been planning. Leave sometime after lunch and get back here by five, okay?"

Hilton grumbled to himself later, snarled in the slow traffic on South Dixie Highway under a hot afternoon sun, which had prevailed over the clouds. It was his birthday, and yet he'd somehow ended up on the road with a list of a half dozen chores that would take him all over the city. He had to return Dede's library books downtown, get his car washed, replace a floodlight that had burned out on the patio, who knew what else.

He should have held firm, surprise or no surprise. There's no way he should have allowed them to send him away for so many hours, today of all days. Complacency was a dangerous thing.

Trapped behind a white and blue Express Mail van stopped with its hazard lights on in the middle of the right-hand traffic lane on Flagler, Hilton was so annoyed he thought about turning around to go home. But he'd already driven twenty minutes to get downtown, and the library was so close it didn't make sense to go back now. The uniformed driver carried box after box out of the belly of his truck, stacking them in front of an electronics store. Traffic was so dense that Hilton couldn't budge to change lanes. Why the hell did the post office make deliveries on Sunday, anyway?

He tapped his car horn. "Could you move it?" he called out his window to the young driver, who shrugged and motioned for him to drive around.

Asshole. Like Hilton hadn't thought of that already. Finally, Hilton cut off a BMW to bolt into the neighboring lane. He heard the driver behind him brake and curse at him in Spanish. Goddammit, he hated driving on Flagler and dodging its tourists and bargain-hunters. On top of that, the sun had turned truly merciless, rapidly draining what little energy he had. Some birthday.

Hilton grew more calm as he climbed the tile steps leading to the palatial Spanish-style library building and its patio with benches and tables beneath umbrellas, a small oasis on the crowded city street. A woman in sunglasses sat watching her twin sons chasing each other in a circle while they laughed gleefully. Two shabbily dressed older men napped leaning against each other on one of the benches. Silently, without waking them, Hilton slid a ten-dollar bill into each of their shirt pockets. The woman in sunglasses smiled at him as he walked past.

It was a beautiful day, after all.

Inside the library, Hilton lost track of time, browsing without particular interest in an aisle of travel books. The sun was still bright when he returned to the patio. The woman and her sons had left, but the homeless men still slept. Hilton bought a cherry Popsicle from a vendor and sat on one of the shaded benches, aching for a small rest. Sunlight always made him so drowsy.

And why not? Hilton curled his legs onto the painted wooden bench and savored the cool spot he'd discovered. He could hear car horns and sirens around him, but he felt untroubled. Maybe he could nap safely today, just for a time.

"... *how many of them in the house? ... we'll need dental records for a positive ID, if we can salvage that much ... looks like maybe everybody wasn't home ... Nobody comes within fifty feet, including the reporters ... it's James, J-A-M-E-S ...* "

When Hilton woke up, his shirt was sagging with cold perspiration and he shivered despite the heat. He sat, confused and alarmed. Where was he? He recognized the patio benches and the two homeless men sleeping across from him, but something was different. The late-afternoon sun had dipped out of sight behind the library building, and something indescribable and sinister hung in the air. This place, where he was now, was another doorway.

He had slept, and a balance had shifted somehow, just like Andres had said. Something was wrong.

sweet dreams, baby

Dede's whispered voice was so clear behind him, he turned to see if she was standing there before he realized the voice was only in his head. In a flash that burst into a staggering headache, Hilton knew with agonizing certainty that he would never see his wife again. Something had happened, was already in motion.

He wasn't sure about Kaya and Jamil. He ran toward the pay telephone across the patio, digging for change in his pocket.

The phone seemed to ring forever, each interval launching Hilton's heart into a more frantic pace. Kaya answered on the sixth ring. "Hello, James residence."

"It's me. Put your mom on the phone," Hilton said, so relieved to hear her voice that he thought he would collapse. His voice shook with urgency.

"What's wrong?"

He couldn't explain. He wasn't sure himself. "Nothing, sweetheart. Just please put her on."

"She just left. She had to go to the market."

Distraught, Hilton had to stop himself from pounding the receiver against the phone booth. He was breathing heavily, thoroughly soaked, and his mind was in such a severe whirl that he could barely stand. Gone. She was gone.

"You sound funny, Dad. Are you sure you're okay?"

What now? Hilton tried to catch his breath, covering the mouthpiece so Kaya wouldn't hear his panting. Oh, Jesus,

Jesus. Something was horribly wrong. He had to control himself somehow, or it would all be lost. All of it.

"Kaya . . . are you and Jamil in the house alone?"

"Yeah, Dad. Everything's fine."

"Are the doors locked? Did Dede activate the alarm?"

Kaya paused. "I guess so. I'm not sure about the alarm. Dad, I'm worried about you. You sound awful."

i'll huff and i'll puff

A voice again, from beyond his dreams. He'd heard it this time. I'll huff and I'll puff. Goode's note.

Hilton's hand was trembling as he grasped the phone. "Listen carefully to me. Make sure all of the doors are locked. I want you to set the alarm, okay? Don't let anyone in the house. Has anyone come to the house?"

"Uhm . . . " Kaya began, hesitating. "Just a mail guy, right after Mom left. But he's gone already, and he didn't come in—"

and i'll blow your house down

A mailman. Goode. Hilton left the receiver dangling on its metallic cord and ran, racing across the length of the patio and flying down the steps so fast he had to cling to the arm rail to avoid stumbling. He ran two blocks, pushing his way past passersby until he found his car in the parking lot, a ticket tucked beneath his windshield wiper. He turned his key in the ignition so hard that the starter squealed like a dying child.

"Help me, Nana," he heard himself say, roaring to the street. Nana had shown him what to do, in a dream. He only had to remember. "Please don't let me get there too late," he wheezed as he sped beneath a red light and a chorus of car horns objected. Hilton felt dizzy as hidden knowledge began to storm his psyche. Doorways. He could feel the unfolding rows of doorways all around him like a divine vision, a kaleidoscope. In some of them, he was still asleep on the bench. In some of them, he'd just awakened and was peering around the library patio, confused. In some, he was still talking to Kaya on the telephone. He could hear his own voice, Kaya's voice, faintly from the fringes of his reason, inside a unison of voices sharing a splintered moment of possibilities in time.

. . . Don't let anyone in the house, okay? . . . Has anyone come to the house? . . . It's me. Put your mom on the phone . . . Hello, James residence . . . Dad, I'm worried about you . . . Are you and Jamil alone in the house? . . . Hello, James residence . . . A mail guy came right after Mom left . . . Don't let anyone in the house . . . Hello, James residence . . .

Hilton shook his head to clear it, hot tears streaming down his face as he wove in and out of traffic on South Dixie Highway. He alone controlled the events of this moment, this doorway. Had he found the right one? What if he hadn't?

Maybe this wasn't real. Maybe he wasn't real at all.

Hilton's head pounded with frustration. Did all of the sleep doorways lead to a reality, or were they just options that were meaningless so long as his true consciousness lived in this moment, driving in the car? He should have talked to Andres more about this to try to understand. He had to believe in one genuine reality—in this reality—or it was all pointless. Running was useless, the doorways were useless. It wouldn't matter what he found when he got home because it would be different everywhere else. He couldn't bear that thought.

What had Andres said? Wherever the spirit rests is that moment's reality. Wherever the spirit rests. He was the spirit.

Hilton lost his concentration, his foot jerking on the accelerator as he sensed his nightmares coming true. Explosions. One after the other, in sickening succession. His mind showed him walls of fire, burning wood, collapsing concrete. Explosions were all around. In some of the doorways, he was too late already.

The realization made Hilton's lips quiver as he drove: he'd made a deadly mistake. Instead of telling Kaya and Jamil to lock themselves inside of the house, he should have told them to run. Goode wasn't there. Goode wasn't the danger. The danger was in what Goode had sent in the mail.

His speedometer told him he was driving eighty-five miles per hour, and his tires screeched as he steered around the cars crawling in front of him. Perhaps he would finally die in his car after all. It was just like Nana had told him; she only thought she had fixed it, but she hadn't. She'd failed to save him, ultimately, and he couldn't save them. What's done is done is done is done.

His street was silent except for the call of birds hidden in the tangled tree branches and the whine of his own brakes as he rounded the corner. The shadowed street was deserted.

Hilton had never seen such a beautiful sight as his own coral wall and the archways of the house intact, still standing undisturbed. Dede's Audi was gone and the driveway was empty. A light was on in the living room, and he could see a banner strung across the picture window inside of the house as his car lurched to a stop at the curb. Charlie was in the backyard barking wildly, standing against the fence on his hind legs. Even Charlie could smell the danger. He could smell it in the air, just as he was trained.

Hilton started to run up the walkway, but he halted after passing the aluminum garbage can left standing at the curb. He stared at the can, and his heart leaped. Yes. This was in his dream, he remembered. Was the answer here?

He fumbled to lift the lid. He was disappointed when he found the can empty except for mildewed paper crushed finely at the bottom. Goddammit. It was in the house.

Hilton unlocked the front door and burst through, not bothering to deactivate the alarm panel, which flashed a red warning. Police would be notified within thirty seconds. Good. The police would need to be here.

The living room was decorated with red, black, and green streamers and balloons, liberation colors. Now inside, Hilton could see that the multicolored banner hanging across the picture window was for him. HAPPY BIRTHDAY, DAD, it said.

"Kaya? Jamil?" Hilton shouted hoarsely. He'd lived this moment a million times before, in his sleep.

As he ran down the hallway, he heard the clatter of silverware. The house was warm from the oven. Dede must have been cooking. The smell of simmering foods was so thick that Hilton felt sick.

He found Kaya and Jamil frozen in the dining room as they set the table, as though they'd been startled in the midst of a crime. The table was laid out with the lace tablecloth they usually only brought out at Christmas and Thanksgiving, with freshly cut blossoms from the yard propped in small glass vases. Kaya was wearing a housecoat, her hair still uncombed, and Jamil was only half dressed in an African ensemble Hilton had never seen before. They looked crushed to see him.

"You're not supposed to be home yet, Daddy," Jamil whined.

Kaya didn't speak, transfixed by the expression on Hilton's face as his eyes searched the room. He saw a pile of wrapped gifts in a chair beside the china cabinet. Other boxes of streamers and gift-wrapping paper from the garage were lined on the floor. Hilton could barely hear anything except his own heartbeat.

"Mom's not home yet?" he gasped.

"Not yet, but I locked the door. Did you turn off the alarm?" Kaya asked. "We got cut off on the phone, right?"

Hilton didn't answer, running to the kitchen and then the living room to search for a box that didn't belong in the house. Had his senses fooled him? Had he imagined everything he'd seen and felt? "We were trying to surprise you," Kaya said in a somber tone, following closely after him. "What's wrong?"

Out of the corner of his eye, Hilton saw Jamil's back as he scampered out of the dining room. "Hey, where are you going?" Hilton called after him.

"Nowhere," Jamil called back, giggling.

Hilton tried to slow his breathing and wiped perspiration

from his face with a dishtowel from the kitchen. "We need to get out of the house," he said to Kaya. "Where's the package?"

"What package?" Kaya asked. He gazed at her and realized she was being coy, trying to hide something from him.

He walked to her and put his hands on her shoulders firmly. He had to make himself clear. He didn't have time for anger or games or panic. "Kaya," he began, "I'm not playing. I need that package. I need it now."

Kaya made a face, studying Hilton. She sighed. "Didn't you even notice the decorations we put up, Dad?"

"They're wonderful," he said, struggling not to shout because he thought it would be worse to scare her. "Where's the package?"

"We wrapped it. We put it with your other presents, in the dining room."

Jesus Christ. Hilton ran, stopping in his tracks when he reached the dining room entryway from the kitchen. The chair beside the china cabinet was empty now, the stack of gifts gone. That couldn't be. He hadn't slept or dreamed. What the hell happened to the gifts?

A movement caught Hilton's eye, and he saw Jamil's grinning face retreating from him as his son walked backward, his hands behind his back. He'd been running back and forth and was breathing hard. He'd been hiding the goddamn gifts.

"Hi, Daddy," Jamil said playfully.

Hilton couldn't believe, after everything, that it was coming down to this. His legs wobbled beneath him. He didn't have the energy to lunge at Jamil the way he needed to. His windpipe felt clogged, as though it wouldn't permit any words to leave him. "Jamil," he said, "what's that behind your back?"

"Nothing," Jamil said, still grinning.

"He knows, Jamil. Just give him the package," Kaya sighed. She started to walk toward her brother, but Hilton grabbed her arm hard and held her at his side, ten feet from his son.

"Stay back," Hilton whispered to her. She looked up at Hilton and then back at Jamil, her expression changing with a taste of monstrous knowledge. Her face looked gray, drained of blood.

"It didn't say who sent it. It just said 'Happy Birthday,'" Kaya said in a tiny, unsteady voice. "Dad, is it from—"

"I don't know," Hilton said, shushing her. He had a bigger problem on his hands: What would Jamil do if he panicked? Would he drop it? Would he fling it away? Carefully, mustering all of his strength, Hilton took two steps toward his son. Jamil stepped back, still smiling, oblivious to the grave look on Hilton's face.

"The surprise is over now, okay? Give me the package. I mean it, Jamil. This isn't a game. You're making me angry."

"Give it to him, Jamil." Kaya's voice was adult, shaken.

Jamil dropped his eyes, bringing a basketball-sized box from behind his back. It was wrapped in shiny striped Snoopy paper, covered with Happy Birthdays. "You ruined our surprise," Jamil said, pouting, still clasping the awful package against his chest.

boom

Hilton took another step toward Jamil and held out his arms, which felt as leaden as the day Raul hypnotized him. His eyes were glued to the package's ridiculously cheerful wrapping. "Is this the one, Kaya?" he asked, his jaw shaking as he spoke.

"Yes, Dad," she whispered. He heard her take a step back.

Hilton's fingertips were almost close enough to touch it. Almost. "Jamil, don't move. I'm going to take it. Then I want you and Kaya to run out back as fast as you can. Don't you move."

Jamil gazed up at Hilton, wide-eyed and bewildered, just as he'd been that day at the birdcage. He was frightened. Hilton realized his son couldn't move now if he wanted to.

Hilton pressed his palms firmly to either side of the box and gently lifted it from Jamil's grip. His arms twitched, and he felt a slight resistance. "Let go, Jamil. All the way."

He had it. It was heavy. But he had it. *"Run!"* he shouted at his children. "Get out!"

In an instant, they were gone. He heard the French doors fling open from the kitchen as they ran to the back patio. The mad pounding in Hilton's chest hadn't let up, and his breathing was still heavy as he held the box in his hands. He closed his eyes, bracing for an explosion.

Nothing.

He had to get out of the house, as far from Kaya and Jamil as possible. Hilton took painstaking steps across the floor, breathing through his mouth as he read the label Kaya had affixed to the wrapping in her girlish script. To: Dad. From: A friend.

He didn't dare shake the box to better judge its contents. They'd wrapped it, bless them. Charles Ray Goode had mailed a bomb to his house, and his children had gift-wrapped it.

The distance from the dining room to the front door seemed endless, but Hilton breathed a little easier once he was outside. Charlie was still standing against the fence, barking his furious warnings. Hilton's extended arms ached horribly. He looked right and left, up and down the emtpy street. What now?

Beyond the coral wall, Hilton saw the aluminum garbage can and remembered. It was all happening just as Nana had shown him in his dream. Had he won, at last? Was it finally over?

Gently, gently, he eased the box into the open container. Once it rested against the bottom, he slammed the can's lid down and jumped back. The adrenaline coursing through his system made him feel as though he were flying, soaring above the scene and looking down at the garbage can and the man who'd dropped a bomb inside. He had really won.

Hilton laughed, filled with an overwhelming relief and hysteria. Jesus, maybe he was just crazy, as Raul kept telling him. For all he knew, Curt or Raul or Stu had mailed him an expensive gift and he'd just chucked it into the garbage can. It wouldn't be the first time his father had mailed a gift instead of bringing it. Anything could be in that package. The thought made him double over with laughter. He felt so light, so light.

hil ton

Hilton's head snapped up. He thought he'd heard someone call his name, a woman, but all he could hear now was Charlie's barking. He turned around to look at his house; he saw the door he'd left ajar, the light in the window, the birthday banner. He started to trudge toward the backyard to search for Kaya and Jamil.

come, hilton

But no. He heard it again. A woman was calling to him.

Hilton smiled despite his emotional exhaustion, cleansed in a contentment he'd never known. What's done is done is done. He wasn't thinking or feeling anything at all when he walked back to the garbage can and wrapped his fingers around the lid's handle. He only knew that this was where he was supposed to be, and this was what he was supposed to do.

Hilton never heard the explosion that rocked the street, shattering the living room's windows, slamming his car against a tree like paper, and blowing to bits the coral wall that had stood for thirty years in front of his house.

EPILOGUE

A traveler can tell many tales, but he cannot explain all that he has seen.

— Ghanaian proverb

Hilton hears a horrible scream suffocating him until he realizes it is not human, but the mechanical squeal of brake pads grinding against rubber. He feels a jolt in the darkness. He lurches and then lunges until he is flying, flying

Glass is breaking around him. he is flying through a wall of glass. He bounces against something solid and hears the thump-thump of his arms falling limply on either side of him

He is here for a long time, surrounded by voices that sound far away, too far for him to hear clearly. He doesn't recognize the voices. He only hears the Dolphins playing on the radio

The Dolphins?

After minute-hours, he feels himself sliding down, down across a smooth surface until he is unsupported, flying again. He is somersaulting into emptiness

He plunges into a cold bath of water, which plugs his ears and his nose. he can feel bubbles swirling all around him. He is still falling, falling into the depths. He tastes salt in his mouth. When he tries to spit it out, the water invades his mouth and he begins to choke, thrashing in the dark pool. No no no no Nana, he tries to call. Where is Nana?

He begins to swim furiously, propelling his body upward with powerful strokes of his arms. There is a light above him; it must be daylight. He must be dreaming again.

He swims toward the light until the water grows more and more shallow, and he feels a sandy surface beneath his bare feet. He gasps, finally breaking his head free from the water's prison. Land. He drags himself across the sand and struggles to stand. When his stinging eyes are clear, he can make out the figure of someone standing on the shore, waiting.

A woman. She is wearing a dress and a scarf that billows in the wind. Nana beckons to him. He can see her smile, her youthful face. Her black, black hair. "You did good, Hilton," Nana says, taking him in her arms. His head only reaches her waist and the folds of her dress there, sinking into her soft belly. He is smaller than he imagined next to her, but it is right this way.

Bit by bit, she wipes sand from his back and shoulders. "You did good, boy."

"Where we going?" he asks in a high, piping voice.

She points. Of course. He can see her house and its porch at the top of a steep, craggy hill, glowing from inside with bright lights. He already feels himself growing sleepy. He hasn't slept in so long. "Come," Nana says, taking his head. "Supper's on."

As they walk together toward home, Hilton feels his heart growing more and more light. He hopes she has a sweet-potato pie waiting. He hasn't had one in ages, or her coconut icing. She always gives him sweets when he's been good.

"Nana, is this real?" he asks, looking up at her face as he clasps her warm, soothing hand. "Can this be real?"

Nana doesn't answer, smiling.

> they caught him, baby
> we're okay, daddy

Voices?

Hilton feels a sharp sting in his palm and opens it with a start. He finds a small silver pin there, a winged staff with two serpents wrapped around it. Suddenly, his insides tremble with joy. He has done something, he's not sure what, to make everything all right.

A dear playmate gave him this pin. No, more than a play-mate. Someone he loves. He cannot quite remember her name or her face, not yet, because this is something that only comes with time. But he knows with certainty that she is a very great woman, a famous healer he knew once, long ago.

ACKNOWLEDGMENTS

I always knew I would publish a book someday. I just never imagined it would be today.

Thanks to the people who taught me to believe before I knew there was any such thing as *not* believing: my parents, John and Patricia Due; my maternal grandmother, Lottie Sears Houston; my paternal grandmother, Lucille Ransaw, whom I wish had lived to see this book; my aunt, Priscilla Kruize; my uncle, Walter Stephens; and my sisters—and best friends—Johnita and Lydia.

Thanks to my agent and voice of reason, Janell Walden Agyeman at Marie Brown Associates, who knew what we had before I did and made me see it, too. And my editor at HarperCollins, Peternelle van Arsdale, for her enthusiasm and gentle hand.

Thanks to my first readers for their candid advice: Muncko Kruize (love you, Cuz), Robert Vamosi, Olympia Duhart, Grace Lim, Mirta Ojito, Milana Frank, Nigel Horscroft, and Anthony Faiola.

For much-appreciated assistance during the journey, thanks to Mitchell Kaplan, Jay McLawhorn (there *will* be a cure), Juan Gomez, John Lantigua, and Ellen Anmuth, LCSW. And Inez Gaffoglio, who saw the future and whispered it to me.

Also, many thanks to my creative-writing instructors at Northwestern University, who helped me in ways I'm still discovering—Janet Desaulniers and Sheila Schwartz.

It takes more than words and advice to write a book, it takes friends helping you navigate through the joys and pains of life. Thanks to Ivan, Luchina, Kate, and Craig, for being a part of mine.

Lastly, thanks to Anne R., who opened my mind.